Muffins Masks Murder

Tai Chi and Chai Tea

Santa Shortbread

Cold as Ice Cream

Changing Fortune Cookies

Hot on the Trail Mix

Recipes from Auntie Clem's Bakery

Zachary Goldman Mysteries

She Wore Mourning

His Hands Were Quiet

She Was Dying Anyway

He Was Walking Alone

They Thought He was Safe

He Was Not There

Her Work Was Everything

She Told a Lie

He Never Forgot

She Was At Risk

Parks Pat Mysteries

Out with the Sunset (Coming Soon)

Long Climb to the Top (Coming Soon)

Dark Water Under the Bridge (Coming Soon)

AND MORE AT PDWORKMAN.COM

SKUNK MAN SWAMP

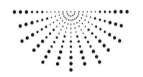

SKUNK MAN SWAMP

REG RAWLINS, PRIVATE INVESTIGATOR #10

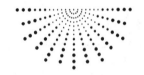

P.D. WORKMAN

ISBN: 9781774680919 (IS Hardcover)

ISBN: 9781774680902 (IS Paperback)

ISBN: 9781774680926 (IS Large Print)

ISBN: 9781774680872 (KDP Paperback)

ISBN: 9781774680889 (Kindle)

ISBN: 9781774680896 (ePub)

pdworkman

AND MORE AT PDWORKMAN.COM

For friends who are a little different

CHAPTER ONE

*R*eg realized she had become distracted and stopped hearing Damon. He had been talking about the Spring Games—apparently the magical equivalent of the Olympics—at least since Yule, but over the past few weeks it had become more and more central to his conversation, until it was practically the only thing he talked about. And she couldn't listen for long before tuning him out and going on a little mental vacation. Normally, she was good at looking attentive but this time she had apparently failed.

Damon was looking at her in exasperation, waiting for her to say something. His dark eyes drilled into her. She wasn't sure if he had asked a question or told a story that demanded some kind of polite social response. She searched his face for some clue. His dark eyes drilled into her. The reddening aura around his head told her that he was angry. Damon was usually laid back. It took a lot of provocation—or Corvin—to get him angry.

"I'm sorry," she said, hoping that an apology would get her out of this. "I got distracted. You were talking about the Spring Games...?"

What else would he have been talking about?

"Yes, I was," he agreed. "But I guess you're not interested."

"I'm interested," Reg objected immediately. "I was just thinking about something else. A client," she bluffed. "This one has me a little puzzled."

1

He gazed at her for another moment. Being a diviner, he would know she was lying, even though Reg was a good liar with plenty of practice. Her face warmed and she wished she could stop the blush.

"So, you are interested?"

Interested in what? In the Spring Games?

"Of course. Just tell me that last little bit again."

Damon scratched the stubbly whiskers of his goatee. He was handsome. Dark hair and eyes. Like Corvin, and yet nothing like Corvin. She couldn't compare her magnetic attraction to Corvin to her friendship with Damon. Damon's physical appearance couldn't compete with Corvin's magical charms.

"There are some indications that he could be in the Everglades," Damon told her.

"In the Everglades." Reg repeated this part of the statement, rather than asking, *Who?* She was clearly supposed to know who he was talking about.

"That's right. So I figured that you could help me find him with your psychic abilities, and I would split the reward with you. It would be a real coup to get him to the Games."

Reg's head spun. She had no clue who he was talking about or what it had to do with the Spring Games. She shook her head, her red box-braids swishing around her face. "You want me to go to the Everglades to find this guy?"

"Well, unless you can look in your crystal ball here and just tell me where he is. Yes. I want you to go with me to the Everglades to find the missing wizard."

Reg rubbed her temples. She looked over to her crystal ball on the shelf, considering. She could try seeking whoever this missing wizard was in her crystal ball. It was possible she would be successful. But if she did something as simple as that, would Damon still feel like she had earned half of the reward? He made it sound like he was expecting it to be quite a bit of money.

Reg had the money she needed. In fact, she hadn't shared the gems that she had received from Calliopia Papillon's parents with those who had helped her on her quest to save Calliopia. She hadn't even *told* the others in her company about the gift. Reg had learned the value of money during the lean years, when she had struggled to keep a roof over her head and food in her belly. She didn't like to think of herself as a selfish person, but she couldn't think of any other way to spin the fact that she had decided to keep all of the reward for herself.

Of course, the more people who knew about the gems, the higher the chances that someone would break into her cottage or attack her in order to get them. Valuable, easily transportable goods that could not be traced were a burglar's dream. Reg really should get a safety deposit box in a bank rather than leave them in the little wooden box under her bed.

But the crystal ball might be a way for her to find out more about the missing wizard Damon was talking about without letting on that she had been ignoring him. She stretched her stiff limbs. She had been sitting in the wicker chair listening to Damon go on about the Spring Games for too long. She made her way across the room to get her crystal ball from the shelf. She put it on the coffee table as she sat back down.

Damon watched her, looking slightly amused. Did he sense that this was just a ploy? She had to assume that he was taking her at face value and couldn't know what she was thinking. He could put visions into her head, but he couldn't read what she was thinking independently of him. Reg rubbed her hands together as if trying to warm them up.

"Starlight?" she called. "Do you want to join me?"

She heard her familiar jump down from the window in the bedroom, and the black and white tuxedo cat came padding out to see her. He blinked at her, first his blue eye and then his green one. He looked at Damon and rotated his ears around so they were facing backward. He didn't usually object to Damon, so Starlight either didn't appreciate her waking him up to participate in the impromptu reading—which, admittedly, Reg did not need her familiar for—or he could read the room and knew that Reg was anxious and Damon angry.

"Come on, Starlight," she invited. "Help me focus on the crystal."

He sat and washed. Reg waited. Rushing him or picking him up would not help. If he had decided he needed to wash before the reading, then he needed to wash before the reading. She had to respect his process. There was no way he was getting around it anyway.

Damon rolled his eyes. "Why don't you just go ahead?"

"No. I'll wait until he's ready."

They both watched Starlight, who gave no indication that he was going to be finished any time soon.

"Why don't you tell me a little more about this wizard while we're waiting?"

She mentally patted herself on the back for this stroke of brilliance. He would give her more detail, and she would be able to fill in the parts of the conversation she had missed and decide whether she were going to do anything more for him than just look in the crystal.

Damon stared up at the ceiling. "I'm not sure how much I can tell you or how useful it will be. I know his name, like I said, Jeffrey Wilson. He's a brilliant wizard, but he just dropped out of sight. No one knows where he went. But there is a reward for finding him and getting him to attend at the Spring Games and I thought... why not? I'll bet that you could find him, and it would be great publicity for both of us, me with my security business and you with your psychic stuff. And it pays well. I might not be able to pay you an hourly rate, but if you take it on contingency, I'll give you half of what I get. And I'll fund the travel for us to go to the Everglades and rent an airboat and a guide, all that stuff."

It sounded a lot more complicated than Reg had imagined.

"The Everglades is just a little way away from here, right? I think I was in part of it when I went out to see Letticia before Corvin's hearing?" They wouldn't need to book a bus or plane to get there. Reg had just driven in her car.

"Yes, you can get to the edge of it from here. But it's a very big area—a million and a half acres. And a lot of it you can't get to by car. You need a boat."

"Oh." Reg nodded. She watched Starlight, who eventually came over to sit at her feet. He gazed up at her. "Hey, Star." Reg didn't criticize him for taking so long to get ready. She knew better than anyone else how hard he could be to deal with if he were grumpy or someone insulted him. "I'm going to gaze into the crystal and it might work better if I had your help. I'm trying to find a lost wizard."

Damon watched with some amusement. He shouldn't have thought that there was anything funny about it. He had seen Starlight in action before. He had seen what Reg could do. It wasn't like it was an act just for his entertainment.

Except that it kind of was.

Reg patted her lap and Starlight jumped up. He turned around a few times, looking for a comfortable position, and then started kneading her with his paws, his claws pricking her through her dress. She petted him and pushed him gently down. "Okay, enough. Just relax now."

He settled in. Reg rubbed her leg where he had needled it.

"Now, we'll start."

CHAPTER TWO

*R*eg leaned in closer to her crystal ball, petting Starlight and feeling the strengthening and stabilization of her powers. She stared at the outside of the crystal to start with. The shining surface reflected back her own face. After a few minutes, she was able to look past the surface of the crystal into its dark depths.

Wizard Jeffrey Wilson.

She thought his name. It was strange that it should be such a common-place sounding name. Almost as if he had picked it to be anonymous. But he was a wizard. Not just a mediocre wizard, but according to what Damon had said, he was pretty powerful. There couldn't be that many really powerful wizards named Jeffrey Wilson. She let her eyes defocus and waited, feeling Starlight's warmth on her lap and his comfortable aura enveloping her. Damon shifted restlessly. Reg tried to tune him out.

Where is Wizard Jeffrey Wilson?

Is he in the Everglades?

She remembered the trip to Letticia's house. The area she had traveled through had been very wild. Untamed. Everything was lush green. But she hadn't been to the swampy areas that one could only reach by boat. She had just driven to Letticia's. On increasingly ungroomed roads, but there had been roads of a sort all the way there.

She imagined herself going farther into the Everglades. Where there were no roads, but only boats. She had seen episodes on TV of some of her favorite crime shows that had investigators skimming over the surface of the water and long grass to find a body or some other clue that had been nearly swallowed up by the swamp. Was that what it was like? She couldn't imagine anyone staying lost in those kinds of conditions for very long.

She didn't imagine them *surviving* for very long, anyway.

A picture started to form in her head. She could see a shape pushing its way through long grasses and weirdly-shaped trees dripping with green moss. It was a tall, cloaked man. Reg focused on the vision, trying to sharpen the details. She could see his face under the folds of the hood. A craggy, lined face. Frightened. Looking for a way out.

Maybe he should have just stayed in one place rather than continuing to wander through the emerald jungle. Stayed still so that someone could find him. But he kept going, trying to get out. How could an old man like that be expected to walk out of a one-and-a-half million acre maze?

How had he gotten there? She hadn't thought to ask Damon when he was telling her the few details that he knew. Did Wilson drive in? Take a boat? Was he on his own when he disappeared or was he with a tour group? Had he crashed there in a plane? Was he searching for some rare plant or animal? Sight-seeing?

She felt moved to help him. It was a very strong pull. Reg's instincts were usually for herself over anyone else, so the feeling that she needed to help him was surprising. Without regard for her own needs or how much the payout Damon had been talking about was, she wanted to drop everything and rescue the wizard.

CHAPTER THREE

There was a shredding pain in her leg. Reg yelled and the vision was shattered. Starlight jumped down from her lap, but not before biting her arm too.

"Ouch!" Reg shouted after him. "What was that for?"

Like some wild creature, Starlight jumped up at Damon, making him start back in alarm, putting his hands out in front of his face for protection. Starlight nipped at his leg, then skittered out of the room, heading back for Reg's bedroom in the back of the cottage.

Damon rubbed his calf, blowing out his breath in a surprised whistle. "Wow. Oh, that stings. What was that all about?"

"I don't know. He doesn't usually act like that. Maybe I squeezed him when I had my vision." Reg shook her head, trying to understand. "He just doesn't do that, normally."

"I would hope not." He continued to rub his leg. "You wouldn't stay in business long with a familiar like that."

"Do you want me to get you something for it? Alcohol wipes? A bandage?"

"Stitches?"

"Is it that bad?" Reg frowned at Damon's leg, hoping he was joking.

"No," he admitted. "I'm sure a bandage will be all that it needs. Maybe not even that. I'm not sure if it's even bleeding."

"I'll get some stuff for it. Do you want to pull up your pant leg and I'll take a look?"

Damon wrestled to pull his tight-fitting jeans up over his calf to have a look. Reg leaned closer. There were a couple of fang marks, red but not bleeding freely. Reg had gotten worse bite marks just playing with Starlight with a string.

"That doesn't look too bad. I'll be right back."

She went to the bathroom to gather together the supplies she needed. When she returned, Damon was straining his neck trying to get a good look at the injury.

"You don't think it needs stitches?" he asked worriedly. "What about a tetanus shot?"

"It's not that bad. I've got some ointment, and we'll put a bandage over it. A day or two, and it will be fine."

He would probably live to regret the bandage. After applying the ointment, Reg pressed it down well over long, coarse hairs to make sure it would adhere to the skin underneath. It would hurt worse when he pulled the bandage off, yanking all of those hairs with it. She suppressed a smile as he groaned.

"There. All fixed up." Reg returned to her chair. She sat down and waited for Damon to stop bellyaching and continue with their conversation. "So…"

He looked at her blankly for a moment, then realized that he hadn't asked her the question. "Did you see anything in your crystal ball?"

"Yes. Or in my head. Doesn't matter where I saw it; the crystal is just a tool to focus the energy. But yes… I saw him in the Everglades."

"So he *is* there." Damon sounded eager and excited. "That confirms it. And if you can see him from here, then when we get close to him, it will be all that much easier, right? We'll have no trouble tracking him down and bringing him back."

"Well… there's no guarantee of that," Reg warned. "But yes… since I was able to see him, I wouldn't think it would be too hard to find him if we were close by."

"That's excellent. So will you do it? You'll take it on contingency?"

Reg considered. She didn't have anything that she couldn't leave for a day or two. And it was always nice to be able to pick up a little extra cash to pad her bank account. She didn't want to always have to worry about how to cash in precious gems, hoping to liquidate them whenever she wanted to and getting a good price for them. Even a psychic couldn't predict what was going to happen with the economy.

"How much is this reward for bringing him back?"

"Five hundred thousand dollars."

Reg didn't immediately jump into it. Two hundred and fifty, her share, wasn't as big as she had hoped when he had talked about the prize. Maybe seeing billboards with sweepstakes giving away tens of millions of dollars had influenced what she considered a lot of money. Especially when she already had all of those gems. What she had in the little box under her bed was worth a lot more than two hundred and fifty thousand dollars.

Damon eyed her. "I know it's a lot of money, and you might not want to make a snap decision, but... well, the Games are not very far away, and we would have to bring him back in time to participate in order to earn the reward."

"So you want me to make a snap decision. You come here today and then expect me to leave with you tomorrow, off on some wild goose chase?"

"Well... it would be really good if we could get an early start, yes. But you know it's not a wild goose chase. You know you'll be able to find him. You know he's there, just like you saw in your vision."

"Yes... I'm just not sure. I had other plans for the next few days..."

"Other plans worth more than two hundred and fifty grand? A quarter of a million dollars?"

"No. Obviously not. But that doesn't mean I want to go. It's like... swampland out there, isn't it? What if there are snakes?"

"You can be sure that there will be snakes. But they're not going to eat you."

"And gators. Or are they crocs?"

"Well, both," Damon admitted. "Maybe the only place in the world you can see gators and crocs in the same habitat..."

"And don't try telling me that they won't eat me. They're just waiting for someone to stop in the wrong place and get out of their car. Or boat."

"We'll get a guide. They'll make sure that we are not in any danger. Yes, there are hazards in such a wild area. But you have strong powers. You can probably just tell them to stay away with your mind."

"Yeah, right. I'm not relying on my psychic powers to keep alligators away! Isn't there... pepper spray or something?"

Damon chuckled. "I don't know about pepper spray. The guide will know all about precautions to take and what products are out there. Alligator repellent." He laughed again. "So does that mean that you'll come? Please?"

"I don't know. Let me think about it."

Damon sat there, staring at her. Reg wasn't going to let him rush her into a decision like that. Putting her life on the line for two hundred and fifty thousand bucks? She wasn't sure that was wise. She didn't need it to survive.

"I need a couple of hours at least," she told Damon. "Why don't you go home, and we'll talk later? When I've had a chance to think about it."

Damon sighed, his shoulders dropping an inch. "Fine. I don't see the problem, but please... let me know as soon as possible. If you're not going to do it... I'll have to see if there's someone else I can get to help."

There were plenty of other psychics around. Reg wasn't the only game in town.

"I'll let you know."

CHAPTER FOUR

hen Damon was on his way, Reg found Starlight in her room and scolded him roundly for clawing and biting her and biting Damon.

"Is that any way to treat a guest? He's a paying client, too. Well, maybe, if I decide to take it on. You can't behave that way, or we won't be able to get any business."

Not that she needed more business now that she had the gemstones. Starlight stared at her reproachfully. She didn't know what had provoked him to attack her and Damon, but he had clearly had his reasons, and he wasn't the least bit sorry for what he had done. Reg could tell. She shook her head at him.

"No more behaving like that. I'll get a reputation. And then we won't be able to afford your kitty food."

He stared back at her. He didn't believe a word of it.

Reg sat on the side of the bed.

"Do you think I should take it?" she asked him. "Go and find this wizard out in the middle of the swamp? I would say no, but I did see him. How hard could it be? I'll go out there for a day or two, track him down, bring him back to the Games, and then we'll get our reward. Easy peasy."

But when was the last time she had declared something would be easy peasy and it actually was?

* * *

She went up to the big house to talk about it with Sarah, the witch who owned the property. Sarah shrugged and told her to go. Why not? What harm could it do? The worst that could happen was that they wouldn't be able to find the wizard, and since nobody else had found him either, how could anyone judge Reg for not finding him?

"Well, I am a psychic," Reg pointed out. "This is how I'm supposed to be making my living."

"Even a psychic cannot be expected to find what she is looking for every time. That's not the way it works."

"No," Reg admitted. There had been other things she had not been able to find. Sarah's emerald necklace for one. And everyone had told her not to be so hard on herself for not being able to find them. Reg had different expectations for herself from what she would have for anyone else. If Marian or some other psychic had said they could not find a lost object or person, she would have thought nothing of it, but with herself it was different. "So... just go? You don't think there's any danger?"

"I lived in the Everglades for a while," Sarah said casually. "Back when they were trying to drain the water and reclaim it as farmland. But they found out... it isn't as easy as you would think. Working against Mother Nature is never a winning proposition. She has every reason in the world—literally—to protect herself."

"And you never had to worry about alligators or snakes when you lived there? They were more afraid of you and stayed out of your way?" Reg suggested.

"Oh, no. Why do you think I left?" Sarah asked with a ringing laugh.

Reg next phoned Officer Marta Jessup about it, because she didn't really have any other friends to get advice from. She and Jessup were always a bit at odds, with Reg's history as a con and Jessup being the long arm of the law. But they maintained an uneasy truce. Jessup was more cautious than Sarah had been.

"Damon seems like a nice enough guy, and you already know what it's like going on a trip with him—"

"Only, this time, I won't have a caffeinated pixie and two cats with me."

"Right. So in that way, it will be easier. But do you really want to be alone with this guy in the Everglades? Have either of you been there before?"

"No… but he says we'll get a guide, so I don't have to worry about that."

"Huh… I'm not sure it's that easy. Is this guide going to know how to find a lost wizard? You don't even know what part of the park he's in. It's a huge area."

"That's why I'm going; I'm the one who is going to find him. I already saw him in the crystal ball. It's not going to be that hard once I get there. I'm just worried about… you know… predators."

"Well, Corvin isn't going with you, is he? He's the predator that I'd be worried about."

Reg rolled her eyes and shook her head. "No, no Corvin this time either. Just me and Damon, a quick trip in and out. And the wizard, when I find him."

"How did he get lost there in the first place? How did Damon know that's where he was?"

Reg readjusted the phone and looked in the fridge for something good to eat. There were a few takeout clamshells but she wasn't sure what she wanted. Starlight yowled, having heard her from the bedroom. He told her how hungry he was and how she was remiss for having let him go so long without any food.

Reg pointed to his bowl of dry kibble. "What's that?" she demanded.

"What?" Jessup asked on the phone.

"Oh, sorry. Just talking to the cat. I don't know how Damon got a line on where this wizard is, but it was good information, because that's where I saw him."

"And how many other people are going to be out there looking for him? Are you going to end up in a big competition seeing who can get to this guy first? With prize money like that, you can bet that Damon's not the only one interested in finding the old guy."

Reg nibbled at a cold fried chicken leg. "I don't know. He didn't say other people were looking… but I guess you're right. There are bound to be others looking for him too."

"Yeah. I don't know if I would take it if I were you."

Reg took a larger bite of the chicken, nodding, even though Jessup couldn't see her response.

"Ah, who am I kidding?" Jessup said with a laugh. "If I was you, I absolutely would go. Even just being me, with no psychic powers, I'm thinking… I could get a few days off of work. I'm a trained investigator. I have just as many chances as anyone else of being able to find him. Why not me?"

Reg laughed. She snorted unexpectedly and then tried to tamp down the giggles at her own response. She felt the same way. Even though she knew she should be cautious, she wanted to go. She was ready for another adventure. One that didn't involve serial killers or weird accidents. Just a good old quest, like when they had gone to the mountains.

CHAPTER FIVE

*I*n the evening, Damon had been thrilled when Reg had reported her decision to go with him to find Wizard Wilson. Reg suspected he had known all along that she would decide to go. She was a little too predictable when it came to joining a cause or chasing down some challenge. Sometimes literally. They'd been through enough adventures—investigations—together that he knew how she would react.

He promised to take care of all of the arrangements.

Reg began packing some clothes and overnight things. They would hopefully only be two or three days. If they were there longer, she might have to buy another change of clothes or hand-wash stuff in the hotel sink.

There was a knock on the door. Reg left her packing and went to see who it was, expecting it to be Sarah. Maybe she had some kind of ward or talisman to help keep Reg safe in the Everglades.

But she felt a peculiar resistance as she approached the door. Like there was a force on the other side that she didn't want to encounter. A push like two magnets with the same poles pushing away from each other. She leaned in to look out the peephole. But the door was warm as she leaned into it, and she knew who it was before she put her eye to the lens.

She put the chain on the door and opened the door the two inches the chain would allow. A warlock stood there, his handsome face shadowed by the hood of his cloak. Short, dark goatee. Dark, penetrating eyed.

"Corvin."

"Regina," he purred.

Now that she could see Corvin's shadowy form outside her door and breathe in the pheromone-laden air around him, it was like the magnet had shifted poles, and she was now drawn toward him. She leaned against the wall, basking in the warmth that surrounded him. She had been distracted by her packing, and it was probably a good thing that they had a door between them so his charms couldn't pull her in.

"What are you doing here? I wasn't expecting you."

"Well, a little birdie was telling me about your newest quest…"

"Would that be a little bluebird?"

She could barely see Corvin's face, hidden in the shadows of his cowl. But she saw his mouth curve upward in a slight smile.

"Yes, a little bluebird," he admitted.

Despite Jessup repeatedly warning Reg away from Corvin, Jessup had a professional relationship with Corvin as a consultant or informer. They talked all too often for Reg's comfort, particularly when the subject matter was her.

"She didn't have any right to tell you about that."

"I don't think she broke any confidences. Why shouldn't she tell me that you're going on a little jaunt to the Everglades?"

"I didn't intend for her to spread it around to anyone else."

Reg was irritated, not only because Jessup told someone else her travel plans, which left Reg's cottage and gems open to burglary—as a law enforcement officer, Jessup really should know better—but also that she had told Corvin in particular. And now the warlock was on her doorstep. Reg knew what was coming next.

"It really isn't safe for you to go with him all by yourself," Corvin crooned. "I think that would be a bad idea."

"He isn't you. He isn't a predator."

"He isn't the same kind of predator," Corvin corrected. "But you have no idea whether he is safe in other ways. Just because he doesn't have the same nature as I do, that doesn't mean that he is… harmless."

"I can take care of myself."

"A woman, alone on the swamp with a warlock…"

"You seem to forget that I looked after myself before I came here. I'm not some damsel in distress. I can take care of myself. Even against *you*."

Despite herself, she was still leaning into the wall, almost sticking her nose out the door to breathe in the heady scent of roses that seeped from his pores. But with a physical barrier between them, she didn't have to be as careful. She didn't have to use her powers to stop him. That would take energy, and she needed her energy to finish packing and getting ready for the trip.

"I'm sure it won't take you long to pack," Corvin said.

"Get out of my head."

But thinking about packing distracted Reg from his visit and she started thinking about what else she would need to take with her. She had a leash for Starlight this time. She would need to pack other essentials for him.

"You can't take the cat with you."

Reg glared at him. She focused on putting up mental barriers to keep him out of her brain. But the two of them had shared too much in the past and there was always a conduit between them. She could shut the door, but she couldn't stop the light from getting in underneath and around the edges. "Why not?"

"It wouldn't be safe, Regina. The Everglades are wild. Full of animals and cryptids and all kinds of magic that you haven't encountered before."

"Cryptids?"

"Cryptids are… creatures that are not accepted by the scientific world. Creatures whose existence has not been properly proven to academia."

"What does that mean? Some kind of rare frogs?"

He laughed. "Well, certainly, they are always discovering new species of frogs and insects. But generally, it means things like… Bigfoot and the Loch Ness Monster."

"Oh." Reg thought about that for a minute. "There's a Loch Ness Monster in the Everglades?"

"That was just an example. Although there could possibly be a creature of that size in the Everglades. There are sharks and manatees."

Reg thought about Starlight. What was she thinking? If she took him with her, she'd just have to leave him in the hotel when they went exploring the Everglades. If they could even find a hotel that would let them keep a cat. Not all hotels liked pets. She couldn't exactly get Starlight in based on the fact that he was her familiar. That wasn't included in the statutes on assistance animals that couldn't be barred from commercial businesses.

She was going to have to find a pet sitter to look after him while she was gone. A heaviness settled in her middle at this thought. She didn't want to have to leave Starlight behind. He would think that she had abandoned him, even if she tried to explain it to him.

How had she gone from a carefree wanderer to someone who couldn't bear to leave her cat at home?

"Well then… I guess I have to make arrangements, so I don't have the time to visit with you," she told Corvin. "I'll see you in a few days when we get back."

He shifted, sending another wave of scent over her. "You should have someone else with you. Someone who knows more about the Everglades and who can make sure that Damon… doesn't take any liberties."

Reg laughed. "You want to be my chaperone now?"

Usually, he was the one she couldn't be alone with. She wasn't sure how many times she'd had to find a friend to join her so that Corvin couldn't use his charms to overcome her.

Corvin's shoulders shrugged under his cloak. She couldn't see his expression, but she could feel his irritation at being laughed at.

"I'm serious, Reg. You have no idea what you are walking into here. Does Damon know anything at all about the Everglades?"

"Well… I don't know. It sounded like we could just get a guide. Hire someone to drive us around, you know."

"A non-practitioner? They might know their way around the tourist sites, but they aren't going to know anything about the… darker areas of the swamp. Or about the magical creatures or dangers that lurk there. People disappear in there, Reg. They disappear and are never seen or heard from again."

"But if we had a guide…"

"Where are you going to get this guide? Just grab someone from the first boat rental place you see? Some college student making a few extra bucks driving tourists around?"

"I don't know."

"You need someone who has studied the Everglades. Someone who knows all about the river itself, the creatures there, the magic. There are curses and spells you wouldn't even dream of…"

"And I suppose you are an expert on the Everglades."

"I would never call myself an expert concerning something so ancient and complex, but…"

Despite his humble words, she felt his ego swelling behind them. Of course. He was offering himself as an expert. Her personal guide and escort. Making sure that she didn't get too close to Damon, who she supposed Corvin saw as a rival.

"If you want to come along, you'll have to talk to Damon. This is his thing, not mine. And I'm not splitting my prize money with you."

"I am not concerned with the prize money." Corvin paused to let the words sink in. "I am concerned with your welfare."

"Oh, I see. That's very generous of you."

"It's true, Regina." He sounded hurt that she wouldn't believe him, but Reg could feel his emotions. He wasn't bothered by her sarcasm.

"Something could happen to you. I don't trust Damon to be able to take care of you. He's young and untrained. He's not familiar with the dangers of the swamp. And if he is... then he would know to leave well enough alone. Don't try to solve the secrets of the Everglades."

The more he warned her off, the more interested Reg was in going. She wanted to prove herself and what she could do. She wanted to find out what he was talking about. She wanted to hit the road and start the adventure. And, as with most of the people who told her she couldn't do something, she wanted to prove him wrong.

"And he doesn't know about *you*," Corvin added.

Reg stared at him. He was smug, pleased with himself.

"What do you mean he doesn't know about me? He knows all about me."

"Does he?"

Reg started to protest. She had known Damon almost as long as she had known Corvin. Corvin had the advantage of having been inside Reg's head and of holding her powers for a short time. But other than that, he didn't have any more insight into Reg's life than Damon.

Then she knew what he was talking about. Their walk on the beach. When Reg... hadn't been herself. She swallowed.

"That hasn't happened again. I think it was just... a weird one-time thing. I was tired."

He laughed. "You were tired. I don't think that's what happens when people get tired."

"Well, maybe for me it does," Reg maintained stubbornly.

Corvin said nothing.

"Or it was the ocean," Reg said. "I won't be anywhere near the ocean."

"I wouldn't say you won't be near the ocean. You can't escape the ocean in Florida."

"But it isn't *in* the ocean," Reg argued impatiently. "Nothing is going to happen."

"You don't think that there should be someone there to keep an eye on things? Someone who can intervene if… you encounter something that the two of you and your *expert guide* can't handle?"

"Like I said… talk to Damon. He's the one you'll have to convince."

Corvin gave a nod. He took his phone out of his pocket and glanced down at it. "My battery is getting low, and I suspect this is going to be more than a two-minute conversation. Mind if I come in to charge it?"

"No, you are not coming in to charge your phone. Nice try. Go see if Sarah will let you in," Reg nodded to the big house at the front of the property, "or charge it in your car. Or better yet—go home!"

Corvin growled in dissatisfaction at her response and turned away from her. "See you tomorrow, Regina."

CHAPTER SIX

*C*orvin had clearly been able to talk Damon into allowing him to come along on the quest, because they were both there in the morning to pick Reg up. Damon's movements were jerky and his expression stormy. Reg looked over at Corvin, then back at him.

"What are the travel arrangements, then?"

"Separate vehicles," Corvin said. "We decided it would not work well for us to travel in one vehicle. So you can choose which warlock you would like to travel with..."

Reg knew very well that he wanted her to ride with him. And of course, it was a temptation. But for that reason alone, she knew that she couldn't ride with him. She needed to be with Damon, where she was safe. She could manage Corvin in small quantities, but she didn't know how long they would be in a car together and didn't want to be exhausted from resisting his wiles for hours on end.

"I'll go with Damon," she said breezily. "You both know the way, I assume?"

Damon nodded. Corvin didn't. He didn't say a word, but turned on his heel and stalked back out to his car. Damon smiled at Reg and extended his hand. "Can I help you with your luggage?"

"I can carry my own."

He shrugged. "All right. Your choice."

Reg hadn't packed a lot. It was only going to be a couple of days, and then they would be on their way back. If she could find the wizard as quickly as she had in the crystal ball, it would be no problem at all. Just a matter of the distances they needed to cover. She grabbed her duffel and she and Damon walked out to the front sidewalk. Corvin was in his white compact and Damon in his big truck. Reg was surprised he would use such a gas guzzler for the trip to the Everglades. It wasn't like they were off-roading. When they had gone to the mountains, they hadn't been sure what kind of conditions they would encounter, and the truck had made sense. But when they were just going to a park? One well-equipped to handle tourists? It seemed like a bit of overkill. But maybe it was just a statement toward Corvin. Male posturing. *My truck is bigger than yours.*

She threw her duffel into the second row of seating inside the cab, feeling a little pang that she didn't have a couple of cats and a pixie to liven up the trip this time. It had been a wild ride. Probably best that she didn't try to recreate it.

"Last call," Damon warned, buckling himself in, "Bathroom break? Turned off the stove?"

She looked at him. "Why would I have the stove on?"

Damon chuckled. "Some people use them to prepare food."

But he knew that Reg didn't really do any of her own cooking. Sometimes Sarah cooked for her. Sometimes she had takeout or went to the Crystal Bowl to eat. Or sometimes she warmed something up in the microwave. But she didn't think she had used the stove since she had moved there.

Damon pulled the truck out into the street and Corvin followed. They traveled close together for the first little while, but Corvin put on a burst of speed and whipped by them when they reached the highway. Damon's foot pressed down on the gas in response. Reg watched his speedometer creep up.

"You really want to get pulled over for speeding? I'm sure Corvin would love that."

Damon looked at her, then slowly backed off the gas, letting their speed reduce gradually. "Aren't you worried about *him* getting pulled over by the police?"

"He's got that whole charm thing going for him. He'd probably get a woman cop and completely bamboozle her. He has influence over men too, though I don't know how much. Probably enough to get off of a speeding ticket."

Damon let out a sigh of frustration. "You're probably right. And that's probably why he did it, too. So that I would get a ticket and he could just laugh at me about it."

Reg shrugged. She wouldn't put it past Corvin.

She watched out her window, letting her thoughts drift. She didn't want to think about Corvin. She didn't want to get tense about his going with them and she didn't want to get inside his head. She would just maintain the separation between them, and she would be able to be calm and relaxed. She needed to be open to inspiration when she got to the park, and she wouldn't be if she spent her time being irritated about Corvin.

Damon turned on the radio and flipped through his saved stations looking for something to listen to. "You don't mind, do you?"

"No, not at all. It's your truck."

"If there's something that drives you crazy to listen to, let me know. My tastes are pretty eclectic. If you don't like something, I'll switch over to something else."

He kept scanning through the stations to see what they were playing. It all sounded pretty homogenous to Reg. Mostly rock. Eighties. A few classic rock songs thrown in. Maybe a bit of heavier metal, but still pretty run-of-the-mill.

People said eclectic when they were trying to show off. Use big words and make you think that their tastes were varied and discerning.

She waited for him to settle on a station. Rock. Eighties. Who would have thought?

Damon looked at her sideways one more time to make sure she was okay with it. Reg shrugged. "Yes, this is fine."

"Good. Nice to have something on in the background. We can talk too, if you want. I'm not trying to drown out conversation."

"I think I'm just going to close my eyes for a few minutes. I'm not usually up yet at this time of day."

He didn't argue and point out that it was already past nine. Not like it was before dawn. But anything in the morning was too early for Reg. She was happiest when her day started at about lunchtime. After all, she was often up into the early morning with seances or other psychic readings.

Damon had a job with more conventional hours, so of course he was ready to start before she was.

But Reg didn't close her eyes. She continued to watch out the window, wondering how she would get through two or three more days with both Damon and Corvin so close together. The part where they were driving in separate vehicles was just fine. She could stand that. But when the two warlocks got onto a boat together and had to sit within a couple of feet of each other? That was going to be ugly. One of them might just end up in the river.

CHAPTER SEVEN

*R*eg hadn't actually expected to fall asleep. That had just been an excuse for not carrying on a conversation with Damon. But someone was shaking her by the arm and the truck was no longer moving. Reg blinked and yawned and looked around.

"Are we there already?"

"We're here," Damon agreed cheerfully. "This here," he leaned and pointed toward a shack with a touristy sign outside proclaiming various types of tours—gator tours, history tours, mystery tours, singles tours, and the like. "This is where we're meeting our guide."

Reg blinked and rubbed her eyes. That little shack? It was worse than Corvin had suggested.

"This is where you're getting a tour guide? You think they know what they're doing?"

Damon took off his dark glasses and looked at it. "I know it doesn't look like much, but Corvin knew a guy…"

Reg rubbed her forehead, which was starting to ache. She hated being woken up from a nap. She always felt groggy and headachy if someone else woke her up. She got out of the truck, and Damon did too. The shack didn't look any better close up.

"This is Corvin's guy?"

Damon nodded. He looked at her. "You don't think it's some kind of joke, do you? Setting us up with someone who doesn't know anything?"

"Who knows. Where is Corvin?"

"I don't see him." Damon looked around. "Maybe he *did* get pulled over."

"Let's go in. We might as well get started, whether he's here or not. No point in waiting around for him. Maybe he went to check in at the hotel first." She looked around but didn't see any close by. "Where is the hotel?"

"Hotel?" Damon shook his head. "There's no hotel."

"That we're staying in tonight. When we've done as much looking as we can today."

"No. There's no hotel. We're camping out." Damon indicated the bed of the truck. Reg turned her head and looked at the plasticky tarp spread out to cover the bulky items underneath. She lifted the edge and found herself looking at a rolled-up tent and other pieces of equipment.

Camping. No hotel.

"Didn't you bring a sleeping bag?" Damon asked.

Reg looked at her duffel in the back seat of the cab. He'd seen her stow her things away. He knew that the only thing she had was that bag. She supposed there were sleeping bags that could be collapsed down to tiny packages, but she didn't have one of those in her duffel bag. Just a few toiletries and changes of clothing.

"No. You never said to bring a sleeping bag."

"I guess... I just assumed you understood that part. It's a park. If you want to be spending a few days here, you need to be ready to camp."

Reg felt dismay at the thought. They were going to sleep on the soggy, cold ground? "I thought we'd sleep in a hotel and go into the Everglades during the day."

"That would limit how far we could search during the day. By at least half. There's a lot of ground to cover; we can't be going back to a hotel every day."

That was great. Just great.

Reg silently led the way to the tour shack. An early start. Sleeping on the cold, wet ground instead of sleeping in a dry, warm space. Two warlocks fighting over her. Unless Corvin had already gotten himself lost. If he were lost, maybe she would have one less thing to worry about.

She pushed in through the light, flimsy door of the shack. It was dim inside. And hotter than outside. No AC running. Reg waited for her eyes to adjust to the dark.

There was a spindly-looking table with a couple of wooden folding chairs pushed up to it. A cloaked warlock sat in one of the chairs. Reg looked around for the tour guide. Was he supposed to be there waiting for them? Was their tour scheduled for a particular time? She didn't want to miss a minute of their first day of searching. If she was going to have to sleep on the ground, she wanted to spend as little time in the park as possible.

The cloaked warlock stirred and looked around as if he had just noticed the arrival of other tourists. Reg saw that it was Corvin.

"Oh. You're here already."

Corvin made a show of pushing back his cloak to look at a watch. "I thought you'd be here an hour ago. Did you run into an accident?"

Reg reached automatically for Damon, wanting to make sure that he wasn't going to react in anger and start a brawl. At least give them a day of searching before they came to blows.

"Don't worry about him—" she started to warn.

"I don't care what he has to say, Reg," Damon said in a flat voice. "He can try to aggravate me as much as he likes. I'm not here to compare... life experiences. He can come on the search with us, or he can go back home. If he gets in my way too much, he'll be on his way home."

Corvin rolled his eyes, and he mentally nudged Reg. *Can you believe this guy?*

Reg didn't like talking about Damon in a way that he couldn't hear. If Corvin were going to mock Damon, he was going to have to do it verbally so that Damon could hear him. Reg wasn't going to participate in mocking him behind his back. She pushed Corvin away as much as she could.

"So, is someone meeting us here?"

Damon looked around for their guide.

"He's already outside," Corvin advised. "He wanted to get started on preparations. I told him that I would wait here and watch for you." Corvin looked at his wrist again. "He should be ready by now, I would think."

Reg turned back toward the door. She wanted to get out of the dead, stifling air and back outside, where at least there was a mild wind blowing.

She led the way out. She looked around but couldn't identify which boat held their guide. Several boats appeared to be ready to go, most with someone on board, either talking or tinkering with something.

Corvin pointed to one of the boats. Reg couldn't see the face of the guide who was aboard. He appeared to be a little on the short side, but solidly built. He wore khakis, mirrored sunglasses, and an outback hat with a broad brim to keep the sun out of his face. Most of the tour guides in the boats at the dock were dressed in a very similar fashion. Some were more formal, some with brighter-colored or flowery shirts, but all very similar.

Damon strode forward confidently as if he knew the guide well, instead of it being someone that Corvin had suggested.

"You must be Mr. Tybalt," he greeted heartily.

The man turned his head to look at Damon more closely. "Just Tybalt," he said in a gravelly voice with an accent that Reg couldn't quite place. "You Damon, then?"

"Yes. I'm Damon, and this is—"

"All aboard, then. We're wasting daylight. It was my understanding that you wanted to spend as much time as possible searching for this... person."

Damon nodded briskly. "Right." He agreed. "Let me just grab my gear, and we'll be on our way."

He hurried back toward his truck. Corvin went to his car, popping the trunk with the key fob on the way. As Damon got his camping gear out of the truck bed, Reg went over and grabbed her duffel from the cab. She wasn't going to let Damon forget it. She was still going to have to figure out what to do about a sleeping bag, but she wasn't going to have any of the rest of her stuff left behind.

She took it to the boat and tossed it in. The tour guide looked up at her as if she had done something she wasn't supposed to.

"What? That's my stuff. We need it."

"Needs to go in the hold." He gestured to a hatch behind him.

"Oh, sure. No trouble."

It wasn't as if he had opened the hatch for her and she had expected him to act as a porter. Reg climbed from the dock onto the flat little boat and relocated her bag. The boat rocked and tipped as she moved around.

"You don't have any gear, do you?" she asked Tybalt. "Damon didn't exactly tell me that we were camping. I didn't bring a sleeping bag."

He looked her over slowly. His face was broad and round. His skin was pale. Almost a green or gray cast to it. He scratched the back of his neck as he considered her question.

"I don't usually supply guests with supplies."

"No. That makes sense. It's just that… I'm going to need somewhere. Is there somewhere near here I can go and buy one? Or somewhere close to where we'll be touring? I'm sorry to be such a pain. Like I say…" She watched Damon struggling to scoop everything up and bring it to the boat. "Damon didn't tell me we were camping. I thought there would be a hotel."

Tybalt shook his head. "There are no hotels in the park."

"Okay. I know that now. But before we got started, I just assumed. I figured if it is this big, then there must be hotels. You get lots of tourists through here, don't you? Wouldn't it be better if there was a hotel?"

He spat over the side of the boat. A glob of spittle hit the side of the boat next to him and slowly started to slide down the surface. "I don't like hotels."

"Okay… well, I guess that's why you live here. You can do your job and you don't need to pay for a hotel. That's great for you."

Corvin got back to the boat before Damon. He had a few bags and handed them down to Reg, who put them into the hold.

"Did you bring a sleeping bag?" she asked him.

Corvin raised his brows. "Of course."

"Damon didn't tell me to. So I'm trying to figure out where I'm going to sleep."

Corvin's mouth curved into a smile. "Why, of course I'd be happy to share my sleeping bag with you, Reg."

"I'm not sharing a sleeping bag with anyone."

"I do have a… deluxe size. I like to have freedom of movement. And, of course, the opportunity to rescue a lady in distress."

Reg remembered how she had told him that she wasn't a damsel in distress. And already, before they had even started the tour, she had run into problems and she was asking him for help.

Well, she hadn't exactly asked him for help. Just explained her dilemma and asked whether he had a sleeping bag.

"I don't need your sleeping bag. Maybe you and Damon could sleep together and I could borrow his."

"That's not nearly as attractive an idea."

Damon struggled up to the boat, unbalanced under his load, and was going to drop it all if he weren't careful. Reg tried to take things from him one at a time, but that didn't work and he just dumped everything on the edge of the dock and down onto the boat. Reg picked up what had fallen onto the boat and put it into the hold.

"We've decided that you and Corvin are going to share a sleeping bag," she told Damon. "Since you forgot to tell me to bring one. And I can use yours." She looked over at Corvin. "Corvin's is deluxe size and he said he won't have any problem fitting both of you."

Damon looked at Corvin. Corvin rolled his eyes and shook his head. "You know I said no such thing."

Damon gave a gasp of shock. "You lied to me, Reg?"

Reg grabbed a few more items from him and put them into the hold. "How much of this stuff do you need? You must have packed half your house!"

"I like to be comfortable when I camp."

"Then you should camp in a hotel. No wet ground or snakes."

CHAPTER EIGHT

*T*hey were finally on their way.

No one had killed anyone yet. Though Reg had certainly wondered at times whether they were going to be able to avoid bloodshed. How Corvin had managed to convince Damon to allow him to come on the trip, Reg didn't know. There was no love lost between the two of them. Reg suspected that Corvin had been one of the bullies in school and, while Damon was not a small man, he might still have been bullied as a boy, or had seen other people bullied by Corvin. That would explain a lot.

Except that they were not, as far as Erin could tell, the same age. That sort of threw a wrench into that theory.

Maybe Damon just recognized a type. Corvin wasn't exactly a shrinking violet.

Their guide took them out into the water and immediately started a practiced patter about the Everglades as he first circled the inlet and then pulled out into the river. He gave some basic tips on boat safety—mostly logical stuff like not trying to rock the boat, not all rushing to one side at the same time, and not drinking alcohol to excess. They were all given life jackets, but when Tybalt said how shallow most of the Everglades River was, Reg and the others put them aside. What was the point in wearing a life jacket when you could touch the bottom?

Except maybe to shove in the mouth of any alligator that tried to eat them.

Reg scanned the water ahead for alligators. Why did she have to go somewhere there were alligators and crocodiles? Why couldn't the wizard have gotten lost in Disney World? Lots of people went to Disney World.

She was sure that each fallen or floating log was the elongated body of one of the predators. She didn't hear much about what Tybalt had to say about the plants they were passing by and the animals that they might see.

"The Florida panther is nearly extinct," he told them. "You aren't going to see one of those. They're too shy of people."

"I would be too if someone was killing off my species," Reg muttered.

She saw Corvin look at her. He raised one brow. She thought about her own statement, wondering why he cared what she said. Then she remembered several different times when Corvin or one of the other people who knew about him had told her that his kind was dying out. She was glad of it. She didn't think there was a place in their society, even in magical society, for a predator like he was, always on the prowl to steal powers from people like Reg. It was good that they were a dying breed.

But Corvin probably didn't think so.

Reg looked back in the direction the boat was traveling, trying to listen to Tybalt's patter and take in everything he had to say. Like Corvin had said, she needed to know about the Everglades and have a guide who knew what he was talking about if they were to find Wilson as quickly as possible.

She moved from her seat to one that was closer to Tybalt. He looked at her, waiting for an explanation as to what she wanted.

"Have you ever heard of anyone getting lost in the park?" she asked.

The guide laughed.

Reg didn't see what was so funny about her question. She stared at him, trying to silence him with her icy gaze. "Well?"

"Anyone getting lost in the park?" he repeated. "Yes, of course. People get lost here all the time."

"I don't mean just for a few hours, or a day, or whatever. I mean… for days…"

"The park swallows people whole," Tybalt said. "There are people missing here all the time. And the swamp doesn't give up its secrets. Once you are lost in the Everglades, you stay lost."

"Lots of people get lost here?"

He nodded. "Probably more than we'll ever know about. There is a ghost village where Seminole once lived, but then they all disappeared. There have been many men, women, and children lost. There have been planes that have crashed here, and all of their passengers have been lost. The swamp swallows them all up."

"Oh." Reg turned and looked at Damon. "If that many people disappear here forever, how will we find the wiz—Wilson? I thought…"

"That's why you're here," Damon pointed out. "Everybody else who is searching does not have a psychic with them. If you're just wandering through the park looking at random places, then of course you aren't going to be able to find someone. It's too big to do an effective grid search, and there is too much water for scent dogs to follow anyone for long. But we can overcome all of those obstacles because we have you."

Reg turned to look forward again. She had sort of forgotten why she was there. She was thinking the guide would take them to the place they were to search, and they would do just what Damon had said—wander around randomly looking for him. But of course, that was never what had been intended.

She closed her eyes to focus, and sent her senses out into the park around her, searching for the wizard. She knew he was there. She had already seen him in one vision. So she recalled that vision. She remembered the cloaked form, the wrinkled face under the hood. She breathed in deeply, letting the feelings grow inside of her, reaching out in all directions with all of her senses.

She could feel something. Like a beacon in the darkness, pulsing on and off, glowing in the darkness and then disappearing. She couldn't see him clearly this time because she didn't have her crystal ball and Starlight there to amplify the signal. But she could still sense something.

Reg looked back over her shoulder to Damon, unsure what to do next. "I think… we should go that way." She pointed.

Damon raised his brows. "We're going to the location he was last seen."

"Okay… but what if he isn't there? How long has it been since he was seen there?"

"Why don't you think he's going to be there? Or at least in the immediate area."

"I think we should go that way." She pointed again.

She didn't want to make a big scene in front of the guide. She didn't know if he was a practitioner or not, and she didn't like to talk too much about her powers in front of the non-magical community. Damon had already outed her, talking about her psychic abilities in front of the guide, but Reg didn't want to emphasize the point. Many people believed in psychic powers in a vague, uncertain way. Few actually thought they could get clear answers to their questions through paranormal powers and fewer still demonstrated their abilities in front of others. Unless they were part of a show.

Talk too much or too confidently about having psychic powers, and a person was asking to get herself thrown in the loony bin for evaluation.

Again.

Reg would prefer to avoid that.

Damon considered. Then he shrugged. He had, after all, brought her for her expertise. He leaned forward and tapped on the guide's shoulder, raising his voice to be heard clearly.

"We would like to go that way." He pointed in the direction Reg had indicated.

"There's nothing over there," Tybalt said, shaking his head. "Just tourist stuff. If this guy has really disappeared into the swamp, you're not going to turn him up in some gift shop or gator farm."

"You never know where we might find him," Damon disagreed. "We don't know whether something happened to him or whether he took off on his own."

"You said the guy was lost."

"Well, we think he is."

"I've seen people looking for lost loved ones. They don't go to tourist traps to do it. They look where it is wild."

"We're going that way," Damon insisted. "I'm not sure what we're going to find. Maybe nothing. But we're paying you to be our guide, so you go where we say."

Tybalt turned to glare at Damon. He held his gaze on Damon for an uncomfortably long time. Reg held on to the side of the boat, anxious about his not looking where he was going.

"You hired me for my expertise," he told Damon. "So why aren't you taking it? If you just wanted someone who would go wherever your whims dictated, there are plenty of youngsters out there who haven't got a clue what they are doing and will go wherever you say."

"It's not one or the other," Corvin said, leaning forward and inserting himself into the conversation. "We need the combination of your expertise and our knowledge. Regina believes we have a better chance of finding Professor Wilson if we go that way. It doesn't hurt you to give it a try. I'm sure there are plenty of places to look over there, despite it being a more populated area."

Tybalt rolled his eyes. He turned the wheel of the boat, and they skimmed over the water in the new direction. Reg tried to stay focused on the pulsing beacon in her consciousness and to keep them pointed toward it.

CHAPTER NINE

*R*eg tried to pay attention to the sights as they skimmed their way toward the quarry. There were all kinds of plant and animal life that the guide was chattering about as he drove. He'd clearly been a guide for a long time and was serious about his work. He pointed out birds, clumps of what just looked to Reg like grass, and wove in a little history of the park into his narrative.

But she wasn't nearly as interested in his patter as she was on homing in on the missing wizard. Maybe she could actually get it done in a day. They could find the wizard, make arrangements to get him back to Black Sands and the Spring Games, and collect their reward money. Not bad for a day's work. And maybe they could avoid the part about camping.

The scent of the water was alluring. She hadn't noticed it at first, but as they flew over the water and a fine spray kicked up into her face, Reg grew more aware of it. It smelled more like the ocean than like a river, at least to her. She sniffed, trying to analyze it. It was swampy or marshy, like she had expected it to be. She could smell the rich mud under the river, the green plants growing under the surface and rising out of it. And there were animals.

She couldn't *really* smell the animals, but she thought she could. Frogs and fish. Unseen things that were bigger and older and had been in the water for many years.

They followed a bend in the river and the breeze that had previously been blowing in her face was now coming from the side. It brought her the scents of Tybalt and Damon. She hadn't been aware of their unique scents before that. Damon had good hygiene. It wasn't like he smelled rank. But Reg could detect his musky odor, his salty sweat, and earthy undertones that she couldn't quite identify. *Eau de Damon.*

Their guide, on the other hand, did have a much ranker smell. She was surprised she could smell anything of Damon or the water itself with his stench blowing into her. She readjusted her position, pulling back from him slightly and turning her head to the side to try to avoid breathing his scent any more than she had to.

Tybalt smelled like… dead things. It was a smell Reg associated with funerals and cemeteries. A musty odor of mold and decay. She gagged, moving closer to the side of the boat to get away from the smell and be able to throw up over the side if she couldn't control her reaction.

"Regina?" Corvin's voice was curious. "Something wrong?"

She tried to school her face to keep from screwing up her expression to give away her disgust.

"Just… a minute. Just give me a minute."

He watched her. She could feel his eyes focused on her back. She could feel him beginning to press in on her, to try to catch onto her thoughts. She pushed back. He didn't need to know how much their smells disgusted her.

Corvin's scent… If the breeze had been coming from the other side, then it would be his scent washing over her, and she knew his scent intimately. The cloying roses that she smelled when he was charming her, his body warming and sending out waves of pheromones and the scents intended to attract her and pull her closer to him. But the wind wasn't blowing that way. It was blowing Tybalt's foul stench into her nostrils.

"Do you want a drink?" Corvin offered.

Reg saw the soft-sided cooler filled with water bottles beside his seat. "Yeah. Hand me one of those."

He pulled one out, cracked the top, and gave it to her. Reg drank a few swallows. It wasn't ice cold, but it was still cool, the bottle sweating in the muggy heat of the day. Reg tipped her head back and trickled water on her face as well, hoping it would help combat the nausea she was starting to feel at being trapped in the boat with the three men. She wished she hadn't moved into the seat next to Tybalt and wondered if it would look rude if she vacated the seat for one of the others. Next to Corvin? Next to Damon? She wasn't sure which would be the better scenario. Maybe she was better off not sitting beside either of the warlocks.

The water over her face seemed only to increase the restlessness she was feeling. She decided that she needed to switch seats, whether it looked rude or not. Tybalt wasn't anyone she would ever run into again. What did she care what he thought anyway?

She stood up and carefully made her way to the seat by Damon. He smiled.

"You doing okay? You're not seasick, are you? I didn't think you could get seasick on an airboat."

Reg settled into her seat. She took another gulp of water. "No, not seasick, just…" She wasn't sure how to explain her heightened sense of smell to him. It was just some trick of the Everglades air. Or maybe a side effect of reaching out with her psychic senses. She poured a little water into her cupped palm and rubbed it all over her face.

"Too hot?" Damon suggested. "I thought you were acclimatized to Florida and this wouldn't be a problem. But you have to be careful of heat-stroke. Dehydration."

Reg lifted her water bottle slightly to show that she was keeping herself hydrated.

"Do you need anything else? You should have a better hat. Something with a wider brim. That red-head complexion…"

Reg touched the ball cap she had grabbed at the last moment before leaving the cottage. He was probably right, but the ball cap was keeping her face shaded from the sun. "No, it's fine."

He shifted closer to her, sending another wave of scent Reg's direction. Her breath caught in her throat. He smelled *so good* she couldn't help leaning toward him, drinking his smell in like a fine wine. How had she never noticed before how good he smelled?

Damon raised his eyebrows, looking at her uncertainly. Could he read what she was thinking in her face? How weird was it for her to be so entranced by his smell? Corvin, sure, his enticing scent was one of his charms, designed to lure the unsuspecting in. But she had never noticed how great Damon smelled.

"Regina."

The single word from Corvin was a warning. Reg froze, then looked over at him. What was he doing, interfering with her business? He didn't have any right to be in her territory. She cut a glare toward him.

"Reg, think," he said in a quiet tone, hardly audible above the sound of the airboat's engine. Or maybe it wasn't audible; maybe it was inside her head. "I think that the... *humidity* is getting to you."

She shook her head at him in irritation.

"I don't think the water on your face is a good idea," he warned.

"What are you going on about, Corvin?" Damon asked, turning his head to look at the older warlock. "What's wrong with water on her face? You think it's going to wash off her sunscreen?"

"I just don't think it's a good idea," Corvin said, giving Reg a significant look. "Try to stay out of the spray. Maybe move back here with me." He nodded to the empty seat next to him.

He clearly just wanted to get her closer to him. He was always trying to take advantage of the situation at hand and to trick her into allowing him close enough to use his charms to convince her to give up her powers to him. But they both knew that she could turn the tables on him. She could use her powers on *him*.

Like a switch had been flipped, Reg suddenly realized what he was talking about. Water on her face. It was somehow triggering her siren instincts. Her unexpectedly enhanced sense of smell. How delectable Damon smelled when she had never before noticed any particular smell around him. She glanced over at him.

Even understanding what Corvin was warning her about, it was difficult to make a decision based on logic instead of instinct. Every cell in her body wanted Damon. Wanted him close, warm against her body, his neck right under her nose, blood pulsing...

Reg took another drink, her mouth dry and her tongue sticking to the roof of her mouth. Was that all it took now? The spray of the river water or the spring water she had dribbled and wiped over her face? The last time she had been in the ocean, and the instinct had been so powerful that she had barely been able to resist it, and it was lucky that Corvin was as strong as he was and quick to understand what was going on.

Damon was still shaking his head, not understanding Corvin's warning or what the two of them were worried about.

"I'll... maybe I will come back there with you," Reg suggested.

Corvin nodded and moved the cooler and a couple of other items out of the way so that she had plenty of room to sit comfortably.

"Watch out for him, Reg," Damon warned. "Don't let him get away with anything. You know how dangerous he is."

Reg settled into the seat next to Corvin and looked at Tybalt to see if he had heard this. He would have to be wondering what was going on too. Why Reg was acting so bizarrely and what she had to fear from Corvin. Even if he were a practitioner, he might not understand what Corvin was. And he had no way of knowing what Reg was. She was still trying to figure it all out.

"Are you sure?" Damon persisted. "If you just want to sit at the back of the boat, Corvin could move forward. Up here beside Tybalt. I'm sure they'd find lots to talk about." He looked hard at Corvin. "Didn't you say that one of the reasons you were coming along was to study the creatures native to the Everglades? Ones that you couldn't find anywhere else in the world?"

Tybalt turned his head, looking interested at this. "Are you a zoologist?"

"No," Corvin said shortly. "It's just one of the areas of study I find very interesting. I'm a professor. History, mostly, but the animal world fascinates me. Especially the... less common species."

They all exchanged looks at Corvin's "less common species," which obviously meant the magical variety. Their guide considered this information. His eyes went to each of them in turn. "I assume, by what has been said and done here, that you all... have an interest in the unseen?"

Reg nodded, glad to finally have it out in the open. It was difficult for her to know what to say and not say and how to determine whether someone was a magical practitioner or not. It all seemed very complicated, and she had not grown up in a community like Black Sands, where there were so many practitioners in one place. No one had known of her talents back then, so she hadn't grown up learning how to deal with the divide.

"There are indeed many species in the swamp that you will not find in other parts of the world," Tybalt said. It was an invitation for Corvin to join him at the front of the boat so that they could discuss the details. But Corvin didn't stir from where he was.

"I look forward to discussing the topic with you at length tonight."

Tybalt looked at him for a moment, one eyebrow raised, then shook his head and turned to look ahead of the boat again, concentrating on the navigation.

Damon looked frustrated with Corvin and Reg. He had done his best to fix everything, but Corvin and Reg made no move to separate from each other. It was understandable that this concerned him. He knew what kind of a predator Corvin was and how he had taken advantage of Reg in the past. But he didn't know how strong Reg had grown and that she didn't have to worry about Corvin overcoming her again.

At least, she didn't think so.

She knew who and what he was now, and he wouldn't find a way to trick her again. She hoped.

Corvin studied Reg's face. After a few moments, he bent over and rifled through the supplies he had kept close to himself. He found a towel and handed it to Reg. She took it from him and considered it for a moment. Did water on her face really make that much of a difference to her nature? Or was there something more that had triggered a resurgence of her siren nature? Being in close quarters with three potential prey? Being stressed or hungry? Maybe just the length of time it had been since it had happened last, a phase of the moon or a certain tide?

She raised the towel to her face and dabbed the water off.

The wind seemed to slacken slightly, and her chest and shoulders relaxed. She hadn't realized she had been holding herself so tense. She avoided looking at Corvin, just gazing out over the water. The restlessness she had been feeling gradually diminished. She took a few deep breaths, and when she looked back at Corvin, she felt normal. She shifted her gaze to his throat and was not drawn to the pulse point.

She gave him a little nod and went back to staring at the scenery.

CHAPTER TEN

*R*eg had thought that when they got closer to the wizard, her feelings about where he was would get stronger, but the opposite seemed to happen. She felt more muddled the closer they got to larger populations. When they pulled up to the dock that was close to where she had felt the wizard earlier, she couldn't focus in on him. It was like she had been focusing on a single signal, but when they got to the area, she was suddenly getting nothing but interference.

Reg rubbed her temples, looking at all of the tourists bustling around. Tybalt gave her an *I-told-you-so* look and sat back with his arms folded across his chest. Damon ignored both of their reactions and was cheerful. Way too cheerful.

"Well, we know he's around here somewhere. Just because you can't immediately identify where he is, that doesn't mean that he's not here. You need something to eat—we all need something to eat—and some time to center yourself, and then I'm sure it will be much easier."

Reg decided that eating something was not a bad idea. The nausea she had felt earlier when she'd been able to smell Tybalt was gone and she could definitely eat something.

"We'll meet you back here?" she asked their guide. "In… how long? A couple of hours? Or should we call and let you know?" She looked at Damon and Corvin for guidance.

"We'll call," Corvin said coolly, looking at Tybalt. "I expect it will be at least two hours."

Tybalt scowled at them. He waited for them to get what they needed from the boat and disembark. Then he turned up the engine and pulled away from the dock, speeding out into the center of the sheltered cove.

"Did we insult him?" Reg asked. "Should we have invited him to lunch?"

"You don't invite someone like him to lunch," Corvin said in a tone that Reg thought was a little stuck up. *Someone like him?*

She opened her mouth to argue with him and demand to know what exactly he'd meant by that. Damon walked into the breach, holding up his hand in a "stop" signal and putting himself partway between them physically.

"Where do you want to go?" he asked Reg. "Anything in specific that strikes your fancy?"

Reg looked around. There were a few eateries in view, mostly little independent places, not big chains. She wasn't sure what to expect from any of them, but she was not a picky eater. She'd eat just about anything. She reviewed the options. There was a fish and seafood place with a striped blue and white awning. She pointed to it.

"How about there?"

No one objected. The three of them started walking toward it. They were walking along an actual boardwalk, built above the surface of the marshy ground to give them dry, secure footing. There were too many people moving back and forth over the boards for her comfort. She didn't like to be crowded. She liked to be able to see any approaching danger. There were too many people to watch.

As they got to the end of the first block, her gaze was drawn to the right, where another street opened up and she saw a garish sign painted with the letters "Skunk Man Saloon" and the roughly drawn figure of what looked like a reddish-brown Bigfoot. She stopped and looked at it.

"What's that?"

"Skunk Man?" Damon asked. He laughed. "Just a local legend. Every nature preserve needs its mythical beast."

Reg looked at Corvin. "Is this what you were talking about?"

"In the boat, when we were talking with Tybalt about rare creatures? That's one of them, yes."

"And at home, when you were talking about… creepers?"

"Cryptids," he corrected. "Yes, Skunk Man definitely qualifies as a cryptid."

"What is he?"

"Why don't we go in? I'm sure they'll be happy to tell you all about him."

Reg hesitated, then nodded. "Yeah. Let's do it."

Damon rolled his eyes, but didn't seem to care that much that Reg had changed her mind about where they would eat. Or maybe just get a drink; Reg didn't know if the saloon sold food or just drinks. They moved as a group down the branching boardwalk and entered the little shop.

The lighting was dim. The walls were covered with pictures and plaques and various kinds of memorabilia. Plaster casts of feet, bits of hair or hide. Other displays that Reg couldn't make out at a distance. A bar ran the length of the back, and a few tables and chairs were set up in the floor space. There was a hand-lettered sign that advised clientele to seat themselves, so they picked one of the two tables that had not been taken. There was a couple with a young child in a highchair at another table, and three older, retired-looking gentlemen sharing a meal at another. Reg looked at them as she put her hand on the back of a chair to pull it out.

"Go ahead," said one of them with a friendly smile. "Bess will be out to take your order in a minute or two. They're short-staffed in the kitchen today."

Reg smiled and nodded. She pulled the chair out and sat down. She looked at the other guests curiously. She hadn't expected to see families with young children in the Everglades. It didn't seem like the kind of place that was made for little children. The retirees made some sense. They all looked like tourists, with colorful shirts and wide-brimmed hats that looked brand new. Out enjoying their retirement savings. It wasn't the Museum of Natural History, but it was an interesting place to visit.

She picked up one of the menus left on the table and started flipping through it. She found the layout confusing, with information about the Everglades and the Skunk Man interspersed among the groups of menu items. She wasn't sure if the passages were supposed to be read in conjunction with the descriptions of the food options or whether they were supposed to read them while eating the courses referenced. Either way, Reg wasn't much of a reader and the dense panels of text were a bit much for her.

An older woman came charging through the bat-wing doors that connected to the kitchen. She was overweight, busty, and sweating, her hair damp at the temples.

"Sorry, sorry," she called out to them. "Hope you made yourself comfortable. We're just a bit understaffed today, but you're still going to get your food and be joining up with your tour again in no time. Trust me. Have you had a chance to look at the menu? Drink orders?" She held a notepad at the ready, waiting for one of them to dive right in.

They each placed their drink orders. Corvin and Damon were flipping through their menus, looking at the various offerings, but Reg's head hurt and she didn't have the patience to sort out what to order. She liked menus with lots of display pictures of the food, but this one didn't have room for them, with all of the side panels and Bigfoot pictures.

"Do you have a special today?"

Bess glibly recited a "catch of the day" meal.

Reg nodded. "Yeah, that sounds good."

"Good choice!" Bess told her. Damon ordered, then finally Corvin, closing his menu slowly. Bess gathered up the menus.

"Can we get refills?" the man at the retirees' table called out to her before she could disappear into the kitchen. He gestured to the glasses at their table.

"Of course," Bess agreed, and then was gone again. Reg sat back.

"You know that the 'special' and 'catch of the day' is just the stuff in the kitchen that's going to expire and they want to get rid of, don't you?" Corvin suggested.

Reg shook her head. "What? No."

He nodded. "You're just being a sucker if you order the special."

Reg shrugged. It was just like Corvin to act like a snob about the little restaurant.

"Oh, I was going to ask her about the Skunk Man," Reg said. She looked around at the memorabilia mounted on the walls. "I guess Skunk Man is just like the Florida version of Bigfoot?"

"The legend of the Skunk Man goes way back," the round-faced, balding man at the retirees' table contributed, inserting himself into the conversation. "Back to legends of the Indians that lived in these parts. It's pretty much a Sasquatch. But one that smells really bad."

Reg nodded. Many of the pictures on the wall showed dark figures that could have been a Sasquatch. or could have been a man in an ape suit or a bear. It was hard to classify them all. Some looked more Sasquatch-like than others. "So is there just one? Or are there a bunch of them…?"

"They aren't seen very often, but since the Indians have been seeing them for hundreds of years, there would have to be more than one," the man suggested. "Humans don't live that long, so I can't imagine that a human-like animal would. Not without modern medicine."

"They could have medicine. Or they could be magical."

The man laughed. "They could be magical," he repeated. "Well, I suppose I can't argue with you there. Maybe that's how they keep from being seen. Maybe they can turn themselves invisible, and it's only when they forget to that we get a picture or a sighting."

It could happen. Reg had seen other creatures who could make them-selves invisible or transport themselves to a different location. Pixies. Davyn, the firecaster who was mentoring her. Elves. Even the gnomes sometimes seemed to blend in so well with their surroundings that they might as well be invisible. Why not Bigfoot?

The other two men at the table immediately began to argue with the first, insisting that the Skunk Man was real, and that they had seen him, or had a friend or relative who had seen him.

Bess brought out a tray of drinks for Reg's table and the retirees. The couple with the child asked for their bill. Reg looked at the preserved Bigfoot footprints on the wall. It was hard to tell at that distance exactly how large they were, but they definitely looked bigger than a large man's footprint. Maybe there was something to the legend.

The talk at the retirees' table had somehow shifted to aliens and UFO sightings. Reg listened to them for a moment before turning back to Damon and Corvin. She sipped her cola. She knew it wasn't good for her, but the sugar and caffeine would do her a world of good. She was lagging and in need of a nap. Her head hurt. And she still had to look more for the missing wizard. If she were right, he was there somewhere in the small settlement. She just wasn't sure where. She hadn't seen anyone who was dressed like or looked like the man in her vision.

She sucked down several swallows of the drink through her straw and tried to relax, letting the sugar do its thing.

"So what else lives in the Everglades?" she asked Corvin. "Bigfoot and what else?"

"Lots of things." He spread his hands apart to indicate a wide variety of choices. "There is talk of gator men, but I think that's just fanciful. Swamp goblins. Foxfire. Many of the species that you will find in other parts of the world. And the animals that you are more familiar with. Crocs and gators, Florida panthers, many endangered species."

"What are gator men?"

"Torso of a man, hindquarters of an alligator."

"But you don't think they exist?"

He shrugged. "I haven't read anything convincing. And when you think about it, the scariest part of an alligator is the front end, not the back. It would make more sense if it had the jaws of an alligator and the legs of a man."

Reg shuddered. "I don't like the sound of either one."

"I don't think that's one you need to worry about."

"But goblins? You think there are really swamp goblins?"

He nodded slowly. "I've seen a goblin or two in my time. I don't doubt that there are some around here. There are many other phenomena to beware of in the Everglades as well. Like our guide says, a lot of people disappear here. Sometimes whole boats or planes. You've heard of the Bermuda Triangle?"

Reg nodded. "So… why? Is it because of bad luck? Or just because it's a big, wild area? Or the water?" She couldn't see the river from her seat in the restaurant, but she stared out the window toward it. If there were big creatures in it, like Corvin had said, then it must be deep.

"In most places, it's not more than a few feet deep," Damon contributed. "You could stand up in it with no danger of drowning."

"But the Everglades still has its secrets," Corvin warned. "Sometimes, the secrets are just below the surface."

Reg took a few more swallows of her soft drink, starting to regret that she hadn't ordered something stronger. But with the way she had been feeling, she wanted to keep her wits about her, not to dull them.

CHAPTER ELEVEN

*a*ny sign of you-know-who?" Damon asked, keeping his voice low.

Reg frowned at him. "Who?" She immediately thought of Voldemort in Harry Potter, but was pretty sure Damon didn't mean him.

"The one we are looking for," Damon said, an edge of impatience entering his voice.

"Oh, okay. I just didn't know..." She frowned. "He's not evil like you-know-who, is he? We wouldn't be looking for him and taking him back to the Games if he was evil."

"What are you talking about?"

Maybe actual magical practitioners didn't watch movies about magic. It would be like cops watching cop shows and complaining about all of the inaccuracies. Reg's face warmed.

"I don't know." She closed her eyes and again pictured the figure she had seen in her vision. Where was he? That tall, dark-cloaked figure had to be close by. She had felt drawn there. She knew that's where he had been. But everything was fuzzy and confused when she tried to focus on his image. "I'm sure we're in the right place. He was close by. But... I don't know where he is now. Maybe... he can cloak himself. Maybe he knew someone was looking for him."

Damon sat back, frowning. "Maybe," he agreed. "But if he's lost in the swamp, why would he not want to be found? Why would he be cloaking himself?"

"He could be in danger," Corvin suggested. "Not from us, of course, but he could be trying to avoid some other person or creature. It might just be a coincidence that he hid himself as we got closer."

Reg looked around. "If he was here, then he's not exactly lost, though, is he? I mean? He's in civilization, not lost in the swamp."

"Unless…" Damon thought it through, "someone else is hiding him. What if he was captured or kidnapped? He could be here, but within a force-field or held under some kind of spell."

Corvin nodded. "It's possible he's under someone else's power."

"I thought he was this powerful wizard. If he's so powerful, then how does someone kidnap him and keep him under their control?"

"Power is relative. Just because you are powerful, that doesn't mean there isn't someone more powerful." He raised an eyebrow at Reg. This was something that Reg had experience with. On several different occasions.

"Okay, yeah," she agreed. She had thought that they wanted the wizard at the Spring Games because he was the most powerful, but maybe someone else didn't want him to go to the Games, and that person—or creature—was stronger. "So do you think he is here? Or came through here? Do we spend our time looking for him or…?"

Damon considered this thoughtfully. Corvin and Reg watched him, waiting for his decision. The waitress brought their dishes, asked briskly if they needed anything else, and then hurried away before they had time to answer.

They all tasted their meals and made appreciative noises. Reg looked around and waited for Damon's answer.

"I think that if he is here or has been here, then we need to trace him backward and try to get more information. The rumors were that he was closer to the Ghost Village. It will be easier to trace him backward than forward, maybe get some more intelligence as to what's going on, enough information to predict his movements and be able to home in on him."

Reg looked at Corvin to see what he thought of this. If the wizard were nearby, then it would make more sense to try to find him there.

"Why go backward?" Corvin asked, echoing the sentiment.

"We know where he's been. We don't know where he's going."

"Isn't that why we have a psychic with us?"

Damon looked at Reg, then nodded. "Yes… and if Reg has an idea of where he was going next, that would be great, but…" He trailed off.

"We can at least look around here for him," Reg pointed out.

"Well… I wouldn't know where to look. Do you?"

"We can walk around this development, or hamlet, or whatever you call it. See if we see him or can pick up his trail." Reg met Corvin's eyes again. He was nodding in agreement. "It's stupid to go looking for him somewhere else when we know that he's here."

There was silence for a few minutes. Reg looked down at her plate and pushed the food around. She wasn't very hungry. She was more angry than hungry. Why would Damon bring her along, beg her to come with him, if he wasn't going to listen to her when she connected with him?

"The thing is," Damon said slowly. "We don't *really* know that he is here."

"Yes, we do. I—" Reg stopped speaking and just looked at him.

He didn't believe her. He didn't think that Wilson was there at all. He'd gone along with her, but he hadn't seen any sign of the wizard and didn't think they were going to find him in a tourist trap like that. He thought she'd made a mistake.

"You say you think he is here. But if you knew where he was… you would go to him. Or describe where he was. Or tell us what he could see. Something. But once we got close to the location you thought he might be, you said you couldn't see him anymore."

"Yes," Reg agreed. "But that doesn't mean—"

"I know these things aren't always straightforward. You're tired and hungry and Corvin said that the water was bothering you… So it's understandable that you lost the trail. Or realized that you'd gone the wrong way to start with. That's fine. We'll just backtrack until you… pick up the scent again."

"I'm not a hound dog."

"I know you're not. But if you can't feel him here, then we can't find him here. We should go to where he has been recently so that we can track him."

"I suppose," Corvin said grudgingly. "As long as you're not going to try to go all the way back to the beginning and start all over. If Reg could tell that he's been in the area, then we shouldn't have to go back too far to pick up a solid trail."

Damon shrugged, looking uncomfortable. Why would he want to go all the way back to the beginning? That didn't make any sense at all. Unless he didn't trust Reg's psychic senses at all.

He didn't think that Wilson had ever been in the area.

Reg stared at Damon, trying to vaporize him with her eyes. He looked away.

"So you don't believe me," Reg said.

"It isn't that."

"You think I was wrong. You don't think he was ever anywhere near here."

"Other rumors and sightings put him north of here. By quite a bit. I don't want to waste time looking somewhere he isn't, letting the trail go cold."

"You don't think he's here. Or ever was."

Damon shook his head, not answering aloud.

Reg slammed her palm down on the table with a loud crack that made everyone jump. She stood up and stalked across the restaurant to the public restrooms and shut herself into the ladies' room. She hit the wall several times before her anger dissipated enough to do some deep breathing and try to calm herself down. Her palms were warm, and she didn't know if it was from hitting the table and the wall, or because of her internal fire. She didn't want to end up burning the place down. Light Damon's hair on fire, maybe. But then, she'd tried that once and he'd simply put it out with his own magic.

She paced back and forth across in front of the stalls, muttering to herself. How could Damon invite her along, beg and cajole for her to help him, and then ignore her advice when she gave it? Yes, it was true that she hadn't been able to point directly to Wilson and say, "There he is," but that wasn't usually how psychic vision worked. It was vague. It needed work. The person the vision was for had to put some effort into interpreting it. She wasn't a GPS tracker.

The woman from the couple with the young child came into the restroom and looked worriedly at Reg, frowning at her unusual behavior. Reg ducked into one of the stalls and closed the door, as if she had just walked in the door and was there to use the facilities herself. After a moment, the woman's footsteps walked to the stall at the opposite end and she shut the door.

Reg flushed after a short time, washed her hands, and returned to the table. She stood beside the table, looking down at Damon, not returning to her seat. He looked up at her.

"Uh, Reg. I'm sorry. I didn't mean to imply that... I mean, I do trust you, and I know that you're doing your best to help find him. And I didn't expect to find him the first day, so it isn't like you let me down. I just hope you understand that..."

"You're a jerk," she snapped.

Both men looked up at her awkwardly. None of them had finished eating, but Reg was no longer interested in food. She stood there for a moment, then shrugged. "I'm going outside. I'll see you when you're done."

She walked out of the restaurant.

Reg looked around. It would take a few minutes before Damon came out after her. Even if he decided to pay his bill right away and chase after her, he still had to get the waitress's attention, use the machine or his credit card to pay, maybe box up the rest of their meals, and then look for her. Corvin could chase after her sooner, but he probably didn't care to. He would be more civilized and not want to rush his meal.

She wandered down the boardwalk, looked up and down the street, and did a slow circuit of all the areas around the restaurant. She looked for any sign of the missing wizard or anywhere he might have gone. *Wizards R Us* or wherever wizards would go in the area. It might just be a tourist trap, but wizards took vacations too. There had to be a reason for him to be in the area. Someone might have seen him. He might have left his imprint on a place or an object. Just because Damon didn't have any faith in her psychic power, that didn't mean she was wrong about Wilson being in the area.

It was twenty minutes before Corvin came out of the restaurant and wandered through the settlement or followed her scent until he came upon her. Reg looked around for Damon, but he was nowhere in sight. Had he ditched her? Or was he still stubbornly waiting in the restaurant, expecting Reg to return and apologize?

Well, she wasn't going to apologize for being angry. She had every right to feel the way she did.

"He's just settling up," Corvin said, raising his hands in a calming gesture. "He'll be out shortly."

Reg blew out her breath and nodded. She looked toward the water, the direction they had come in from. "How long before our guide is here and we have to go?"

"If you want to look around for a while longer, we can do that."

Reg grunted, irritated. But she probably would have been annoyed at any answer he had given her. He didn't say she had to leave or that she had to stay.

A few minutes later, Damon joined them. He didn't try to explain or excuse his actions, but he didn't start accusing her or saying that he didn't want her around anymore, either. They both looked at each other.

"Did you have anywhere else you wanted to look?" Damon asked grudgingly. "Or… is there anything we can do to help?"

She had a sneaking suspicion that Corvin had something to do with the questions. He'd put Damon in his place and told him to start behaving like a respectable warlock. Like someone who knew how to deal with a psychic.

"Do you have anything that belonged to him? You said you have information about where he was last seen; maybe you should share what you have. It's sort of dumb to keep it to yourself and then expect me to work blind."

"I… don't have anything that belonged to him. Sorry. I know they do that sometimes… but since I'm just someone trying to find him, I don't have anything from his family."

Reg nodded. She had expected as much, but she also knew he wasn't telling her everything he knew. She waited for the rest.

"I told you he was seen north of here," Damon offered.

"Yes."

"I don't really know much more than that. I thought that we should go to the last place that he was seen. Ask some questions. See if maybe… you can pick up something there. He might have left some kind of clue or some kind of imprint on the place, right? Something that you could feel?"

"Yeah, maybe. Depending on how long he was there and how long ago it was."

"That's what I'm hoping. Your psychic powers are prodigious…"

If they were so prodigious—assuming "prodigious" meant she was good

—then why didn't he trust her when she said that the wizard was there? She knew Wilson was close by, even if they couldn't see him.

Reg was silent. Corvin and Damon waited. Damon scratched his jaw, waiting for some kind of reaction or direction from Reg. Finally, she shrugged. "I guess if you want to go somewhere else, then we go somewhere else."

CHAPTER TWELVE

*R*eg was quiet as they walked back to the dock where the boat had dropped them off in. Damon called Tybalt and they sat on benches in the shade awaiting his return. Reg didn't have anything to say to Damon and didn't feel like talking. So they all looked at their phones, ignoring each other, until Tybalt pulled the airboat in once more. Reg took a seat in the back so she wouldn't get the spray from the river in her face.

Just as the boat started to pull out, she realized she was hungry.

How stupid was it to go out in a pout and not eat her meal? How childish. And she knew better. After living hand-to-mouth for so long, she knew better than to give up a meal for something as stupid as pride. She had to take food where she could get it. Even though now she had the money to buy food, they were out on the water; there was nowhere to buy it.

Corvin looked over at Reg. He nudged a bag with his toe. Looking down at it, Reg realized he had packed up the food and brought it with him. "Did you bring a fork?" Reg asked in a low voice, not wanting Damon to overhear. He was up at the front, talking animatedly with Tybalt. Telling him where to go or some other story about the lost wizard, she assumed. Tybalt looked at the river ahead of him, nodding occasionally, not exactly enthralled at the story.

"There are a couple of forks in there," Corvin confirmed.

Reg picked up the bag and carefully untied the knotted handles at the top. "Thanks. I guess I was too mad to realize how hungry I am."

"Take care of yourself. Don't let pique get the better of you."

It was what Reg had just been thinking, though not in those words, and it bugged her that he thought he needed to advise her on it.

"I know," she said evenly.

He shrugged, one side of his mouth curling up into a small smile. "Red-heads are known for their temper, aren't they? I have found most of the redheads I know to be… passionate."

"Watch it, or I'll make you sit in the front."

His smile broadened. He watched her tease the bag open and check the boxes within to find her own lunch.

"I should eat all of these."

"Go ahead. It isn't like they're going to last. You can't leave food in this heat for long. That's just asking for food poisoning."

"Why did you bring it all, then? Planning to feed the fishes?"

"We could. You never know what might surface to eat it."

Reg had a sudden vision of slimy things swimming up from under the murky water and shook her head. "No. Ew. No."

She found her catch of the day and dug in, trying to quiet her grum-bling belly. "There must be all kinds of fishing around here. Unless it's banned in a national park."

"No, there's fishing—quite a lot of it. There's a very wide variety of fish in these waters. Both fresh and saltwater."

"Because it's so close to the ocean."

He nodded. They sat, watching as the airboat raced down the river. It was all so green. And wet. And it smelled like… Reg couldn't quite put a name to the brackish scent. She didn't like it, but it wasn't horrible. It would probably smell better if the water moved faster, but it seemed to practically stand still.

"Does it flow when it rains?" Reg asked.

"The flows were all altered when they tried to drain the land to make it into farmland," Corvin explained. "They have a project on the go to try to rehabilitate the flow again. I'm not sure what kind of changes that will cause to the ecosystem, and whether it will restore any of what has been lost." He shook his head. "They're hoping so, but only time will tell." He raised his brows. "Or a psychic. Any predictions?"

Images flashed before Reg's eyes, but they were gone too fast for her to make sense of them. She blinked rapidly, trying to catch snapshots of a few of them, but they were all too fleeting.

"Uh... no. Things will change. But I don't know... whether that's good or not."

"Things always change." Corvin looked out over the water. "Like the river, if things don't move forward, they get stagnant."

After eating her lunch, Reg could hardly keep her eyes open. She had been up much earlier than usual that day, and the sun on the water made her eyes want to close for protection, and as soon as she closed them, she would start to drift, her thoughts jumping illogically from one thing to another.

Eventually, she decided she would just let her thoughts wander as they would and have a nap. It wasn't particularly comfortable in her seat on the airboat, but she'd slept under far more physically uncomfortable conditions before.

Even as she slept, she was aware of the water around her. But in her mind, she could see far more than she could when she had kept her eyes open. She could see some of the things that moved beneath the surface. And some things that didn't move. Not only garbage and fallen trees, but bones buried there long ago. People who had ventured out into the Everglades and never returned. She was glad that it wasn't like the enchanted lake in Harry Potter, where the dead things came to life again and tried to catch them.

Was the wizard down there with the bones? Had she been wrong when she saw him at the last settlement? Or had she been right about the location, but had limited herself by looking for the tall, cloaked figure when his body was under the water or the soggy ground?

* * *

Reg nearly screamed when long, cold fingers wrapped around her arm.

She jumped awake, pulling away and putting her fists up to protect herself. The air crackled around her like static electricity on a grand scale. Corvin snatched his hand back, his eyes wide.

Reg swore and blew out her breath. "Holy crap! Don't grab me like that. What are you doing?"

Tybalt and Damon looked over their shoulders at Reg. Everyone was acting like she had done something surprising when she had just reacted to a perceived threat. Anyone would have reacted the same way when jerked out of a dream like she had been.

Reg unclenched her fists and slowly lowered her arms. The air around her still crackled with electricity.

"Sorry," Corvin said mildly. "I was just waking you up to let you know that we're going to pull in here to set up camp tonight."

Reg looked around. The sun was low and the sky starting to darken. Tybalt was guiding the airboat closer to the shoreline, though Reg wasn't sure where the river ended and the dry land began. "Dry land" was kind of a misnomer. She didn't know how far they would have to walk before they reached land that was dry enough to set up a tent. It looked swampy for miles.

"Here? How are we going to camp here?"

"Same as you would camp anywhere else. Damon brought the gear."

"There really aren't any hotels around here?" Reg dug her phone out of her pocket to search TripAdvisor. But she had no cell signal. "No bars? How can there be no bars?"

"We're too far away from civilization."

"Well... did it occur to anyone that it's called civilization for a reason? Why do we have to camp?"

Tybalt ran the airboat aground. Sort of. He threw out some kind of anchor to keep the boat still.

"Reg, Corvin, can you start pulling stuff out of the hold?" Damon asked. He stepped out of the boat into the deep mud, positioning himself to take items from Reg and throw them onto the land beyond him.

"How are we supposed to sleep here?" Reg complained again.

Corvin was struggling to get the hold open. Reg reached past him and touched the catch to release the door covering. They pulled out the large bags and equipment. Corvin handed them to Tybalt, who threw them over to Damon, who threw them as far onto the land as he could. Reg kept an eye on everything and wouldn't let them throw her bag. "I'll carry that myself."

Corvin looked down at the duffel. "Is this all you've got?"

Reg didn't bother answering. She wasn't too happy about it herself.

* * *

The spot that Tybalt helped Damon pick out did not improve Reg's mood. The ground still squished under her feet, the water table just below the surface. Damon gradually got everything set up. Reg didn't know if they'd even be able to have a fire. But then it was warm. They didn't need a fire. Reg had just never camped without one before. It seemed like a necessity for a successful camping trip.

They eventually were all sitting in a circle on various stumps or fallen tree trunks or coolers. Reg looked at the others. It would appear that Tybalt was planning to stay with them.

"Do you have a family?" she asked him, wondering whether there were children at home who would be missing their daddy tonight.

Tybalt looked startled at the question. "Me? No, no." He shook his head. "No, I'm not that type."

"What type? The type to have children?"

He nodded. "Yes."

Reg shrugged. A bachelor, then. Someone who wasn't interested in starting a family. Or maybe a divorcee who had resolved never to get into that trap again.

"What about you?" Tybalt returned, his voice rough, loud in the falling darkness.

"Me with kids? No."

"Are you that type?"

"No. I don't think I am either," Reg agreed. "I don't know if I'll ever have kids. Seems to me... people need to be more careful of bringing kids into the world. All of this... mess. People shouldn't have kids if they're not prepared to be good parents and provide for them right."

"I think most people would agree with that sentiment," Corvin said.

"Maybe. But I don't think most people are willing to follow through. There are plenty of people with kids who really shouldn't have had them in the first place."

She knew that Corvin was against bearing any children who might be born with the same "condition" as he bore. He didn't want to pass on to them the hunger that could only be satisfied by consuming others' powers. He did not, as far as Reg knew, have any progeny.

Though he had lied to her enough times that she couldn't be sure that anything he said was the truth. He would say whatever he felt would give him an advantage over her. Sympathy for the man with the chronic condition who wouldn't bring children into such an awful world… maybe it was just another line intended to lure her in.

Damon didn't contribute anything on whether he ever planned to have any kids. Maybe he already did. Reg didn't know much about his history. She'd never asked if he'd ever been married or had any children. Seeing as he was a warlock and was probably older than he looked, maybe she just didn't want to hear the answer.

"Where do you live?" she asked Tybalt. "Is your home near here? Is it a commute?"

"A commute," he repeated, and Reg got the feeling that he didn't know what the word meant.

"I just mean, is it a long drive? Do you drive in? Or take your boat in? I haven't ever known an airboat driver before. I don't know how it all works."

He was silent, looking at her.

Reg started to get a creepy, skin-crawling feeling looking at him. She wished they did have a fire. Could she light a fire in a swamp? Is that what foxfire was? Some kind of magical fire that would work there?

"Not far," Tybalt said eventually. He looked around them and repeated it. "Not far."

Reg shivered.

CHAPTER THIRTEEN

*A*fter a while, Tybalt left them.

He had set up his camp a little distance from theirs. At least, it had seemed like a short distance when they had set it up when it was still light out. After the darkness fell, Reg felt a little disoriented, and she wasn't sure if he was too close or too far away from them. It wasn't comfortable having him there.

"You checked his references, right?" she asked Damon.

"Sure. A few people recommended him. Said he really knew his way around the park."

"Okay. Real references? Because it's not hard to set up fake ones…"

"How would I know if they were fake?"

"Well, you could call them, of course. You're the one who is a diviner. You can tell if they're lying to you."

"Of course they're going to lie to me. Everybody lies. Especially job references."

"Then you don't know whether he's really a good guide or not."

"I saw today. He knew his stuff, didn't he? I don't know what you're worried about."

"Just having him sleeping over there. I don't like it. What do you know about him?"

Damon shrugged. "Corvin who recommended him."

Reg looked at Corvin. "Is he… a practitioner?"

Corvin looked to the side, evasive before even voicing his answer. "He is known in the magical community. He's good at what he does. No one knows the Everglades better."

"Why?"

"Why did I recommend him to Damon?"

"Why does he know the Everglades better than anyone else?"

Corvin frowned, puzzled by her question. "I would imagine… because he's been here so long. Because he lives here himself. He spends all of his time here, exploring and acting as a guide."

"And you're not worried about him sleeping over there?"

"Are you upset that he's not staying in our campsite? Or that he's sleeping too close?"

"I don't know. I just don't like him there. Are we safe? Have you set wards against strangers? Outsiders?"

Corvin shook his head. "I can set up a few safeguards. What about you? You have been working on protective spells."

Most of them against Corvin. But Sarah had also been teaching her about imbuing physical objects with protections. It was a lot harder for Reg. Harrison, Reg's immortal godfather, had helped her build a protective barrier around herself, but she had to mentally maintain it, something she couldn't do while asleep or distracted. It was strong enough to keep Corvin back, and he was a powerful warlock, especially since consuming the Witch Doctor's hoard. But what she could do while awake would not help them while asleep.

"Should we take turns keeping watch?" Reg asked. Tybalt was certainly not the only danger in the park. Corvin kept talking about the other creatures and saying that they needed to be careful. "Sleep in shifts?"

"I don't think that's necessary," Corvin said. "Tybalt is being paid to be our guide. Why would he do anything to harm us?"

"I don't know. Maybe he doesn't care that much about the money. He can get money from all kinds of tourists. Maybe he wants something else that we have. We wouldn't know it until it was too late."

"Like what?" Damon asked, looking amused.

"I don't know." Reg looked at Corvin. "Powers."

"He's not like me," Corvin assured her.

"What is he like? Do you know what his powers are?"

"He's a good guide. That's all you need to know."

Reg was starting to feel a chill. She dug a hoodie from her bag and pulled it on. She noticed a small bundle in her duffel that hadn't been there before. She poked at it and then pulled it out. From the silky, tightly-packed material and capsule shape, she assumed it was a sleeping bag. She looked at the two warlocks.

"Is this what I think it is? Did one of you get me a sleeping bag?"

They looked at each other; both shook their heads. Reg undid the tie and pulled the sleeping bag out of itself so that it stretched in a crumpled form along the ground. It wouldn't provide a lot of cushioning from the ground, but it would keep her warm. And Damon had groundsheets and pads that she could use.

"Well, if it wasn't one of you, then it must have been..." Reg looked in the direction Tybalt had gone to sleep.

Corvin chuckled. "What was it you were saying about not trusting our guide?"

"You think he got it for me?"

"I don't think it was swamp fairies," he said dryly.

"He must have done it while we were having lunch," Damon said. "He had a couple of hours to kill."

"Well... I guess I do feel bad, then. I never thought he would do something like that. I can pay him back. He never said anything!"

"Think hard before offering to pay him for it," Corvin warned. "Many races would consider it an insult for you to offer to pay for a gift."

"Oh. Okay, I wouldn't have thought of that. I don't want to insult him."

Reg sat down on top of her sleeping bag, then wrapped it partially around her. It was very cozy and warm. She was finally able to relax.

CHAPTER FOURTEEN

*M*aybe it was because she'd had a nap in the afternoon. Or maybe because Reg didn't normally go to sleep until late at night or early in the morning. Either way, her body did not agree with her decision to go to bed after talking with the warlocks, who wanted to get an early start in the morning. She knew that Corvin often stayed up as late as she did—they'd had more than one late-night telephone conversation when one of them wanted someone to talk to. Since it wasn't safe for Reg to have Corvin in the house, especially at night or when she was tired, phones were the easiest solution.

She had wild and restless dreams for the first hour or two after she finally managed to drop off. Voices spoke to her out of the cool mist that hovered over the swampy ground. They hissed warnings to her. Told her to go back home. Something in the Everglades did not want her there. In her dream, she searched for the boat and tried to wake Corvin and Damon, but they didn't respond, snoring away obliviously as she shook them and shouted at them that they had to wake up.

It was like one of those dreams where she was looking desperately for a bathroom but couldn't find one. Or did find one but it was flooded. Or she couldn't get her pants off because she was wearing layer upon layer.

Her brain knew there was something wrong and was trying to prepare her and wake her up to face it.

Reg finally pushed her way out of the dream. She sat up with a gasp and clutched her sleeping bag to her chest, trying to see through the darkness. There was something out there. Something was creeping around their campsite. She strained her eyes, but the clouds and the mist blocked out any light from the moon and stars. There was no fire. She didn't have a flashlight or lantern. She hadn't even brought a mobile charger for her phone because she had not realized that they would be camping out in the middle of nowhere instead of sleeping in a hotel like civilized people. So she was loathe to turn her phone on and use it as a flashlight, wanting to conserve the power for as long as she could.

Instead, she squinted her eyelids as close to shut as she could, trying to sharpen her vision and see something in the darkness. She remembered Ruan marveling that she couldn't see in the darkness and calling her "blind one."

Then Davyn reminding her that she could use her fire for light as well as warmth. And fire would help to keep wild animals away. She held her hands close together and conjured fire between them. It didn't work the first time, but she focused and breathed slowly and felt the fire growing gradually inside her and, eventually, a flicker of flame appeared between her hands. Reg nursed it into a small ball of fire, then held it in front of her and used it to light the area around her. It was a very small fire, so it didn't light anything more than a couple of feet away very well. She didn't want to make it any bigger and attract attention. She wasn't too worried about burning down the forest. Everything was so wet; there was no chance of a wildfire.

There were sounds outside the radius of her fire. She could hear someone or something out there. She slipped out of her cozy new sleeping bag with regret and moved toward Damon's and Corvin's sleeping forms. She reached Damon first and shook his arm, telling him in a whisper to wake up. He started to move around restlessly, so she left him and went to Corvin.

"Corvin. There's something out there. Wake up."

She touched him, knowing it would cause a jolt of electricity to flow through both of them. Corvin's body stiffened like a plank, but he didn't wake up. It was sort of like in a TV medical show where they shocked the dead guy, and his body jumped up into an arc, but it didn't work. Then they turned up the voltage and tried again and, in most shows, it would eventually work, and he would get up and start talking to them. Maybe it wasn't realistic, but Reg liked the shows where everything worked out in the end. It made her feel better about her chances that everything would work out in her life.

"Corvin!"

He still didn't wake up. Reg went back to Damon. If he were awake, he could help get Corvin up too. She grabbed his leg and gave it a shake. "Damon! Come on. You want to get attacked out here in your sleep?"

She shook harder, and he groaned but didn't wake up. Reg swore under her breath. She looked back and forth between them. Were they both naturally deep sleepers? It seemed unlikely that the two warlocks would both be such deep sleepers that she could not rouse them. Had someone been there? Tainted their food to knock them out? Corvin had brought a bottle of scotch with him, and they had both partaken, but Reg already had a headache and didn't want to wake up in the morning feeling even worse. Was there something in the drink? Or were they both just intoxicated?

She slowly rose to her feet. Crouching hurt too much to sustain the position for long. She moved farther away from Corvin and Damon, looking for any sign of a monster lurking outside the circle of her fire. Would the wards Corvin had placed keep it at bay? Would Reg's fire?

She couldn't see anything, but she could feel a presence close by. It wouldn't answer any of the questions Reg asked as she probed its mind. Either it was keeping her out, or it didn't have conscious thoughts. The same way as she couldn't get clear thoughts from Starlight or other animals. She could sense his mood, understand what he wanted or things he disliked, but he didn't use words in her head to communicate with her.

Thinking about Starlight seemed to help. She felt her mind expand, and the consciousness of the thing out there respond to her. She pictured Starlight, saw herself feeding him and picking him up to scratch his ears or give him love. She thought about how he strengthened her psychic connections and had helped her in the past.

The being drew closer to her, despite her fire.

She could see a shape just at the edge of the darkness. Barely a smudge beyond her fire. She had no doubt it could see her with her face lit up. It was long and low to the ground, animal rather than something human-shaped. She didn't try to use speech to communicate with it, just her mind, emotions, and memories.

Then there was movement from another direction. Behind her and to the right.

They were hunting her in a pack. One out in front of her to draw her out while the rest circled around to trap her.

She turned quickly, the fire flaring in her hands. She was looking down where the creature should be, and instead of the elongated shape she had seen in front of her, saw two legs clothed in pants and boots. A man and his dog?

She didn't have any time to think about it or to take anything else in.

CHAPTER FIFTEEN

*R*eg was encased in darkness.

Everything around her was black. She wasn't even sure she had her eyes open. It was black as the inside of a coffin.

At the thought, Reg started to struggle. She was bound hand and foot, but she was not lying in a coffin. She was not being buried alive. Something beneath her was soft and springy, giving way and bouncing as she moved. She stopped and searched the blackness in front of her again for some crack of light or slightly lighter shade of black. Still nothing, just even blackness. She tried to call out, but her mouth must have been gagged, because she couldn't make a sound. She wanted to call out for help, but she could not. She reached out with her mind, exploring, using all of her psychic senses to build a picture of where she was and what had happened to her.

She didn't remember anything at first. Just falling asleep in the boat while she was so tired. It took time for her to slowly recall what had happened later. They had stopped for lunch. They had talked. They had traveled down the river for a long time in the boat, headed for the last place the wizard had been seen. And they had gone to bed. That was the last thing she could remember.

Her senses told her she was lying on a mattress or pallet. Someone had at least gone to the trouble to make her comfortable. The air moved freely around her. Not a coffin. Not a closet. Maybe a room or cell. She could hear water running somewhere.

All day they had skimmed over the water of the Everglades, and the river itself moved so slowly it seemed to be standing still. Now she could make out a trickle of water, falling over rocks or in a fountain. It made her thirsty. How long had it been since she'd had something to drink? Corvin had warned her against getting dehydrated. She knew that when dehydration set in, it could turn things bad very quickly. She needed water if she were going to survive, even in the humidity of the Everglades.

She lay there for some time, the minutes passing by so slowly it felt like she was there for days before she detected someone's approach.

The stealthy sounds were so quiet she didn't know at first whether it was the person who had trapped her or whether it was a rat rustling around in the darkness looking for something to eat. She reached out with her mind, pressing against it.

Not a rat.

But something familiar. She had seen or felt it before. Reg probed, trying to find out more about it without giving herself away. It was against the rules to enter another being's mind, of course, but it was also against the rules for that being to kidnap her. Reg didn't feel any guilt over what she was doing. She just didn't want him—him? Yes, definitely him—to know that she could touch his mind.

The mind was intelligent. Dark. Cunning. She found the presence of both vast stores of knowledge and a sharp, predatory instinct. Who was he? What was he?

As he moved closer to her room, Reg gathered more details about him. But it wasn't until the air flow shifted that she had new sensory data. A foul, rotten smell clung to the creature—a hideous smell like a hundred dead, decomposing things.

And that was when she knew. When she remembered the scent, she had smelled earlier in the day on the boat that had turned her stomach.

Tybalt.

She breathed shallowly, trying to ignore the smell that made her want to retch. If she ignored it, then sooner or later, she would get used to it. Like a coroner in a morgue. It wouldn't bother her anymore. She would be able to just forget about it and to focus on other things. Things like how she was going to escape his lair.

She tried to speak as he got closer but still couldn't make a sound. What had he done to her? She explored her mouth with her tongue but did not find any kind of gag inside or outside. Everything was black, yet he seemed able to move around with ease. Even cats had to have some light entering their pupils to see in the dark.

He drew up close to her. She could feel him breathing. His eyes were on her, whether he could see her or not. She could feel his watchfulness and attention.

"Reg Rawlins," he said, drawing the words out. He sounded foreign. British, maybe? She hadn't noticed that when he had talked to them earlier in the day. Was he faking an accent now? Or had he faked an American accent earlier?

Reg's mouth opened, and saliva sprang up around her tongue. She tried again to speak.

"Tybalt."

This time the word came out. He had released whatever spell had been keeping her silent. Reg wondered if she should chance screaming for help. Were they close enough to anyone who could help her? Or would she just be angering Tybalt when she needed to keep him happy with her to ensure her survival?

She'd better not do anything until she was sure. Maybe she hadn't understood what had happened to her. Maybe he had rescued her and would take her back to her friends.

"Yes!" He sounded pleased that she knew him and remembered his name. "Yes, Tybalt. You remember Tybalt from yesterday."

Reg nodded. "Of course. I spent a long time with you."

"Ah, but some people don't remember. Or don't recognize me when they see me here. Or *don't* see me here."

"Why can't I see? Why don't you turn on the light?"

"The light is on."

"Where? I can't see anything. What happened to my eyes?"

She tried to bring her hands up to her eyes to rub them. To see if they were open or closed and whether she was blindfolded. She wasn't even sure she had eyeballs anymore. Maybe he had stolen them. Maybe if she could see around her, she would find shelves filled with jars of preserved eyeballs from everyone else he had blinded.

But her hands were bound behind her; she couldn't bring them up to her face.

"You have nothing to fear. It is not permanent."

"What, then? What did you do to make me blind?"

"It is merely a potion. It will wear off."

She was relieved to hear that. She still didn't know how she was going to get away from him, but she'd work something out. She would find out everything she could about Tybalt and their surroundings, and then she would get out. It was bound to work. She and the others had gotten out of worse fixes before.

The others.

She hadn't given Damon and Corvin a thought until then.

"Where are—"

"The others are perfectly fine. I left them there. I didn't want *them*."

"Why did you want me? I don't understand. Want me for what?" Her skin crawled when she imagined what his intentions might be.

She couldn't see him, but she could still feel his shrug and the slight tilt of his head. "I just want a little company."

"You had company. We spent almost all day yesterday with you."

"Yes, but that's work. Don't you want to see people outside of work? Maybe it doesn't matter to you anymore. Maybe you enjoy your mind games so much now that you don't feel the need for any other interaction."

"Well… no. I still want to see other people," Reg admitted. "I have friends. People who come over for a visit, or we go out to a restaurant together. Or… something."

"Yes. You have many friends, don't you? It must be lovely to have so many friends. To pick up the phone and call them and have them come over to see you. To watch TV with them. To go out to restaurants and eat with them."

When she remembered how they had dismissed him at lunchtime when he was probably hungry, she felt ashamed. They should have invited him along. She might not particularly like the guy, but he had helped them out when they needed it, and they had treated him as if he were just an afterthought. Someone who didn't matter, who could just be pushed aside and ordered around at a whim. Would it have hurt them to have invited him to the Skunk Man Saloon too? Treated him to something nice for lunch and a drink with him?

But they hadn't.

This was what happened when you ignored people and let them get lonely and depressed. When you made them outcasts because you didn't have anything in common or because they smelled bad. Reg swallowed, trying to forget the smell again, to keep from gagging with how close he was to her.

"I'm sorry. We should have asked you along."

"Nobody invites me along. You don't take someone like me to decent places. No one does."

"Like you?"

He prowled back and forth restlessly, stirring up the air around them. It was hot and muggy. Already daytime. Where were the others? Tybalt had left them in their camp. Where did they think Reg had gone? Did they know that he had taken her with him? Or did they think it was another creature? Or that she had wandered off? She might have sleepwalked into some slough or she might have decided that she'd had enough of marshes and gone home. She could hitch-hike or find someone to take her back to Black Sands. It wouldn't have been that hard.

"You interest me," Tybalt declared. "What are you? You're a psychic? But you have red hair." He touched her tiny braids fleetingly. "And you have fire. Tell me what you are and from where you hail?"

"I'm a psychic, yes," Reg agreed. It was best not to let him know what all of her powers were. If she could play a human with very little power, she would have the advantage. He would be less careful. He would not know the things she could do. "Sometimes I can talk to ghosts. Under the right circumstances. It isn't easy; it takes a lot of concentration."

"But on the boat, you said that you knew where this lost man was. Were you communicating with his ghost? On the boat?"

"Uh…" Reg was a good actor and did her best to sound sheepish. "Well, to tell the truth… sometimes I have to put on a bit of a *show*, you know? Yes, I'm helping them look for him… I told them I could do it. But… I thought we could just ask around, and I could get some clues, and then I would put them together, and when we found him, I would get the credit…"

"You can't find him? You don't know where he is?"

"You said that lots of people get lost here."

"Yes," he agreed.

"And you know the Everglades. Really well."

"Of course. I have lived here all of my life."

"So, *you* would probably have a better chance of finding him than I would."

He made a nasty, wet sound, and it was a moment before Reg figured out that he was chuckling. "It is a game? You are only pretending you can find him?"

"I have psychic powers. I might be able to find him."

He discounted this immediately, deeming her a charlatan. If she had powers, then she would have used them to find Wilson, and she had not.

"But you had fire," he said. "I saw that with my own eyes."

"Yes," Reg agreed, trying to make her voice sad. "But what good is that? I mean, you can't direct it like a flashlight. In a place like this, everything is too wet to even light a campfire. So you can hold a little fire in your hands. Good party trick, but pretty useless."

"Reg Rawlins."

Reg shrugged. "That's me. I guess… I'm sort of a disappointment if you were looking for someone who was… more interesting."

"You do not have to be powerful to interest me." He touched her red braids again. People liked to touch them. People she didn't even know would approach her and ask if they could feel them, fascinated by seeing red hair done up in tiny box braids. It was so unusual, people overcame their natural reluctance to approach a stranger in order to get a better look.

"I'm not that interesting."

"I don't need *interesting*. I just want company."

"Okay… well… I guess we could visit for a while. And then I want to get back together with my group. They'll be worried."

"Ah. That doesn't matter. They'll forget you soon enough. Everyone is forgotten, sooner or later."

Reg felt a chill climbing her spine. Everyone? How many people had he taken before? How many of those disappearances in the Everglades had been his doing? It wouldn't be that hard for a tour guide. He would have access to anyone who came in for a single tour. And for small groups like Damon's, he could still separate one person from the group and take her away in the middle of the night. Especially if he drugged the members of the group. Or put a spell on them. Somehow he had made them sleep much more heavily than they should have.

Corvin would not be happy at being duped. And Damon would blame himself. They would both be worried. They would try to find her. They wouldn't give up.

But it niggled away at her. How long would they keep looking? Sooner or later, they would have to give up and go back to their lives. Sooner or later, Reg would be just one more person to disappear into the swamps of the Everglades.

"Do you… take a lot of people? You have done this before?"

"No need to worry about that right now. You should try to get some more rest. I don't think you've had enough yet."

"What are you going to do? I want to go back to my party. I want to go home. You can't just keep me here."

"Don't worry about these things, Reg Rawlins. You do not need to concern yourself with anything. Rest for a while longer and we will talk again when you wake up."

Reg opened her mouth to protest, but was overtaken by a blackness pouring into her mind that was even darker than her eyesight.

CHAPTER SIXTEEN

*R*eg had to escape.

She had to get away from Tybalt. She didn't know what kind of power he was using over her. She didn't know if it was a spell that made her sleep or if it was some kind of drug. She hadn't eaten or drunk anything as far as she knew. But there were injections, IV's, patches, and gases. All different ways to administer a potion or poison. She hadn't been able to feel her body well enough to know whether she had been on an IV drip when she had awakened last.

It was a little easier to awaken the next time, with vague memories of what had happened and some returning vision. She could see shapes around her. The bed she lay on. The walls of the room. Or the cave. The walls were much darker and rounder than she had expected. She couldn't yet see enough to be sure, but she thought it was a natural structure rather than man-made. A cave or a clearing. Dim, but not pitch-black like she had thought the first time. There were passages to other rooms, caves, or tunnels, some of them covered by boards.

There was little of interest. She was relieved that she still had her eyes and was not surrounded by jars of eyeballs or any other body parts.

When Tybalt returned to find her awake, he gave a formal little bow and then stood in front of her, looking over her with glittering dark eyes.

The lighting was dim, but Reg could see reasonably well, and the first thing she realized about him was that he was not wearing his outback hat. Of course not. Why would he keep wearing it in his own home when he was no longer taking tourists on his boat. It was to protect him from the sun.

Only it wasn't, she realized. The large, floppy-brimmed hat had served another purpose. To cover his large, pointed ears. Reg gasped sharply. Tybalt looked at her.

"You're... what are you?" Reg asked. The fairies she had seen had not had ears like that, but maybe different families or subspecies looked different. He didn't look like anything she had seen before. How had they not known that he was something other than human? His skin was pallid, especially for someone who had been out in the sun so much. Even without seeing his ears, they should have been able to guess from his skin and smell that there was something different about him.

"Kobold," he said, with another little bow. Reg wasn't sure whether that was a name or a title or whether he was even answering her question. What was a Kobold?

"Knockers," Tybalt tried again. But this was no clearer to Reg. He must be some kind of being that Reg hadn't ever heard of before. There was such a variety of creatures on the earth; was it surprising that she hadn't heard of them all yet?

"I hate the human names," Tybalt said with vehemence. "Why should we have to go by the name another species gives to us? Are we not what we say we are? Do we not have the right to self-identify?"

"Um... yeah. Of course. Why not?" Most of the species she had learned about so far had their own names to identify their people. The Kin. Gnomen. Piskies.

"But you do not know these names. You do not bother to educate yourselves."

"I've had to learn a lot since I got here. I'm sorry if I haven't covered that in my education yet. It's been sort of... haphazard."

Tybalt sighed. He leaned closer to her, his foul stench rolling over her in waves. "I am... goblin."

CHAPTER SEVENTEEN

*I*t was not as much of a shock as it might have been. Reg knew Tybalt was something foul. Corvin had warned her about swamp goblins. Then why had he suggested Damon hire one? Did Corvin even know what Tybalt was? She would have expected someone who studied history and other magical species to be able to recognize one when he saw it.

"A goblin," she said. "I mean—what did you say? Kobold?"

Tybalt nodded. "Gobelin and its derivatives mean 'evil spirit.' Don't you think that's prejudicial? You do not know what kind of spirit a person has until you get to know them. Do you think that all Kobold have evil spirits?"

Was it racist to brand all goblins as evil? Or was it the truth? Tybalt had been a good guide. He had been knowledgeable about the Everglades and had not made any threats against them. He had apparently bought Reg a sleeping bag as a gift, knowing her need. Did that make him evil?

Until they got to the point where he had bewitched Corvin and Damon and kidnapped Reg, holding her hostage in his lair, blind, gagged, and bound hand and foot.

He couldn't exactly claim that was for her health.

Reg looked around, trying to learn as much as she could about the place where she was being held. It seemed to be a cave, but she was not sure it was enclosed on all sides. There were trees along one side, and she didn't know if the trees were growing inside the cave or whether the cave and the trees

78

formed a natural lean-to. If she weren't bound, she might be able to walk right out of there.

But where would she go? Reg had no idea where she was or where his boat was. If she walked out into the swamp, how would she find her way back to her company or civilization? The Everglades swallowed people. They went missing there all the time.

She swallowed. "Do you know what happened to the missing man?" She deliberately did not call him a wizard.

"Which one?"

"The one we are looking for. Jeffrey Wilson."

Tybalt pondered that for a while. "People don't always introduce themselves," he said, with a smile that showed his teeth. Not gap-toothed like a Jack-o-lantern, but there were spaces between them, and his incisors seemed a little too long to be human. How had she taken him to be human? She should have been paying more attention. "Do you have a picture of him?"

Reg shook her head. But his question gave her pause. Why hadn't Damon shown her a picture of the wizard? She understood that he wasn't part of the Wilson family and did not have any of Wilson's personal possessions for Reg to focus on, but why didn't he have a picture? There should have been posters and social media posts all over the place with his picture on them.

"Even if I knew his name," Tybalt said slowly, "I don't remember everyone I meet. I do tours with multiple people almost every day. Sometimes, several different tours. That's a lot of people to remember. When did he go missing?"

"I don't know. Uh... not long, I don't think. There's a reward..."

His eyes glittered. Did goblins care about money? He must have some reason to do tours. If his lair were any indication, he didn't have a lot of expenses. He lived like an animal; what did he need money for?

"That is why you and the witches are looking for him," Tybalt said. "You want to build your hoard."

Reg shrugged.

"Would you recognize this Jeffrey Wilson if you saw him?"

She wasn't about to tell him that the only thing she'd seen of the missing wizard was a brief vision. "Yeah... I think I would recognize him."

He stared down at her for a few minutes, considering. Then he reached down and pulled her up, off of the bed, depositing her on her feet. Reg's stomach tied in a knot. What was he thinking? What did he want from her?

He marched her into a dark passage that branched off from the cave she had been kept in. Reg resisted, her body reacting automatically to being taken into such a dark, close place, where she couldn't see very far ahead of her and didn't know what she was going to find. But Tybalt was strong. He didn't care that she resisted; he just hauled her along, like an adult might pull on the arm of a two-year-old who had been naughty. With her ankles bound, she could only take shortened, shuffling steps, and he dragged her most of the way.

He led her to another room. No door on this one either. It was as dark and dank as a tomb. Tybalt let go of Reg and strode into the room. He lit a match that flared and lit up his face in gruesome grimaces until he applied it to the wick of a lantern. The lamp glowed and lit the room.

Reg wondered if she should have run while his attention was on the lamp. But how could she, when she was still tired up? She looked down at the bonds on her wrists. Not metal shackles or plastic zip ties, just ropes. She should be able to do something about ropes.

Tybalt raised the lantern and moved it toward the wall to Reg's left. There were rows of shelves, floor to ceiling. At first, she couldn't see what was on the shelves. Jars of preserves or pale gray pottery?

But then the light got close enough and Reg's eyes focused on row upon row of grinning skulls. She reared back, an exclamation escaping her mouth.

"Well," Tybalt asked, an answering grin of his own. "Do you recognize him?"

CHAPTER EIGHTEEN

*R*eg choked and coughed, overwhelmed. She backed out of the doorway of the cave as quickly as she could with her bound feet. Tybalt was making that horrible wet laughing noise again.

"They are my friends," he said. "Don't you like my friends?"

How many of the people who had disappeared in the Everglades had disappeared into Tybalt's lair? Reg's whole body was shaking as she struggled to get away from him. She had to find a way to escape and get away from him. She wasn't going to stay and entertain him, wondering just how long she could last before he tired of the game and decided to kill her. Did he eat his victims? She assumed by his stench that he must. The smell of rotting flesh that imbued his pores... She should have known it when they were in the boat. She should have known what that smell meant, but she had doubted herself. She had thought that Corvin and Damon must know better than she did. They were older, more experienced about the creatures that inhabited the world that she was still finding out about. They must have known the habits of goblins and how to recognize them. Corvin especially. He said he had known goblins before? Was Tybalt a different breed? Or only part goblin? How had he been fooled?

"There is no need to be afraid, Reg Rawlins." Tybalt advanced toward her. Slowly, stalking her. The veneer of civility had fallen away, even though his voice was still polite and cultured. She was no longer fooled into thinking that he was something other than *gobelin*.

Evil spirit.

He had told her himself and she had thought it was just the prejudice of humans, believing that anyone different was evil. That everything society judged as ugly must also be bad.

Reg's heart pounded hard and fast. Not just in fear, but in anger. He had stolen her. He had come into her campsite, stalked her, and taken her away. She hoped that Corvin and Damon were still alive and unharmed, but she didn't have any confidence that they were.

Did she really think that Tybalt had told her the truth about anything?

"There is no point in trying to get away from me," he pointed out in a rough voice that was probably intended to sound soothing but which grated on her nerves like fingernails on a blackboard.

He took another step toward her. Reg tried to keep the distance between them, hobbling to escape. The stupid ropes. If she could at least be free of her bonds, she'd have half a chance. Trying to run away from him when she couldn't take a step of more than two inches at a time was futile.

She directed her anger toward the rope binding her feet together. She burned it with her mind, tightly focused on getting it off. In seconds, a flame sliced the cord into pieces and she stepped out of them. She looked down at her hands, forming a fire between them. She made it grow, feeding it with her anger.

"A nice party trick," Tybalt said, recalling their earlier conversation.

"No," Reg said. "I am a firecaster."

He looked uneasy. "You said you had no magic."

"Did you tell me the truth about everything?"

"I told you no lies."

She let the fire play between her hands, let it nip at the ropes around her wrists until they too fell away.

"No!" Tybalt growled, lunging toward her to keep her from escaping.

A fireball burst from Reg's hands, flying away from her like a cannon and hitting Tybalt square in the chest. He fell backward into his mausoleum.

Reg turned and ran, going back the way they had come, back to the half-room where she had been held.

She decided she hated the Everglades. It was dark and spooky and slimy.

Everything was green and dripping. The trees themselves seemed to be melting, forming weird shapes that threatened to cage her.

She pushed through the grasping branches, leaving Tybalt's lair behind her. She looked around, trying to get some sense of direction. There was nothing but water before her, and she didn't know how deep it was and whether it was infested by crocodiles or alligators or some other kind of monster. Corvin had said that there were sharks, snakes, and who knew what else? Everything in the Everglades seemed to be a predator.

She skirted the shore, trying to stay on dry ground. Or at least, ground that wasn't so wet that she sank past her ankles with every step. The thick mud stank and the long grasses cut into her legs like needles despite the fact she was wearing long pants. She would be leaving a nice wide blood trail behind her for Tybalt to follow.

She continued to circle Tybalt's lair, looking for a way to escape to civilization and dryer ground. But there didn't seem to be anywhere to go. She was out of breath, moving as quickly as she could, knowing that he must be right behind her.

If her fireball hadn't killed him, he would find a way to follow her.

Reg looked around her frantically, gasping for breath and stumbling into every puddle and depression in the ground. She was sure she was right back where she had started. Were they on an island? Maybe that was why Tybalt hadn't seen the need to lock her up, feeling perfectly comfortable with leaving her in the half-cave. As long as she was bound, she couldn't get away, and even now that she wasn't, she didn't know how to escape him.

There was only one way, and that was to venture out into the water. It was her only option. And in her circuit of the small island, she hadn't seen any sign of his boat.

It wasn't that Reg couldn't swim. She just didn't like the look of the dark, murky water. There was no way to know what lurked beneath the surface and how big it might be. Reg didn't know where she was and had no idea which way to strike out in order to find her party or civilization again.

But there was nothing else to do. She struck out, keeping Tybalt's shelter behind her and walking straight into the water. Corvin had said that the water was only a few feet deep in most areas, which meant she didn't need to worry about drowning.

There was an angry growl behind her and running footsteps. Reg moved more quickly. Tybalt wasn't disabled. He had just been hanging back, waiting for his prey to wear herself out or give up on being able to escape her confinement.

She used her arms to pull herself forward through the water. Her feet kept getting stuck in the thick mud under the river, and despite its shallowness, Reg flopped over on her belly to try to crawl through the water. With her body at the surface instead of trying to wade through mud, she was able to move more quickly.

The grass was cutting her even more with her face so close to the surface. Death by a thousand cuts.

Come on. Get moving. She knew she could move faster than he could. She could still escape.

But he seemed to be gaining on her. She didn't know how he could be making such good time through the swampy waters. He was a goblin. They probably had webbed feet and skin as thick as armor to protect against the grass.

She felt a hand close around her ankle.

CHAPTER NINETEEN

*R*eg gave a shout of surprise and anger and kicked, trying to escape his grasp. Tybalt responded by lifting her foot up. Gravity compensated by dumping Reg's face and head under the surface of the water. Reg struggled and arched to get her face back out of the water. Now she was really angry.

Really, really angry. She thrashed to escape him, then curled her body around to bring her head and hands closer to Tybalt. He hadn't been expecting that and wasn't quick enough to escape. Reg grabbed him on both sides of the head, hands clapped over his big, pointed ears, and she squeezed like a vise, not letting go.

Tybalt shouted and released her leg, reaching instead for Reg's hands on his face and trying to peel them off. Reg drew herself even closer to him. His smell was so foul she could hardly bear it. He didn't smell good, like Damon or Corvin. Getting *them* into the water would feel completely different. She closed her eyes for just a moment, visualizing it, thinking of how comfortable and complete she would feel if it were one of *them* that she had in the water.

But she couldn't allow herself to be distracted by pleasant visions. She had a terrible creature to take care of, and he was strong and an accomplished predator. Just look at the number of lives he had taken in the swamp. All of those grinning skulls. How could anyone ever discover where they had all come from?

Reg had no intention of being caught like they had been. She was going to be the top dog in this fight.

She readjusted her grip on Tybalt, moving her hands down from his ears toward his throat. She had no desire to hold him close to her body as she had with Corvin. With her siren senses triggered, he was so foul she could hardly bear to touch him. She twisted, trying to push him under the water. He struggled. He was very strong. He had killed many other creatures, pushing them under the water and holding them there until their struggles ceased. But he had never before wrestled with a siren.

The water was not as salty as the ocean, but it was enough to bolster her strength. She longed for the ocean. There, she could just drag him under the water and dive to the bottom, where she would keep him until all of his struggles had ceased. He would become one with the ocean, and it would take away his foul stench and his years of killing. In the swamp, he could get his feet under him and use them as leverage to push back against her and to keep his head above the water.

Reg squeezed more tightly and again tried to twist him to get him under the water.

Was it even possible to drown a goblin? Or did they have gills like a fish or breathe through their skin like some amphibious creature? If she couldn't drown him, then she would have to use another method. She explored his neck with her fingers, looking for the warm pulse point where she knew it was in a human. But despite his similarity in appearance, Tybalt's circulatory system didn't seem to be designed the same way. She could not find the warm, throbbing artery she was looking for.

She dragged him along with her, farther away from the shore of his island, even though the water didn't seem to be getting any deeper.

Reg heard something in the tree above her.

She froze. What was it? She turned her head and tried to see what was up there, but there were a lot of shadows cast by the thick canopy and she couldn't see well enough to make out what it was. Another goblin? Corvin had said that there were swamp *goblins*, not just one goblin terrorizing the swamp like a troll under a bridge. Tybalt might have a mate in the tree above her. Or a child or pack brother. Did goblins live in packs? She had no idea. She had always supposed that they were solitary creatures, but she had made a lot of wrong assumptions about other magical species. She couldn't trust modern fairy tales for the straight goods.

Tybalt struggled. She pressed him again, trying to get him under the water.

The noise in the tree changed from something making its way through the branches to a low, sustained growl.

Reg would have sworn aloud, but was too afraid that it would draw the animal's attention if it weren't already hunting her. So she kept it in her head and probed Tybalt's consciousness, trying to learn what he knew about the swamp and its dangers. What was in the tree, and just how much of a threat was it to her?

A snarl made Reg jump and look up, and loosened her hands just enough that Tybalt was able to wrench free from her grip. She looked at her hands in shock. How had he gotten away? Shouldn't she have suckers or microvilli on her hands to be able to keep a better grip on a slippery prey? Something that had been lost by too many matings with humans, she supposed.

Tybalt splashed back toward his cave, frantic. He was quick and, even with her siren powers, Reg found it difficult to keep up with him. If she were out in the open ocean, she would have been his match and more. But in the swamp, she was out of her element and he was in his.

She watched him stagger up onto the shore out of the water. She didn't want him out of the water. She didn't want to have to track him or overcome him on the land. It would be much more difficult that way.

Reg saw a shape separate itself from the tree above her and fly through the air toward the goblin. She caught her breath, eyes wide, as it resolved itself into the shape of a cat. For a moment, she thought illogically of Starlight, about how more than once he had taken it upon himself to attack a being that he felt threatened her, even before she knew there was a threat. This time she was aware there was a threat, but she had no idea where the cat had come from.

She watched, silent, as the cat shape and the goblin shape wrestled and warred, tumbling over the marshy ground until the goblin shape was still.

The cat shape sat up and began to groom. Reg moved slowly back toward the island for a better look. She stayed in the water where she felt safe, but she wanted to see and thank this new being who had come out of nowhere to help her.

She watched from the water as the big, beautiful panther groomed itself like a house cat. It took her breath away.

After a few minutes of seeing to his face, teeth, and claws, the cat turned his attention back toward her, as curious as she was at this new creature inhabiting his swamp.

Reg tried to push her feelings of gratitude toward him. He wouldn't understand the words, but, hopefully, he would understand the emotion. And hopefully, he had no interest in attacking her. She was in his territory. He didn't appear to have killed the goblin out of hunger. He sat away from the body and showed no interest in partaking of the stinking goblin flesh.

Reg splashed water on her face and rubbed her hands together, trying to get Tybalt's smell off of her. She didn't want to carry it around the rest of the day. The cat watched her.

After a few minutes, he started to prowl around. Reg worried that he wouldn't be able to get off of the island. He had jumped down from the canopy, but he wouldn't be able to jump up that high, would he?

In answer, he ran up the trunk of a nearby tree, easily scaling it until he sat in a branch that was far overhead. Reg closed her eyes and thought a message. She wasn't sure he would be able to help her. Even to understand her. She needed to know how to get out of there. How to get somewhere she would be safe. Back to civilization. She knew there were many other dangers in the swamp, and she didn't want to escape one to be eaten by another.

The cat stood stretched out long on the branch, looking down at her and blinking sleepily. Eventually, he started to move again. Reg tried to follow in the water below. He was much swifter than she was, being hampered by the mud and the grass and other thick vegetation. But he kept an eye on her and slowed and waited when she became entangled or had to take a rest.

Night began to fall, and it was getting darker and more challenging to see him up above. She lost sight of him and reached out again with her mind and senses, trying to locate him and impart to him the message that she could not see in the dark. She heard again Ruan's sarcastic "oh, blind one."

She could hear and sense the panther moving out of the tree to the land. He mewed softly several times. Reg moved toward him, dragging herself up onto the land and feeling like she suddenly weighed a thousand pounds. It was so much more effort to move on the land. Something touched her hand and, at first, Reg made a noise and jerked away, startled. Then she realized it was the cat, trying to guide her in the darkness, and she rested her hand on the top of his head and trusted him to lead her into the night to somewhere safe.

CHAPTER TWENTY

*R*eg awoke to birds and other sounds of the wild around her. She moved around slowly, expecting to find herself in her sleeping bag, but she didn't seem to have one. Had she been sleepwalking? Or had something happened?

She encountered something soft and warm beside her and snuggled closer. There was nothing like cuddling with a cat in the sleepy hours of the morning, as long as the cat would stay put. Starlight always got up and wanted to be fed before Reg was ready to be up and around.

Realizing it wasn't Starlight next to her despite the feline aura nearby, Reg blinked her eyes open and forced herself to look around. She saw the trees overhead, heard the water, and felt the springy ground beneath her. But no sleeping bag. And the cat was much larger than her tuxedo cat.

Reg drew back from the sleeping panther, half afraid and half astonished. She had apparently stayed with the panther until she could no longer walk any farther, and then had lain down and gone to sleep, the cat settling in and keeping watch over her throughout the night.

The cat stretched out his very long body and gave a wide yawn. He turned his head to look at Reg with his bright golden eyes.

"Thank you," Reg breathed. She couldn't believe what he had done for her. She sat up and looked around. Now that she was no longer trying to escape, she was able to keep her mind calm enough to sense her surroundings and to try to establish herself in space. Where exactly was she and where did she want to go to find her companions or a way back home?

She had a vague sense of where she was in the park, but she didn't know the park well enough from the cartoonish maps she had looked at to know what was close by and what direction she should go in.

The cat's head whipped around suddenly, and Reg followed his gaze to see what he had seen or heard. There was a shape back in the trees. A tall man, cloaked, moving slowly and carefully from one tree to the next. Reg stared at him. Could it be the wizard? How ironic would it be for her to find him while she was lost, unable to help either of them get home?

The panther got to his feet. He was watching the shape but didn't seem threatened, only curious.

Reg stretched and massaged her arms and legs and then stood up as well.

"Hello? Can you help me?"

The figure froze, then started to move away from her. Reg jogged toward him, not wanting to be left behind. "Excuse me? I don't want to bother you, but I wonder if you could help me out, just for a minute."

The figure glanced over his shoulder once, then finally stopped, waiting for her. "I'm sorry, I don't think I can help," he said in a male voice, cultured, with an accent—maybe French or New Orleans?

"Please. I don't mean to impose, but if you could just point me in the direction of the nearest settlement. I just need to find my way to civilization."

"There is nowhere near here."

"There must be something. Or if you have a phone or a boat. Anything, please, I need to make contact with my friends and get out of here."

He looked over his shoulder again, then finally conceded to turn and face her, letting Reg get a better look at him.

Not the wrinkled old wizard that Reg had expected. A very tall man, his face nearly covered by long reddish whiskers. A full beard and long hair. His eyes were dark and secretive. Someone who lived deep in the swamp and didn't want to be bothered. He drew the cloak close around him as if he were hiding from her.

"I don't have a phone."

"Then how do you get ahold of anyone? There must be some way to get a message out. Please. I can't just wander around here."

"Where did you get the cat?"

Reg looked down at the panther, who was following her, just a couple of steps behind. "Oh… uh… we kind of made friends last night. He's been helping me out."

The man looked at the cat. "Why did you bring her here?"

Reg laughed. But the hairy man continued to look at the panther as if expecting an answer. The cat tilted its head, looking at him. Reg could not have put words to the communication that was exchanged between the two of them, but the cat imparted feelings and memories from the last couple of days. Reg was surprised to realize that the cat had been there when Tybalt took her. She had been communing with him, the fire in her hands, when Tybalt had managed to sneak up behind her and to knock her out, or whatever it was he had done to overcome her.

He had followed her and Tybalt all the way back to his lair and had waited and watched to see what would happen. Reg stroked his head and scratched behind his ears, the way Starlight liked her to.

"Thank you. If you hadn't been there… I don't know what would have happened. He might have killed me."

The panther reminded her of her ferocious battle with Tybalt in the water. He thought she would eventually have been the winner of that contest.

Reg was glad that she hadn't had to find out. Fighting a life or death battle was not how she had planned to spend her trip to the Everglades.

The tall, hairy man scratched his head, looking at Reg. "I supposed you'd better come with me."

"Thank you."

He turned and started to walk away from Reg. She followed at a bit of a run, feeling like a toddler trying to keep up with an adult. The tall man looked back at her and slowed. Reg looked back at the panther, and he continued to trail them, though getting farther and farther away, until she lost sight of him, somewhere in the trees. He might be up above them, following her from the trees as he had when Tybalt had captured her, but she didn't think he was. She could no longer sense him close by.

"You can communicate with cats?" She tried to start a conversation with the man, who seemed to be content to walk in silence. After her run-in with Tybalt, Reg wasn't going to make assumptions about him like she had about

Tybalt. She wanted to find out everything she could about him, even if he thought her questions were rude.

The man's head bobbed. "Yes."

"What's your name?"

He didn't answer for a while. Then finally, he told her, "Etienne."

"Etienne." Reg repeated it. "My name is Reg. For Regina. Is that French?"

"Yes, it comes from the French."

"Are you French? You have an accent."

"I am not. Some of my people came from there generations ago. But we keep to ourselves, so we have not fully... integrated."

Reg had known other insular populations that had retained their original language and accents, so that made sense to her. She looked up at the tall, cloaked man, trying to determine what she could from his body and manner of dress. It was hard for her to be sure of anything with the cloak around him. It disguised his shape and covered most of his body, leaving only his heavily whiskered face visible.

"Have your people lived in the Everglades long? Or did you move here by yourself?" She was assuming that he was native to the swamp and not just a tourist like Reg. He seemed at home there, and he had talked to the panther.

"We have been here for many years. I was born here."

"Cool. So you must know the park very well."

"Park?"

"The Everglades. It's a national park." Maybe he didn't know that. He might not have any communication with the outside world. If he didn't even have a phone, how would he know about what was going on in the world around him? And what would it matter to him if they named it a park or not? It was to his benefit, protecting the natural habitat he lived in, but that didn't mean that he was one of the people who had lobbied to have it declared a protected area.

"That will cause more people to come here?"

"Uh, no, I don't think you need to worry about that. It was declared a park years ago."

He nodded. "Good."

"You didn't know that? You don't have much contact with... visitors?"

"No." Etienne's head turned in her direction briefly. "I try to avoid contact."

"Sorry. Getting kidnapped by a swamp goblin wasn't really in my plans."

"Then you should not have talked to him."

Reg shrugged. "Well... I guess. But he might have stalked and kidnapped me anyway."

"Goblins usually seek out victims they enjoyed talking with."

"Oh." Reg blew out her breath. So, talking to someone she didn't know was a goblin could be a problem. And what was she doing? Talking to someone else she didn't know. She had no idea whether her companion were just a tall, wild-looking man, or whether he might have powers or an agenda she couldn't fathom. She probed his mind, trying to do it gently so as not to tip him off. He made a woofing sound and shook his head. He looked in her direction again.

"I did not invite you in."

Reg's face warmed. She did know that it was rude to try to read him without his permission. But she was in sort of a difficult situation. Of course, if she asked him, he would say that he didn't have any evil intentions toward her. He hadn't even wanted her to go with him. But that didn't mean he wouldn't turn on her and try to shove her into his oven, like the witch in a fairy tale.

"I am not a witch," Etienne said with a growl.

"Now, who is reading minds without permission?"

"You reached out to me."

"I suppose." Reg looked for some sign of a settlement or the man's house. How far away were they? She hoped she didn't have to hike several miles through the swamp to get wherever he was taking her. And she hoped that there was a way to make contact with civilization once she did. She wasn't sure she would be able to. He said he didn't have a phone. How else was she supposed to get a message to Corvin and Damon if they were still alive and looking for her? Or how was she supposed to find her way back to civilization by herself if they were not there to help her?

"Not much farther," Etienne assured her. "I was just gathering some breakfast."

With his cloak wrapped around him, she couldn't see what he might be carrying. What did a giant gather for breakfast? Nuts and berries? Birds? Bunnies? Larger prey that happened to stumble into his parlor?

Eventually, they reached a small house. The boards were gray and aging. It looked like it had been there for a hundred years or more and might just collapse at any minute. Reg hesitated when he opened the thin board door and gestured for her to enter. Was she going to be trapped? What would happen to her inside?

She hoped that he didn't have shelves full of human skulls like Tybalt.

CHAPTER TWENTY-ONE

*T*he house was dimly lit by the sunlight making its way through the cracks of the walls and under the roof. Reg looked around. No skulls.

There were some animal parts—a fur rug in front of the fireplace, a couple of trophy heads and taxidermied swamp animals that looked like they had been there gathering dust for many years. Etienne nodded to each of them as if he were greeting old friends. And maybe that's what they were —his only friends.

Reg rubbed her arms and looked around. It was cooler in the house than it was outside, and she had a sudden chill. Etienne moved over to a rough plank table and set a satchel onto it. Reg watched as he unbuckled it and started to remove mushrooms, moss, and other lumps that she couldn't identify. Some kind of root? Fungus? This was breakfast. No birds or bunnies. Nothing to be worried about, unless they were to whet his appetite before a main course of psychic wandering in the swamp.

Etienne turned his head toward her slightly. "I prefer not to eat flesh."

"Okay. Good."

She watched his hands as he sorted through his breakfast. They were thick and covered with hair. She had seen men with hair growing thickly down the backs of their hands and knuckles before, but never one with as much as Etienne.

He washed the mushrooms, moss, and some of the other lumps in a bowl of water, and then put them into a frying pan on top of his stove. In a few minutes, he had the fire roaring, filling the room with waves of heat, and the food in the frying pan began to sizzle.

Reg watched the fire, mesmerized, feeling it pulling at the fire within her. She tried to resist it and to think of other things. Davin was her fire-casting mentor and had told her that she was not yet practiced enough to play with fire on her own. She had probably done more than he would have liked the night before, using the fire to light her way, and then letting it get away from her in anger to knock down Tybalt. He had deserved it, of course. And Reg couldn't help it if he had made her react instinctively in self-defense. That wasn't her fault.

Etienne looked in her direction, then closed the front of the stove so that she could no longer see the fire. That was probably for the best. As it grew warmer, he fingered the edges of his cloak. It was warm enough that he didn't need it on indoors. He was ready to take it off, but she could see he was hesitant.

"What is it?" Reg asked.

"I am not the same as you."

"No," Reg agreed with some amusement. "You're different from me in a lot of ways."

"You will be frightened."

"I won't. What's wrong, are you... scarred or deformed? I won't scream or run away."

"I am different."

"Okay. It's up to you whether you take it off or not. Do you want me to... look away? Or shut myself in another room?"

He hadn't invited her to any other rooms of the house, so she had stayed with him in the kitchen. There was a great room with heavy furniture grouped around the fireplace. And there were doorways to other rooms, probably bedrooms, along the side. She didn't know if there was any kind of indoor plumbing. She assumed not, since she didn't see any faucet or indoor pump in the kitchen.

Etienne considered this for a moment, then shook his head. The best thing for him to do was probably just to remove the cloak without cere-mony and to expect Reg to be able to handle it. Prolonging it was just making her more curious and probably making him more anxious.

Reg walked into the great room and made a show of examining the trophies. If Etienne did not eat flesh, why hunt big game? For the sport? Or did they belong to some long-ago ancestor? Maybe someone who was not vegetarian.

She could hear Etienne moving around, and didn't look at him. She continued to examine the trophies as if she were a connoisseur of taxidermy. Eventually, as she heard him pull the frying pan off the burner, she turned back toward the kitchen. The smell of the frying mushrooms and other vegetable matter was making her stomach growl. She couldn't remember what she had eaten since lunch the day before at the Skunk Man Saloon.

She saw Etienne standing there, working over the food without his cloak on, and it all clicked into place.

It probably shouldn't have taken her so long. She had been looking at the Bigfoot pictures in the restaurant's menu just the day before, but it seemed like a very long time before.

"You're the skunk man!"

"*A* skunk man," he corrected. He shook his head grumpily. "Skunk man. Do I smell like a skunk to your sensitive nose?"

"No." Reg was surprised. She took a sniff in his direction. She could smell musk, damp fur steaming dry close to the wood stove, and other swamp smells melding together, but they weren't unpleasant. Rather like the smell of the ground after rainfall.

Etienne's fur or body hair was a reddish-brown. He wore little clothing, already well-dressed in his fur coat, like any primate other than the bare-skinned humans. Just what was necessary for modesty and to carry about a couple of essential tools.

"Homo sapiens smell worse than other hominini," Etienne told her. "Always trying to cover up their natural odors with store-bought scents." He made a sniffling, sneezing sound and shook his head. "But then, it is hard for you to stay clean, with all of those clothes trapping the scents and oils."

Hard to stay clean?

Reg had a sudden vision of Etienne sitting down and grooming himself like a cat and tried to suppress giggles. Etienne looked at her uncertainly. She didn't know if he could see what she had pictured or whether he was wondering. Either way, she wasn't about to explain herself. She looked at the food in the skillet, and the food still on the table, berries and a few other edible leaves and flowers. Her stomach growled loudly.

"Sit," Etienne told her, motioning to a chair.

It was taller than a human's chair. More like a bar stool. Reg felt childish boosting herself into it and letting her legs swing free, feet hanging above the floor. Etienne didn't make any comment on it.

"Are you sure there is enough?" Reg asked. "I don't want to eat your share. You must... get very hungry." She stopped short of saying that he must eat a lot. A human might take that the wrong way. She didn't know how a Bigfoot would feel about it.

"There is enough. I will gather more before dinner."

Reg didn't argue.

Etienne removed two large bowls from the cupboard and divided the hot food between them. He provided Reg with a knife and fork, and a larger set for himself. He muttered for a moment before he began to eat. Maybe a prayer or a blessing. Maybe just irritated by having a guest at breakfast.

Reg had no idea what the mosses and unidentifiable lumps would taste like, but their savory smell filled the little house, so she dug in. It was warm, hearty, and satisfying.

They both ate in silence for a while.

"It's delicious," Reg told Etienne. "You are a good cook."

"We eat simply. We live simply."

Looking at the rustic interior of the house, Reg had to agree. But he said it as if it were a good thing, something to be proud of, rather than sounding like he was being denied the finer things in life. As if he really did enjoy living the way he did.

The food was good, Reg had to admit that. But entertainment? As far as she could see, there was none. It would be a very boring life with no TV, telephone, internet, or other electronics.

"There are books," Etienne pointed out.

Reg had seen several thick volumes on her tour of the great room. And there were probably more in the bedroom. Maybe even books borrowed from the library or other Sasquatches.

"Are there many of you in the park?" Reg asked. "In the Everglades, I mean. I couldn't tell from what it said in the menu whether there is just one *so-called* skunk man in the swamp, or whether there are a bunch of you running around." She looked around what she could see of the house, considering. There must have been a family there once upon a time. And for there to be generations before, there had to have been more than one solitary skunk man in the Everglades for many years.

But much of the habitat had been destroyed. That would have had an impact on the residents. Especially larger ones who needed more food to survive.

"Now? Not anymore. There used to be quite a few. But most have moved away now. There are better opportunities in other places. I did not want to leave."

"What opportunities are in other places? Do you… mix with humans? I would think that a lot of the wild habitats are being destroyed."

"Some choose to mix with homo sapiens. Laser hair removal." He shrugged. "In some countries, it is easier to mix in. But for me…" He ran his hand down a hairy arm. "I would not give up my coat for others. I am… old fashioned. A dying breed… literally."

Reg was sad. She hated to think of the world running out of mythical creatures. Goblins, she didn't mind so much. But Etienne was a pleasant, civilized man who didn't eat humans for breakfast, and the world would be a poorer place without him.

"You don't have… a girlfriend? No one who would like to live out here? There must be others… like you who don't want to move to areas with more modern conveniences. There must be others who would prefer to live simply."

His eyes darted up from his plate to look at her for an instant. She thought she detected a smile under all of the whiskers.

"I am writing to a woman in Russia," he admitted. "Long distant relationships are difficult to judge, but… I think we have a good connection."

"You think she would come here?"

"If her family will allow it and we could make the proper arrangements… I think she would. But a proper courtship in our cultures takes years. Not just a few brief letters over the months."

Reg nodded. It was hard for her to imagine in the modern, fast-paced world full of cell phones, texting, instant messages, and emails. Everything was designed to be quick and efficient. She would hate to have to wait weeks or months between letters. Not to mention the hours it would take her to read her pen-pal's handwritten letter and then compose one herself.

Without the pressure of time, maybe her reading and writing difficulties would not be such an issue. It wouldn't make any difference to anyone whether it took her two minutes or two days to read a letter. No one would know the difference.

"What is her name?"

"Ilka." He hesitated whether to tell her more. Reg didn't press, and eventually, he decided on his own. "Her coat turns white in the winter," he said in a shy, reverent tone.

"Oh! Like a rabbit. But if she came here… it wouldn't turn white, would it? Does it depend on the weather, or does it just happen every year whether she is somewhere cold or not?"

Etienne contemplated the question. Apparently, it was not something he had asked her. "I think it has to do with the length of the days. When she is not in the sun for as many hours."

"Like a tan fading? Or like forcing a poinsettia? I don't suppose you'd be able to lock her up in a closet for eighteen hours to see if it would change."

She was worried when she heard how the words came out of her mouth that she had offended him or Ilka's honor. But he took it in good humor, laughing a soft, puffing sort of laugh that cheered Reg's dark mood.

"I do not think that would be a good idea," he agreed. "The women of our species can be quite… formidable."

Etienne's French accent on the word "formidable" made Reg laugh as well. She could just picture Etienne trying to lock his dark-furred bride away to see if her coat would change, and her vehement objections and reaction.

They went back to eating. Etienne had finished most of his hot food and helped himself to some of the berries and greens on the table. Reg picked up some red berries.

"These are safe, right? They are not poisonous to humans?"

His hairy shoulders raised and fell. "I do not have guests often. Your kind and mine avoid one another."

"You speak English, though. You could put on your cloak and maybe some more clothes and pass as human. Do you ever do that?"

"Rare. I know a few… mmmm… friends. I mostly deal with them, but not unknowns."

Reg nodded eagerly. She popped the berries in her mouth and ate them without further thought. "Do you think that one of these friends could help me to get back to my friends?"

Etienne thought about it. "I suppose. I usually take my mail to Bruce the last Tuesday of each month. I could take you to him then…"

Reg was aghast. "Wait here until the end of the month?"

He nodded. He glanced around his cabin. "It isn't as bad as all that. It's comfortable. Your ancestors would have lived in a place like this."

"I can't wait that long. I was hoping I could get in contact with someone *today*. Get back to civilization."

"Today." It was Etienne's turn to be taken aback. "*Today*. That would be very rushed."

"Please. I know it probably wrecks your plans for the day. But maybe there's something I could do for you… I would offer to pay, but I don't suppose you have much need for human money. If you do… or if you want jewels… I could get you those too."

"I was going to begin work on a new letter to Ilka later this week. But they take much time and attention… I wouldn't be ready to send it to her until… maybe the twentieth?"

"No. No, I need to get back to my friends right away. We need to find the missing wizard and get him back to the Spring Games before that. They start on the equinox, and he will have to make arrangements before then."

"Missing wizard?"

CHAPTER TWENTY-TWO

O h..." Reg hadn't meant to mention aloud that Wilson was a wizard. It had just come out in her panic to explain to Etienne that he needed to get her to civilization right away. But it didn't matter if he knew she was looking for a wizard, did it? He wouldn't have anything to do with the search or the prize and certainly wouldn't be talking to anyone in the human world about it. He wouldn't spread their secret.

"Well, yes. We are here in the Everglades to look for a man who is lost. To try to get him to the magical Spring Games. But we need to find him soon. And my friends will want to know where I am and what happened to me."

"I can't have my letter finished more quickly than that."

"But you don't need to finish your letter to take me to Bruce. You can finish your letter later and take it to him on the day you normally would."

This seemed to be a new idea for Etienne. "I don't know..."

"I know you probably have other things to do today. I don't like to make you drop everything... but is there any way you could help me to get to this Bruce's place today? And like I say... I can pay you if there is anything that would be of value to you."

Etienne stroked his chin, thinking about it. He pursed his lips and looked as though he were going to speak a few times. Reg tried to exude warm, helpful feelings in his direction. He would feel good if he helped her.

She would want to do something for him in return. Everyone would be happier if he would help her to get back to civilization.

"This is unusual," Etienne pointed out.

"I know."

"Bruce knows when to expect me so that we can avoid… the paparazzi."

"Paparazzi?" Reg echoed blankly.

He nodded. "People trying to get a picture of the Skunk Man." He said the name with distaste, wrinkling his nose. "Creature hunters. Cryptozoologists."

"Oh. Yeah, I guess there are probably a few of those around here." Reg suddenly felt guilty at having eaten at the Skunk Man Saloon. Hadn't she seen how they were exploiting him? Someone who just wanted to live a quiet, simple life? Someone who wanted to avoid all of the cameras and prying eyes.

"I'm sure we could find a way to do this without you being seen. You could take me close and then point me in the right direction so that you don't have to go right up to Bruce's house or wherever you usually meet him. I won't tell anyone that I met you here. I won't give away your secret."

"We have to keep moving," he pointed out. "Every few years, the curiosity-seekers find our home, and we are forced to leave there and start over." He looked fondly around the interior of his old, gray cabin. "I was just getting settled here. I don't want to have to move."

"You were… just getting settled? Whose house was it before you moved into it?"

"No one's. My father built this house."

"How long have you lived here?"

He considered the question. "Maybe… ninety years. It seems like just yesterday."

"Oh." Reg nodded. "I see. Well… don't you think we can do this in a way that you are not exposed? I don't want to cause you any trouble."

He sighed. "It would be better to wait until the end of the month."

"For you. But I really do need to get back before that. And I can't just walk away from here and hope to find my way out and not run into anyone or anything that could harm me. I'll get lost and eaten." She tried to make herself sound as helpless and pitiful as possible. She had a sense that he had a soft spot for the vulnerable. That was why the panther had thought to bring her to him. At some time, Etienne must have fed or helped the big cat in some way. "There are so many dangers in the Everglades. And I don't know them like you do."

She might be able to get out on her own, using her psychic senses to try to pinpoint her companions or the closest civilization. But where had that gotten her in finding the missing wizard? She had taken them a long distance from where Damon said the wizard should be, and then she had not been able to find him. Her senses had somehow been blurred or interfered with. Maybe he had some kind of confusion spell to keep people from finding him. Something that he had cast himself? Or had he been kidnapped and someone else was trying to hide him?

Reg wished she'd had more time to search for him in the settlement around the Skunk Man Saloon.

Corvin and Damon should not have been in such a hurry to get her away from there and follow their own plans.

"I suppose." Etienne had been speaking, and Reg had failed to hear what he had to say. She gathered herself together at his last words.

"You will? You'll take me to Bruce? Will you do it today?"

"I suppose I don't want you to fall into the river or hurt yourself in some other way. If we were to wait even just a few days, something might happen to you."

"Yes. It could. Neither of us would want that."

Etienne picked at a few more of the fresh foods on the table. Reg helped herself to some berries but couldn't bring herself to eat the raw greens or flowers that Etienne ate. She just wasn't a salad person.

"You must prepare yourself, then," Etienne announced. "We will leave… in an hour of the clock."

Reg let her breath out. "Thank you. Thank you so much."

"I will require payment."

"Uh—sure. Of course. I said I would pay you. What is your fee?"

"Hershey's."

"Hershey's?" Reg couldn't think of what he meant.

Etienne reached over and took her plate. She saw when he picked it up and stood that it was actually a small hubcap. He took the two plates over to the sink and set them down. He opened a small side cupboard and displayed it to her.

"Hershey's."

Reg saw a small stack of chocolate bars with silver foil and dark brown paper wrappings. Hershey's chocolate bars. She laughed.

"Hershey's. Of course. How many Hershey's do you want as payment?"

"I would think that this is worth at least... two bars."

"Certainly," Reg agreed. "I don't have them on me. What is the best way for me to get them to you when I can?"

He went to a writing desk in the great room and pulled out a block of notepapers and an old-fashioned fountain pen. He wrote carefully and, when he was done, blew gently on the ink, and when he was satisfied that it was completely dry, took it over to Reg. "My address. You can mail it. Bruce brings me my mail once a month."

"The last Tuesday of every month?"

Etienne nodded.

CHAPTER TWENTY-THREE

$\mathcal{E}$tienne had told Reg that she would need to get ready to go to Bruce's in an hour. Once they had come to terms, he explained that she would need to wash before they left.

"You smell like goblin," he said delicately. "And you are cut up from the saw grass. That... and cat... the stagnant water..."

Reg's face burned. She raised her arm to her nose and sniffed. Even she could smell the putrefying scent of goblin. If Etienne's nose was as sensitive enough to also smell the cat and the marsh water on her, she could only imagine how offensive it must have been for her to sit at the same table and partake of food with him.

"I'm so sorry! I'm normally very clean."

He nodded. "I'm sure you are. I don't have any clothes that would fit you, but if you at least wash your body..."

He warmed some water in a pot on the stove and set it in one of the bedrooms with a washcloth and towel for her to clean herself up the best she could. There was an antique mirror over the dresser in the bedroom, and Reg leaned close to it to look at herself. Her face was covered with mud and scabby cuts and scratches.

She looked as if she had crawled through the swamp and fought with saw grass and a goblin.

* * *

Reg hoped that she smelled better when she presented herself to Etienne some time later. The water in the pot was dark and murky, and she couldn't smell any more goblin stench when she held her hands up to her face. The cuts on her face were not as shocking with the scabs and dirt washed away. Only a couple of them had reopened and bled when she cleaned them.

Etienne dumped the goblin-fouled water a distance away from his cabin and left the cloth and towel outside to dry and air. Reg wondered how his people had earned the moniker of skunk man when Etienne was so fastidious. Maybe it was something they had learned after being exposed to humans over the years. Or perhaps some human had mistaken a bear or some other animal for one of the Bigfoots. Or maybe one of them had once been sprayed by a skunk.

Or maybe humans were just mean and prejudiced against beings different from themselves.

Etienne looked her over and nodded. "Now, we will go."

He started walking. Reg followed. Etienne clearly had to go much more slowly than he normally would have, forcing himself to stop and wait for her and take his long strides at a very slow pace. But he didn't complain or rush her along.

They walked through the swampland in relative silence. Etienne was much quieter than Reg, which seemed impossible given his size, but she felt like a bumbling water buffalo beside him. She kept her eyes open for snakes or large reptiles. Or swamp goblins. What other hazards had Corvin warned her against? It seemed like nothing was safe. They should have just stayed at home.

And left the old wizard to wander in the Everglades by himself? Or maybe under the control of some powerful magical creature? Reg had learned long ago to put her own safety first, because no one else would. But she found it hard to know when to help others and when to stay out of it and protect herself. The magical world was a whole new complication that she had never had to consider before.

"You haven't run into this wizard I am looking for, have you?" Reg inquired, puffing a little as she tried to keep up with Etienne.

"A wizard? It has been a while since I have seen a wizard. I try to avoid homo sapiens. They are more trouble than they are worth."

Reg's face burned at his words. She couldn't deny that she was causing him a lot of extra trouble. He would have to gather more food. He had to traipse across the swamp to deliver her to Bruce, the postman. He had to worry about whether she would expose him, and he would have to move out of the house he had come to love.

"Now, there was one," Etienne said slowly, "not so long ago…"

Reg's heart lifted. Maybe he could point her in the right direction, help her to find the lost wizard.

"Maybe just… thirty years…?" Etienne suggested. Then he nodded to himself, confirming. "Yes, I think that was it. Forty at the outside."

"Oh. No, I don't think that's my wizard, then."

Etienne nodded.

"What if… you didn't know he was a wizard. Have you come across any lost non-magical humans lately?"

"No."

They fell silent again. Reg wondered how long it would take them to get to Bruce's house or place of work. Etienne was used to walking there; he didn't have a car. But he didn't have Reg's short legs and was in much better shape than she was. It might take him half a day to walk out there and half a day to walk back when he could go at his usual speed. It was frustrating not to be able to see what was ahead. The vegetation kept her from being able to see any distance. She also thought that Etienne might be intentionally walking her in circles or a roundabout route so that she wouldn't be able to find her way back to his cabin if she wanted to. He didn't want her bringing more homo sapiens back there.

Reg stopped, bending over with her hands on her knees to take a few deep breaths. "How much farther is it?"

Etienne stopped. He looked her over. "We are probably halfway there." He handed her a canteen. Reg opened it and took a long drink of water. That helped. At least she'd had breakfast. She would have had a difficult time on the hike without some calories in her.

"Halfway? Can we slow down a little?"

He nodded. Reg handed the canteen back to him. He put the strap over his shoulder and started walking again. Reg sighed and followed.

* * *

At first, Reg didn't see the shack. Like Etienne's cabin, it blended in with the trees and vegetation. It was not painted, or the paint had long since peeled off, so it was a soft gray that didn't stand out. Reg stretched her arms and shoulders, which she had been holding tense as she walked, worried she would never get there. Maybe Etienne simply planned to abandon her in the middle of the Everglades, knowing she would never be able to make it out on her own. She was relieved to see some sign of another resident.

She looked over at Etienne, asking him the question without words.

"This is Bruce's house," he confirmed.

"Thank goodness. I am not in shape for a walk like that."

"Then you should not come to the Everglades."

Maybe there was something to that.

There was a split rail fence around the back of the house and, as Etienne approached, a small gray donkey trotted over to the side, nickering at him. Reg headed for the front of the house. She would have to explain to Bruce what she was doing there and what she needed from him. Maybe she should wait for Etienne to join her, but they were, at least, dealing with a human being, so Reg didn't think there was any danger in talking to him while Etienne occupied himself with greeting the burro.

She glanced around the front of the house, but didn't see anyone in the garden. She also didn't see a car or mail truck. Bruce was probably still at work. She was going to have to wait there until he got back home. Etienne wasn't going to like that. Either she would have to stay there without him to explain to Bruce what had happened, or he would have to wait with her until it was past dark and too late to walk home.

Reg knocked on the front door anyway, in case she were wrong. Maybe Mrs. Bruce had taken the car out and Bruce himself was still at home. There was no answer. She knocked again.

"Uh… Bruce? Are you home?" she called out, hoping that if she knew his name, he would answer. He would know that she wasn't just some random stranger or missionary. "Bruce? Hello?"

The doorknob was warm and inviting under her hand. Reg remembered receiving a lecture from Harrison on opening doors and locks and keys and their magical significance, and she knew she probably should not open the door to a place she had not been invited to. But she was sure the door was unlocked and that she could just open it just a little way to make sure that there was nobody home. People did that in the country all the time, didn't they? They just walked into the kitchen and yoo-hooed, and if the owner wasn't home, got what they needed and left them a note. There wasn't anything wrong with her just *checking*.

She turned the doorknob and found that she was right. It had been left open. So either the owner was not far away, or he was okay with people walking in. She pushed the door open a few inches. "Hello? Anyone home? Bruce?"

No answer. No sign of anyone. There were dishes in a drying rack next to the sink and the scent of fried sausages hung in the air. He'd been there recently. He'd eaten breakfast, cleaned up, and gone out. He might be in one of the outbuildings or gardens doing chores, but she didn't think so. Not with the car gone.

Reg shut the door again and walked back around the house to Etienne. She was quite proud of herself. She hadn't even been *tempted* to pry into Bruce's private business or check out his valuables. She felt quite virtuous.

Etienne turned his head to look at her as she got around the house again.

"No one home," Reg explained. "What do you want me to do?"

There was another man there, on the other side of the split rail fence, talking with Etienne. An older gentleman with graying hair and a long face.

"Oh! I didn't see you there. I guess you must be Bruce."

His head bobbed up and down in response. Neither of them said anything. Reg looked around, feeling there was something wrong. Something was missing. It took a minute to put her finger on it, but then she was puzzled.

Where was the donkey?

CHAPTER TWENTY-FOUR

*R*eg frowned at Etienne and then at Bruce. "Where…?"

Bruce must have taken the donkey into a barn or another paddock. Reg hadn't realized how much time had passed in going to the front of the house, knocking on the door, and returning. It must have been longer than she had thought. He had returned from his chores, taken the donkey into the barn, and returned to talk to Etienne.

She didn't think he'd had enough time to do that, unless he had superpowers.

Reg looked Bruce up and down. She didn't think there was anything unusual about him. He looked just like any other old man.

"Umm…" Reg shook her head. She looked at Etienne. He didn't offer anything. "So, Mr. Bruce, I was hoping you would be able to take me into… uh, I don't know. The nearest settlement. Or if you have a phone, I could borrow it to try to reach my friends and they could find a way to pick me up here."

Bruce nodded again. He shifted his feet. He leaned a little toward Etienne, the person he was familiar with. Living all the way out there, it would be easy for someone to become unaccustomed to visitors. To be anxious about unexpected visitors. He and Etienne had structured things so that they would know exactly when to meet each other, at the same time every month.

After a reassuring look from Etienne, Bruce coughed and cleared his throat. His voice was low and hoarse. "I can take you to the store," he agreed. "Etienne said that you have..." he coughed again, "been a good guest."

Etienne looked at Reg expectantly. Reg smiled and let out a breath of relief. "I'm so glad. I didn't see a car, and I thought you weren't even home. It must be in the barn or another building?"

"I don't have a car."

"Then... how are we going to get to the store?" Reg's legs ached already from walking all the way there. She sincerely hoped that Bruce had a boat or some means of conveying her to the store, because she didn't think she could walk any farther.

"I will... carry you."

Reg laughed in disbelief. The old man thought—what?—that he could carry her piggyback all the way to the nearest settlement?

Etienne looked at Reg reproachfully. She felt instantly guilty at having laughed at her new host, but still didn't see how he could get her to the store without a vehicle.

"I'm sorry..."

"Bruce is a skin-walker."

Reg looked from Etienne to Bruce, trying to fathom his meaning. She hoped that didn't mean he was a nudist. That would make traveling to the store with him all that much more awkward.

"A skin-walker," Bruce repeated. "I can change my skin." He met her blank look, a little fan of wrinkles appearing next to his eyes as if he were laughing at her. "My form. I am not confined to this body."

"You're..." Suddenly, Reg knew where the donkey had gone. He was still standing right in front of her. Ready to carry her into the settlement. "You're a shapeshifter?"

"Yes." A little cough. "If you prefer."

Recalling Tybalt's anger at his kind not being called by their preferred name, Reg immediately shook her head. "A skin-walker. I just hadn't heard that term before. I didn't know... I've never known someone like that before."

"We do not generally make ourselves known." Bruce looked at his friend. "Etienne believes you are safe."

"I won't tell anyone. If you don't want people to know where you live or what you are. I won't give you away."

"That is most kind." His head bobbed up and down, and Reg found herself nodding with him.

"You're the one doing me a favor. I really appreciate it. Thank you. Um… I can pay you, send you something of value, if there's something you want or need."

"I want for nothing."

"I'm sending Etienne back Hershey's bars. If there's some treat you can't normally get…?"

Bruce considered this gravely.

Reg didn't know if he were the mailman or just a friend that helped carry Etienne's mail back and forth for him, but either way, he could probably get whatever he wanted through Amazon or one of the other online fulfillment companies.

"Maybe… oats?"

"Oats?"

"I quite liked some that I had when I was in the city a couple of years back. Apple and cinnamon. In little packets."

"Oatmeal. Sure, I can send you some oatmeal packages. Apple cinnamon."

Bruce smiled widely. He bent forward as if he were going to pick something up off of the ground, then transformed before her eyes. Reg hung on to the fence for support, hardly believing what she was seeing. She had seen some weird stuff since moving to Black Sands, but she had never expected to see a man turn into a donkey right in front of her eyes.

The animal made a bunch of donkey noises at Etienne, who still seemed to understand him perfectly well. Etienne nodded and opened the gate to let donkey Bruce out. Whatever magic allowed him to change form had also transformed clothing into saddle and bridle. Etienne showed a stunned Reg how to put her foot in the stirrup and then swing herself into the saddle. The donkey was not big, so she wasn't too far off the ground if she fell. But Bruce stood still and didn't seem to want to throw her off. Etienne handed her the reins and gave her a few simple directions.

"Bruce knows the way; you don't need to guide him. But if you see something that worries you, you can get him to slow, turn, or hurry up. Although," he looked at the donkey with a thoughtful expression. "In this form, he can be rather stubborn. Best if you just let him make the decisions."

"Okay." Reg was happy to let Bruce be her guide. She had no idea where to go, and he seemed like a far safer guide than Tybalt had been. "And we can get there all the way by donkey? We don't need to get on a boat or climb a cliff?"

"No. Certainly not."

"Good. Well, thank you very much for your help. And thank you, Bruce," she petted the donkey on the side of his neck. "You have been very kind to me. I keep hearing about how many people get lost around here, how the Everglades swallow people up… and I don't want to be one of those statistics."

Etienne looked around him. "It is a good place to live. It would not be so bad for you to stay."

"Unless I got eaten. Or drowned. Or something else."

He nodded slowly. "Homo sapiens are particularly vulnerable," he admitted. "It is surprising that *they* are not the hominini going extinct."

Reg shrugged uncomfortably. She supposed it was because humans had weapons and Bigfoots did not. Or they didn't choose to use them, since it was apparent that they could hunt and were sometimes in contact with the outside world and able to conduct trade.

Etienne slapped Bruce on the rump. "Goodbye then. I will not see you again."

Bruce set off at a trot. Reg looked back over her shoulder to wave to Etienne, but by the time she was turned around, he was already melting into the trees, a tall, indistinct shape against a green backdrop. Just like in a Bigfoot video.

* * *

The trip to the store was entirely uneventful. Bruce did not buck her off and bolt. She didn't develop blisters on her backside, though she did experience some chafing. The trip went by more quickly than her hike with Etienne and a few times she actually dozed off in the saddle.

She felt cheered when she saw the blocky shapes of buildings up ahead through the trees and heard the sounds of voices and cars. Civilization! Humanity! Bruce stopped some distance from the small cluster of buildings, and Reg had a distinct impression that she was to get off there. He didn't want to be seen delivering her. It would, she guessed, be something out of the ordinary and maybe the people who ran the store and the other businesses didn't know about his ability to change skins.

She hadn't received any instruction in how to get off of the donkey, so her dismount was rather clumsy but, by some miracle, she didn't end up sitting on her butt in the middle of the damp grass.

Reg stroked Bruce's neck. "Thank you again. You're a lifesaver. Etienne was going to keep me until the last Tuesday of the month and send me in with the mail."

The donkey's lips opened in a laugh and he made a coughing sound. Reg left him there and walked into the busy little collection of buildings. She didn't think it could be called a town or even a village, but there were people there, and that was what she needed. She went into the store, a sort of general store like she might have seen a hundred years earlier, carrying bits of this and that, everything a person would need.

Except that the dry goods and necessities of a hundred years before had been replaced with pay-as-you-go cell phones, bulk bins of candy, coolers of soft drinks, energy drinks, and enhanced waters, and the various other things that tourist might need in the middle of a tour of the park. Reg wandered in and looked around.

She spoke to the man at the counter, a youth who might have been eighteen at the outside, earbuds draped around his neck and a permanent eye-roll over everything that his bosses or anyone else over twenty might try to tell him.

"Excuse me… I'm wondering if there is a phone I could use."

"Cell phones are aisle one, right by the window."

"No, not a cell phone. I don't have any money. I wondered about a payphone or landline?"

"A what?"

"A phone… you put quarters in. Is there anything I could borrow?"

"Thought you said you didn't have money."

"Well, I might have a couple of quarters." She started digging around in her pockets. "Or I could call collect."

"Who?"

"I could reverse charges."

He shook his head in disbelief. "We take credit cards, Bitcoin, Apple Pay…"

"I don't have any of those."

"Don't you have your phone? You can tap."

"No, I don't have my phone. That's why I asked if I could borrow one."

"Riiiight." He looked at her, then past her to the next person. "Can I help you, ma'am?"

"No, no, I'm not done," Reg protested, keeping her body between the young man and the woman behind her.

"Could I borrow *your* phone? I only need it for a minute. I need to tell someone where to pick me up."

"Use the Uber app. The water taxi services are on it. You can get anywhere you need to go."

"Okay. Can I borrow your Uber app?"

He looked at her speculatively. "I can't give you my phone," he said in an aggrieved tone.

Reg turned and looked at the people waiting impatiently behind her. "I'm sorry, is there anyone who could lend me their phone for two minutes? I just need to make an emergency call."

"Did you know you can call emergency from any cell phone, even one that isn't on a plan anymore?" one of the men in the line asked. "Any old phone. You just have to charge it up."

"But I don't have my phone. Not even an old one. And I'm not calling 9-1-1; I'm just calling for someone to pick me up."

"You should use Lyft. Way better than Uber," a woman contributed.

She and the man started arguing over the selling points of each ride-share program.

Someone tugged at Reg's sleeve. She looked down into the face of a young boy. Maybe eight or nine years old. He held his phone out to her.

"Thank you!" Reg moved away from the counter to allow the next person in line to conduct her business. "You're a life saver!"

The child stood watching her as she tapped out the digits of Corvin's cell phone. She knew Damon's too if she put some thought into it, but Corvin's came to her more easily, so she tried him first. She just hoped that he would have service wherever he was and hear or feel it ringing. She really didn't want to wait at the store all day, borrowing people's phones as she tried to get ahold of the two warlocks.

There were a couple of rings, and then Corvin's voice. "Yes?"

"Corvin. It's Reg!"

"Regina!" Corvin sounded shaken, a very unusual state of affairs for him. "Reg, where are you? Are you okay?"

"I'm okay. I'm at a store. It's... I'm not exactly sure where it is." Reg looked around for the name of the town or the settlement. The sign on the outside of the store had simply declared, in white letters on a black sign-board, "The Store." She looked at the boy who had loaned her his phone. "Do you know where this is?"

He took the phone back from her and performed some magic on it. He handed it back, showing her a map with a blue dot on it.

"Tell him those numbers," the boy instructed. "He can put them in his GPS."

"Okay." Reg explained this to Corvin and then read the digits out to him.

"Stay there," Corvin instructed. "We'll be there as soon as we can."

"I don't have any other choice at this point. Do you have my phone? My bag? Or did he toss everything into the swamp?"

"Who?"

"Tybalt. Did he leave my stuff there or get rid of it?"

"You left your things here. What's this about Tybalt? He had already gone off to make his own camp when we went to bed. You sleepwalked... we thought you had drowned."

Reg didn't point out that it was highly unlikely that, being part siren, she would drown. But maybe he was only saying that to keep their cover. She hadn't told very many people about her mother's apparent heritage.

"No. Tybalt kidnapped me. He drugged or magicked the two of you and took me away. Back to his lair. And he was going to..."

"His lair?"

Reg couldn't understand why Corvin was being so dense. Did he not even see what was right in front of his nose?

"Tybalt's lair. Tybalt the *swamp goblin's* lair."

Corvin gasped audibly. "What?"

"I thought that you must know, even if no one else did. You had no idea?"

"Well... no, Reg. He had references. Of course I had no idea..."

"Well, I wouldn't recommend you refer him to anyone else. Actually, it doesn't matter whether you do or not because he isn't going to be running any more tours."

"Oh. I see." Corvin's voice was low. "We'd better not say anything more about it until we see each other. We'll get there as soon as we can."

"Thanks. See you then."

Reg ended the call and handed it back to the boy. "Thank you again. So much. I don't know what's wrong with people these days!"

He nodded gravely and slid his phone into his pants pocket. "You were kidnapped by a swamp goblin?"

"Well… yes. But please don't tell anyone else. It's kind of… a secret."

"Like when my brother went out with a witch."

"Uh… yes, that's right."

He nodded and wandered down an aisle and stopped to look at Pokemon trading cards. Reg wondered whether his brother had gone out with an actual witch. Maybe , someone had called her that or something that sounded similar.

CHAPTER TWENTY-FIVE

*C*orvin and Damon were not as close as Reg had hoped. Corvin hadn't given her any estimate, so she had no idea how long to expect. When twenty minutes had passed, then forty, and then an hour, she was very impatient for their arrival.

She didn't want to be the target of any extra attention, especially from any creatures or malevolent human beings. She wondered if Etienne and Bruce had already returned to their respective homes.

She sat on the boardwalk outside the store, watching the people going by, wishing she could transport Corvin and Damon there by sheer force of will, similar to when she had called Calliopia and brought her and Ruan tumbling out of thin air into her reality. But she didn't suppose that they would appreciate it very much. They would lose any equipment they were not holding. She assumed they were in a boat flitting over the top of the water to reach her, and had no idea whether calling them magically would bring the boat with them or leave it speeding along unmanned without them. Besides which, there were a lot of people around who would probably not be too happy to have a couple of men tumbling in from the ether. In Reg's experience, people tended to be irritable and even outright angry when they saw things that could not be explained by their own reality. They would think it was some kind of trick. And anything they couldn't explain was bound to be classified as dangerous.

Calling them there without knowing how they would all be affected was definitely reckless. Better to just wait for them to arrive.

A woman who came out of the store approached Reg and handed her a water bottle.

"Oh... thank you!" Reg cracked the bottle open without demurring about how she didn't need it and the woman didn't really have to do that. She was very hot and thirsty after traipsing through the swamp for so long.

The woman smiled pleasantly and walked away with her friends. Reg heard her murmuring something about homeless people being everywhere as they walked away.

Even after washing up at Etienne's house, Reg still looked homeless? She looked down at her arms and her clothing. Her hands were a little dirty, but other than that, she didn't look so bad. Scratches, but no mud and grime. But there were some holes torn in her pants, and the cuffs and knees were in a shameful state. Wrestling with swamp goblins and crawling through the swamp would do that. Reg sighed.

She had nearly given up on Corvin and Damon finding her. They might have gotten lost despite the GPS coordinates, or been eaten by something in the swamp. Reg might have given them the wrong numbers, inverting some of them as she sometimes did, and they could be miles away looking for her.

"Reg!" Damon shouted, hurrying toward her.

Reg got to her feet. Damon grabbed her and held her close in an embrace. Reg went rigid at the unexpected contact. She put her hands on Damon's shoulders to push him back.

"I'm fine. It's okay."

"We didn't know what had happened to you. I felt so bad. I was the one who asked you to come along, and then you ended up sleepwalking into the river or something. I thought you were a goner. We should have had someone keep watch..."

"I told you something was wrong with Tybalt."

"Tybalt?" Damon shook his head. "He never came back. We figured he must have gotten a better offer from someone else. We had to find someone else to drive us. We were looking for you..."

Corvin joined them. He put his hand on Reg's shoulder. Not so invasive as Damon's hug, but his touch always gave her an electric shock. She pulled away from him too.

"Yes. Tybalt. I told Corvin on the phone. He was a swamp goblin."

Damon took a step back. "A swamp goblin?"

"You know, the kind who kidnaps people and takes them back to his lair to kill and eat them. That's who you hired to guide us."

"I didn't know... he was Corvin's recommendation."

Corvin held up his hands. "I was told he was the best there was. No one knows the swamp better."

"Oh, he knew the swamp all right. But that doesn't make him the best guide."

"No." Corvin rubbed his whiskered chin and looked down. "No, of course not."

"A swamp goblin took you back to his lair?" Damon asked in a tone of disbelief. "What happened? How did you get away?"

"It helped that he wanted to visit with me before he... you know... did away with me. I think... sort of like a cat that likes to play with its prey..." She shuddered, remembering him taking her into his trophy room with its shelves lined with skulls. "He wanted to scare me first."

"I'm amazed that you were able to get away." Corvin shook his head. "Swamp goblins aren't known for... that."

"I used fire to burn the ropes he tied me up with. And... I was sort of angry and knocked him down with a fireball. I ran away, but he still caught up with me. I couldn't figure out where to go. It was on an island... no way off except through the water."

She recalled the fight and wasn't sure how much more she should tell them. That she had communicated with the panther? Run into the skunk man in person? And ridden on a skin-walker? She didn't want any of them to be put in danger because Reg revealed too much about her story.

"Anyway... I got away. But it took me a long time to find anyone who could help. And... I need a bath and fresh clothes, and about ten meals. I want a hot bath. In a hotel."

"Of course," Corvin agreed.

Damon had opened his mouth with an objection on his face, but they both stared him down. Reg was going to a hotel. She was going to have a hot bath. And then he would be lucky if she didn't go home.

* * *

Corvin suggested a hotel in Miami. Once Reg had had a soak in the tub and had on fresh, clean-smelling clothing, she invited Corvin and Damon to her room to talk about the case. She wanted to go home. But she also didn't want to leave without the wizard. After being lost and attacked in the swamp herself, she couldn't just abandon someone else to his fate. Who knew what kind of creatures he might have faced or have yet to confront? He might be held captive, like Reg had been, by something that wanted to scare him before killing him. Or something that was feeding off of his powers or forcing him to perform some kind of slave labor.

"I want you to tell me all about Wilson," she told Damon flatly, thinking about all of the points that others had brought up. "Everything you know about him. Everything you've been holding back."

"I haven't been holding anything back," Damon objected.

"You know more than you say you do. Did you think that if you told me everything, I wouldn't agree to come?"

She saw the guilty look cross his face and knew that she'd hit the nail on the head. There was something about the case that she wouldn't like.

Corvin studied Damon's face, and Reg wondered if he saw the same thing that she had.

"Damon. Tell me or I'm going home. I'm not going to tell you what I have already found out, and there is no way you are going to find him before the Spring Games."

"You can't go home—"

"I almost got killed! I can go home if I like."

"But you don't have any means of transportation."

"Really? You're going to hold back on the car? Fine. I'll get a bus. I'll Uber. I'll do whatever I have to. And you can wander around the park asking all the questions you like. No one is going to tell you anything."

Damon's eyes went up to the ceiling. He scratched the back of his neck.

"I… only know a couple of things that I haven't told you."

"Spill the beans. I don't know how you expect me to find someone when you don't even give me all the information."

"But you're a psychic. You should be able to find him without knowing all of the details."

"That's not the way it works."

He was still reluctant.

"I'm counting to five, and then I'm out of here." Reg didn't slow down to count the numbers out, like she was counting seconds. She fired them off rapidly like gunshots, forcing Damon to make his choice and act. "One, two, three, four—"

"Okay. Okay, don't go. Just listen."

She waited.

"Jeffrey Wilson... has been missing for fifty years."

There was dead silence in the room. Reg stared at Damon in disbelief.

"Fifty. Years."

Damon nodded. His face getting pink.

"You didn't think it was important to tell me that part."

"Like you said... I figured if I told you that, you wouldn't come. A lot of people think he's dead."

"Well... yeah! He walked into the Everglades and didn't come out for fifty years? What do *you* think that means?"

"There have been sightings. And there is a reward. I thought... you're good at finding things. You have strong powers. Maybe you can find him."

Reg ignored the part about her being good at finding things. She hadn't been good at finding things since Calliopia's cursed blade had cut her and Corvin had stolen her powers. Things hadn't been the same after he had returned them. And while Reg's powers had been growing in other areas, she hadn't been strong in finding random objects.

"These sightings... it could be his ghost. If he didn't come home after a year, then you can bet that he's dead. He got eaten by a crocodile or a boa constrictor or a swamp goblin."

"The Everglades hide a lot of things. Just because he hasn't turned up, that doesn't mean he isn't here. There are lots of places to hide. The sheer amount of space, the dense vegetation..."

"Why would he want to hide?"

"I didn't mean that he was intentionally hiding. Just that... it would be easy for someone to get lost. Or to hide someone."

"You think someone has held him captive for fifty years?"

Damon looked down. "I don't know. It's possible."

"Why would someone hold him captive for fifty years?"

"Maybe to use his powers. I don't know. Just speculation."

"This is ridiculous. You don't know if he's still here or still alive."

"You thought that you felt him in the first area we stopped. Where we ate."

"Yeah, but he could have been buried under the floor."

"I don't think he's dead. A lot of people don't believe that he is."

"A lot of people don't believe Elvis is dead."

He frowned at her. "He's not."

"Don't you dare tell me some story of how Elvis was actually an alien and has been living in Florida all along."

"Okay."

Reg stared at him, but Damon didn't take back what he had said or offer any other explanation. Reg closed her eyes to shut out his face and Corvin's curious presence.

She tried to remember everything she could about the vision she had seen before accepting Damon's proposal. She had seen the wizard, so he had to be alive, didn't he? She remembered the way that he moved, the way he was dressed, his wizened face. It was harder, since she didn't have her crystal ball or Starlight to amplify the signal. But she was closer to him; she should be able to have a better picture. She rubbed her temples. She had bathed, but she still hadn't eaten. It had been a long time since breakfast, and she had only had a bottle of water during the interval.

A picture started to form in her head. But this time, there was something different about the wizard. Was he shorter? Heavier? He shouldn't have changed that much in the time since she had seen him last. What was different?

"Damon."

It was Corvin's voice. But he hadn't spoken aloud; the voice was in her head. Reg opened her eyes and looked at Corvin in irritation. She didn't respond to him audibly. But the vision was gone, and she was sure she would not be able to get it back. She was too fatigued. It would be at least a day before she could bring it back again.

"Damon is a visionary." Corvin was still in her head. She didn't push him out. "He is the one giving you that picture."

CHAPTER TWENTY-SIX

*R*eg's jaw dropped and she looked at Damon. He didn't know what Corvin had told her and didn't realize that he'd been caught out.

"What?" he asked in confusion. "What did you see?"

"You know exactly what I saw."

"Why? Because it was the same as before?"

"No, because you're the one that put it there."

The flush that had previously risen to Damon's face drained away. He looked at Reg, glanced over at Corvin, and then looked back at Reg again.

"I... uh... why would you think that?"

"It was different this time," Reg said. "It should have been the same, but he looked different."

"You might just be remembering him differently," Damon bluffed. "It's been a while, and our memories aren't perfect."

"Yours isn't," Reg snapped, "or you wouldn't be *feeding me a different picture* this time!"

Reg got up from the hotel couch and paced across the room. "I can't believe you would do this. You hold back what you know and then you feed me a false vision? That's... unconscionable." She couldn't believe that she was calling someone else out on his moral standards. Usually, she was the one trying to con everyone else. But that didn't excuse Damon's behavior toward her. "And you're shooting yourself in the foot."

Damon's brows twisted, puzzled. "What do you mean?"

"Do you even know what he looks like?"

"Now? No."

She remembered Tybalt asking if she had a picture of Wilson and being surprised that Damon hadn't shown her one. It was no wonder. In the beginning, he had told or—or at least implied—that Wilson's disappearance was recent. Damon wouldn't be able to show her a fifty-year-old picture without tipping his hand.

"Do you have anything to show what he looks like? You've contaminated my mind now with your stupid visions of how you think he might look. And you can't even remember what you showed me from one time to the next."

Reg paced, trying to keep her fury under control. Not only had he lied to her and misled her, but she had made it clear before that he wasn't to put visions in her head unless he had permission. And he'd gone and done it again, pretending that she'd had a real psychic vision of the real Jeffrey Wilson, when it was just a made-up picture.

That was why Starlight had clawed her to end the vision and why he had attacked Damon. Because he knew where the vision was coming from, that it wasn't Reg herself.

Damon dug into his pocket for his wallet and pulled out a snapshot to show Reg.

She'd been right about the fact that he would have given away the con if he'd shown her that photo. It was an old black and white photo. Wilson was an attractive man who looked to be in his prime, unlike the wrinkled wizard he had shown her in his vision. But Damon had done a poor job of aging him; the wizard in his vision didn't look anything like the man in the picture. He would have been better off replicating the photo in the vision and trying to explain the rapid aging later. At least then, she would have been looking for the right man instead of chasing the vision of a man who didn't exist.

"Do you even know how old he'd look now, if he is still alive?" she demanded. "I mean, isn't one of the things about practitioners of magic that they don't age as quickly as normal humans?"

Reg had learned there was no point in judging a witch's or warlock's age by their appearance. Someone like Sarah, who appeared to be in her sixties, might claim to be centuries old.

"Well, no," Damon admitted. "But I figured he would have aged some. Especially if he's been lost or held captive here. The emotional stress can age a magical practitioner more than years."

"I can't believe you would feed me false information and expect me to be able to find him."

"I really wanted your help. It was the best way I could think of to get it. I figured that once we were here, we would talk to some of the people who had seen him, and you would be able to use them and their clues to track him down..."

"And that's where you were taking me. To where he disappeared fifty years ago, or the people who thought they had seen him?"

"Well, to where he had disappeared from first, and then... I wasn't sure if I'd be able to find the people who had seen him or not..."

"Why not?"

"Well... people who are vacationing, they don't stay around here, but I thought I might be able to find something out from the locals."

"So you don't have anyone here that you know has seen him."

"No, but people must have. If he's been here for fifty years, then it shouldn't be hard to find someone who knows him."

"Shouldn't it." Reg shook her head in disgust. "You can get out of my room now."

Damon's mouth tightened. "Well, since I paid for it, it's not exactly your—"

"You want me to go home right now?"

He was clearly fighting back fury. Though what he had to be angry about, Reg didn't know. He had lied and misled her. She was the injured party, not him.

"No," he snapped. "Fine. It's your room and I'll get out. I'd appreciate it if you'd let me know your decision in the morning."

Reg nodded. "Fine," she echoed.

Damon looked at Corvin, clearly expecting him to leave. Corvin didn't make any move, and Reg didn't tell him to go. Damon looked back and forth between them and decided he wasn't going to be asked to act as a chaperone or bodyguard this time. He left the room without another word. Reg turned her attention to Corvin.

She was still angry, and she could take the remainder of her anger out on him, pointing out the fact that he wasn't supposed to be getting into her head without her permission, and that he was the one who had made the disastrous recommendation of hiring a swamp goblin to be their guide.

But it wasn't his fault that Damon had not been upfront about the details of his search. If Reg spouted off at him, that would be why, not because Corvin had done her any harm.

"Dinner?" Corvin suggested, his tone light.

Reg breathed out, slowly pushing out all her air, hopefully along with the anger and frustration.

"Okay. Yeah. I know I need something."

"There happens to be a very famous restaurant and bar here. We will be able to make it for the show. How does that sound?"

She wasn't sure she was interested in any bar entertainment, but at least it would take Corvin's attention off of her and she would, hopefully, be able to relax.

"Okay, sure," she agreed. "Let's check out the floor show."

CHAPTER TWENTY-SEVEN

*R*eg stared at the sign in the elevator as they went down to the main floor. She wasn't sure how she had missed it on the way up. She supposed she had been too focused on a hot bath at that point to notice anything else. She skimmed the headlines on the poster, together with the picture, and looked at Corvin in disbelief.

"A mermaid bar?"

He nodded, grinning. Reg took a quick look around to make sure that no one was eavesdropping on their conversation.

"They're not... real mermaids, are they?"

She had seen a real mermaid for the first time in Black Sands while she was on the hunt, and Reg didn't want to get anywhere near any real mermaids.

Corvin shook his head. "Of course not."

"Oh." Reg let out her breath. "Well, good. So you just want to see some women in seashell bikinis while you're eating."

"They do a dance and everything."

"I can imagine."

"Soon, you won't have to imagine. You'll be able to see it for yourself."

Reg didn't care. Corvin ogling the mermaids was just fine with her. She didn't want his attention focused on her. Especially while she was trying to sort things out and figure out what she was going to do about Damon.

Was she still in? Was there any point in trying to locate a wizard who had been missing for fifty years, even if she did have a picture now? There wasn't any guarantee that the picture Damon had given her even *was* Wilson, or that he looked anything like that. But she had more now. If she went to where he had been lost and where people had seen him, then even without talking to witnesses, he might have left enough of an imprint there for her to get some kind of read. She had thought that she'd gotten a location on him once, even without a picture and with the wrong image in her head. Now that she had the right information...

* * *

"Reg?"

Reg focused on Corvin. They were sitting at the bar having a pre-dinner drink while waiting for a table to open up. With his glass, he indicated the scantily-clad woman who was waiting for them. "They're ready to seat us."

"Right. Yeah. I'm right with you."

She took her drink and followed the hostess, with Corvin bringing up the rear like a gentleman. The curvy woman stopped at a booth that was right up against the side of the huge aquarium and gestured to it. "How's this?"

Reg shrugged.

"That's just fine," Corvin agreed. "Thank you."

She fluttered her eyelids at him, brushing by him just a little more closely than was strictly necessary. Even when he wasn't trying to, Corvin often charmed the women around him.

Reg sat down and Corvin sat across the table from her.

"There, this is nice."

"As long as they've got food, that's all that I care about."

Corvin glanced around at the other tables. "It would appear so," he observed dryly.

Reg picked up one of the menus that the hostess had left at the table. She flipped it open and was glad to see that it wasn't full of pictures of mermaids, but had photos of some of their signature dishes alongside the descriptions. That made it so much easier than trying to puzzle through all of the descriptions. She would still be reading when Corvin was finished his meal. Although with the distraction of the mermaids, maybe not.

"Order whatever you like," Corvin advised. "I imagine the seafood is the house specialty."

"The seafood is the house specialty at every restaurant in Florida."

"Well… pretty much," he admitted.

Reg browsed through the pictures. Nothing ever looked exactly like the picture when she got it, but as long as it was close, she didn't care. She just needed something edible to boost her blood sugar. It had been a long time since Etienne's mushrooms and berries.

Corvin had barely glanced over his menu when he folded it back over and set it to the side. He must have been there once before, to have made a decision so quickly.

"So… tell me how you managed to fight off a swamp goblin," he suggested.

Reg looked at him. She considered whether to tell him about the panther or not. He knew there were panthers in the Everglades; he had told her so. It wouldn't exactly be a surprise.

"I admit I had a little help."

"Oh?" His lids were half-lowered as he gazed at her. She wondered how much he could sense from her thoughts. The two of them had shared powers and energy too many times for her to keep him completely out. At least he wasn't trying to charm her; she would have known by the scent of roses around him. "I would be surprised if you had not. Swamp goblins are physically powerful, even if their magic is not. But then, so are sirens."

"I'm not a siren."

"No," he agreed. "But… you definitely have siren in your blood."

Reg shook her head. "I don't want to talk about that. Do you want me to tell you or not?"

He sat back slightly, his eyes never wavering. A lightning bolt of heat shot through Reg. "Yes. Do tell me."

"Well, I don't know how happy with the answer you'll be, since you don't like cats."

"Cats? What do cats have to do with it? I don't imagine you ran into a clowder of cats out there in the swamp."

"A clowder?"

"I believe that's the right term for a group of cats."

Reg had never heard the word before. She shrugged. "No. Just one cat."

"Not a house cat, then."

"No. Did you know that when you were snoring away the other night, feeling all safe in your sleeping bag, that a panther was prowling around outside the camp?"

"No." He raised his brows. "I had no idea. But the panthers around here do tend to be quite shy. I wouldn't really have worried about one of them approaching the camp. It would have avoided us."

"Yeah, lots of things around here would avoid us if they could. Well, I was talking to him. Sort of. Communing. When Tybalt kidnapped me. I guess Tybalt never saw the cat, and the panther never gave himself away. He just followed us."

"Why? And what did you say when you were talking to him? I wouldn't think it would be particularly safe to be having a conversation with a large cat out in the swamp in the middle of the night."

"I thought you said that he would avoid us."

"Until you start messing with the natural order of things. Like communicating with it."

"Well… I didn't say anything. Not in words. I was just thinking. Thinking of Starlight and home and being safe. I guess he was… curious."

"So he followed you, and then when you got free of Tybalt…"

"He helped. He's the one who… took care of things."

Corvin nodded slowly. He sipped his drink. "You always seem to have well-placed friends," he observed. "Even when you were brand new here, you always seemed to have someone close by looking out for your interests."

"I don't know why he decided to help. I don't think he eats goblin. But he did help me; I don't think I could have fought Tybalt off on my own. Or gotten off of the island and to… safety."

"This creature escorted you all the way to where we found you? That was the nearest civilization?"

Reg shrugged. She was saved by their waitress, who appeared at the side of their table, looking a little harried, to take their dinner orders. Reg indicated a picture of a burger with fries on the menu.

"The Angus burger?"

The waitress nodded, chewed her gum, and wrote it down. "And you, sir?"

Corvin rattled off questions about their offerings, then placed his order in exacting detail. The waitress made a couple of notes and took the menus from them.

Corvin started to ask Reg a question, but then the lights dimmed and music started, and it was time for the floor show. Or the aquarium show, since the mermaids weren't actually on the floor. Reg looked into the big aquarium beside her as mermaids swam down from the top and in from the sides, which were out of view. They didn't look much like the real mermaid she had seen, and that was probably a good thing. She didn't want to think too much about that evening. It had been quite disturbing to see the mermaid and siren out hunting together, and the image had stuck with Reg.

Their dance was nicely choreographed and the mermaids were undoubtedly attractive. They had been fitted with long flippers that helped to propel them through the water. Corvin had said that not many mermaids had flippers anymore; apparently, it was a recessive trait that was dying out.

It was amazing how long they could hold their breaths, especially while doing all of that physical activity. Reg found herself holding her own breath, seeing if she would be able to stay under the water as long as they did. It wasn't even close. But what would happen if she were really in the water? Would the siren traits she had inherited allow her to hold her breath for longer? Or, as a siren, would she be hampered by her human characteristics?

She tried to breathe normally. Her sudden breath in was too loud, and Corvin's eyes were drawn away from the mermaids to her.

"They're quite good, aren't they?" Reg asked.

"Yes. Amazing. It all seems very natural."

Reg nodded.

She had the uncomfortable feeling of someone looking at her and turned her head to sweep a glance at the people seated behind her. Her senses told her that it wasn't Damon, but someone else she should know. She didn't see anyone on the initial glance and looked again a minute later, studying the faces more carefully. Who was there? Who was watching her?

"Something wrong?" Corvin inquired.

"No… just… someone watching me."

"They're probably just watching the mermaids, looking past you."

"No. I can feel it. Someone is looking at me."

He looked at the various people in the direction she had looked and shook his head. "No, I don't see anyone suspicious."

Reg wondered if Bruce the skin-walker could change himself to look like other humans, instead of the form she had first seen him in. If he could... then he could be almost anyone.

But then she saw him.

CHAPTER TWENTY-EIGHT

*I*t was one of the men she had seen at the Skunk Man Saloon. One of the group of retirees, with a round face and a fringe of white hair.

He was probably just as surprised to run into her again at the mermaid bar as she was to see him there.

Then again, she didn't suppose there was a lot of night entertainment in the Everglades. People would have to look farther afield. And an older man like that, he might not want to go very far. So they both ended up going to the nearest convenient place. Reg because she needed a hotel room, and the man because he wanted someone to talk to, or to see all of the sites, or maybe he had booked a room for the night too. There weren't a lot of hotels close to the park, and as Damon had discovered on their way there, many were already booked up for some kind of sneaker convention.

"There," she said to Corvin, indicating the man, "he was at the Skunk Man Saloon."

Corvin looked. "Was he? You have a good memory."

"Yeah." She nodded. "I have a pretty good memory for faces. Maybe that's from going to so many different foster homes and schools. If you don't remember who is supposed to be picking you up at the end of the day or which kids are in your class…"

"That could be rather awkward," Corvin agreed with a nod.

"I guess when different people are all touring the Everglades, you probably run into people over and over again."

"I've noticed that at other places. The same way as when you keep passing by and getting passed by the same cars on the highway, or running into the same person on different aisles at the grocery store. It's just natural that if you're in the same space, you're going to keep seeing each other."

Reg took a sip of her drink, wondering when the waitress would be bringing their food. They probably shouldn't have arrived right in time for the floor show. It was probably the restaurant's most busy time. They should have just ordered from room service.

But staying alone in the hotel room with Corvin was really out of the question. She would have had to kick him out and eaten alone. She wasn't sure, after all she had been through over the last couple of days, that she wanted to be alone.

So she had to wait a little longer for her meal.

She closed her eyes briefly to rub her forehead, just above and between her eyebrows. She hoped that once she had some food, her head would start to feel better. But maybe it was sleep she needed more. It was hard to tell.

When she opened her eyes and raised them again, a man was sitting in the seat next to Corvin, who appeared to have been shoved several inches toward the aquarium. The space that Corvin had been occupying had been taken by a man who was familiar with Reg, but who she hadn't expected to see again. It was no chance meeting of two tourists who had booked the same hotel or entertainment.

He was tall and broad-chested. He looked vaguely like the lumberjack in a TV commercial—handsome and rugged.

"Weston."

"Hello," Weston greeted. He spread himself out to take up more space, forcing Corvin to hug the wall of the aquarium. "How is Regina Rawlins today."

He said it in a flat tone with no inflection to indicate that it was a question. Maybe something that someone had told him he should say, but he didn't understand why.

"What are you doing here?" Reg demanded, not bothering to answer.

"I am sitting here with you." He remained focused on her as if he couldn't even see Corvin, the man who had been sitting with her before his arrival.

"You can't just barge in here like that!"

He cocked his head slightly. "Clearly, I can."

"I don't want to see you. Why did you come here? You don't belong here. And you can't just appear and disappear into thin air. You'll freak people out. They won't know what's going on."

He looked around, but no one seemed to be paying him the least bit of attention. Everyone was still watching the swaying, swimming, dancing mermaids. Weston looked back at Reg, brows raised. Reg pressed her fingers into her temples, trying to figure out what to do. Where was Harrison?

As soon as she thought of him, he was there beside her. On the inside of the bench, against the aquarium, so that the two immortals were sitting kitty-corner to each other. Tall like Weston, but slim, and with a mustache he twirled and fidgeted with while he thought. While Weston's outfit was fairly normal, Harrison was wearing a bright orange silk shirt with a kind of a gangster hat. The type Reg thought might be called a porkpie.

"Ah, there you are," Harrison said to Weston.

"Why is he here?" Reg turned her question to Harrison this time. "I thought it was part of your job to protect me from him."

Harrison shrugged. "You do not appear to be harmed."

"If you can't keep track of him, then how are you going to make sure of that? He could have taken me somewhere else. Or some *time* else. Isn't it a rule that he has to stay away from me?"

"No," Harrison said slowly. "Not really. When you were a little girl, you were more vulnerable and we had to protect you from Destine. But Weston?" He gave a careless shrug. "You are his blood. I cannot keep you apart."

"That's crazy. I thought there was this whole balance of power thing and he has to stay hidden now."

"I'm right here," Weston pointed out, apparently annoyed at being talked about.

"Then go somewhere else," Reg snapped.

Weston raised his eyes to watch the mermaids. He tipped his head from one side to the other.

"I don't think those are real mermaids," he said eventually.

"No, they're not."

"They are good, though." Weston looked at Harrison. "Perhaps we ought to make some more mermaids. Someone said there weren't very many of them left. They were always a fascinating species."

"You can *make* mermaids?" Reg asked. But she supposed she shouldn't have been surprised. They could appear and disappear at will, transport her from one place or time to another, teleport food from a restaurant, break curses; why not create mermaids or some other species? They had to have come from somewhere. She shook her head and changed her question. He had distracted her, intentionally or unintentionally. "Why are you here?"

Weston smiled. "To see you."

"Why? You haven't come to see me before."

"Then maybe it is the right time."

"Why here? Why now?"

"This is where you are. If I wanted to see you, then this is the place to come." He rolled his eyes at the mortal's dimness.

"It is difficult for humans to understand," Harrison explained to Weston. "Their understanding of time and space is so limited."

On one hand, Reg wanted to take advantage of the opportunity to learn more about the immortals, and Weston in particular. But she remembered the difficulties they'd had with Weston and the Witch Doctor before him. Considering all of Francesca's warnings about not having anything to do with the immortals, she knew it was probably wiser to either get them to leave, or to leave herself.

But she wanted to eat and wondered where her food was.

Harrison motioned to the table in front of her, and Reg looked down to see the burger she had ordered. She was pretty sure she hadn't missed the waitress delivering it.

But she was hungry and didn't care where it came from. She picked it up and took a bite. "Why do you want to see me?"

"Ah." Weston tapped the table thoughtfully. "You are in the Everglades."

"Yes."

He nodded as if that were his answer.

"You're here because I'm in the Everglades? But why?"

"You will have to ask your companions if you do not know. I would also like to know why."

Reg tried to follow his meaning. "You want to know why *I'm* in the Everglades?"

He raised his brows and nodded. Reg looked at Corvin, sitting against the aquarium but no longer interested in the mermaid show.

She didn't ask him what she should say in so many words, knowing that Harrison and probably Weston too could read at least some of her thoughts.

Corvin gave a slight shake of his head. Reg looked back at Weston and didn't tell him why she was in the Everglades.

"It's been an interesting trip so far," she said. "Have you ever been here before?"

"Of course. I have been many places."

She studied his face and tried to read him. Immortals were more difficult. It was like reading another species without conscious human-like thought. Like when she had reached out to the panther. Immortals' consciousness felt more scattered. Operating on another plane.

"Why have you been here before? To watch the mermaids?"

"Humans are much more amusing than mermaids."

"So, you came to watch humans?"

His eyes slid over to Harrison. "There are no rules about watching humans," he said. Even without inflection, she knew it was a question. Making sure he hadn't broken immortal rules before telling Reg anything about it.

Harrison spread his hands. "Watching, no. As long as you're not producing progeny."

Weston chuckled. "Their males are too delicate to incubate offspring."

Males. So he hadn't been there to watch a woman or a group, but a specific man.

"Who? What man?"

"I did not ask his name. Humans, like immortals, can go by many names. I did not need to know."

Reg rolled her eyes, frustrated. She dug into her hamburger, taking a bite that was much too big and required plenty of chewing and straining to swallow it down. Reg chased it with several swallows of her drink.

The waitress returned, carrying a platter with their meals on it, and looked at the plate already on Reg's table in consternation. She served Corvin his meal and looked at Reg, not sure what to say.

"Uh… did someone else bring this?"

"Yes."

Reg didn't give the waitress any details, and she apparently wasn't sure how to pursue it. She looked at Harrison and Weston.

"And… did you gentlemen want anything?"

"I am here to see Reg Rawlins," Weston said, nodding toward Reg.

"Uh… okay. And you…?"

"I would like that one," Harrison pointed at one of the mermaids in the aquarium.

The waitress's jaw dropped. She looked into Harrison's face, trying to understand the joke. "Ha… ah, I mean, do you want something to eat. Something on the menu."

"Do you have chocolate cake?"

Reg remembered Harrison devouring a black forest cake he had made appear in her cottage.

"Yes," the waitress agreed "Nothing for an entrée?"

"Just cake."

She nodded. "Okay. I'll bring that to you shortly."

The poor waitress returned to the kitchen with the burger she had brought out for Reg.

Reg was getting tired of trying to find any logic in Weston's appearance. He wanted to see her because she was in the Everglades. It didn't make a lot of sense. As far as she could tell, he didn't have any special connection to the Everglades. He had been there before, but apparently didn't remember much about it. Maybe he was just sightseeing. Curious as to what she was up to. Since he had been released, she had always been in Black Sands. Perhaps just the fact that she had left Black Sands had drawn him to check on her.

"So you just wanted to see me?"

Weston looked at her, but his eyes were distant, as though his thoughts were far away. "Eh? What's that?"

"You just wanted to see me. That's why you came here."

"I want many things."

Reg didn't know how that could be true. He could, seemingly, go wherever he wanted and have whatever he wanted. How could he want for anything?

She had seen in people before, though, the tendency to want more, the wealthier they got. A poor, struggling person wanted food in her belly and a roof overhead. Her wants were dictated by what her body needed. A wealthy person, who had everything his body required, had lists of material possessions he wanted and was never satisfied with what he had. Maybe it was that many times magnified for Harrison. He could have anything, so he wanted everything.

"Do you remember Lethe?" Weston said suddenly.

"Lethe?" Reg shook her head, wondering if that was a person's name and how Reg was supposed to know her. "I don't know who that is."

Maybe someone she had known as a child? A friend of her mother's? A neighbor who had taken care of her when her mother was passed out? The neighborhood cat?

"Who!" Weston chuckled, sharing the joke with Harrison. "Not a who."

"Do you mean the river Lethe?" Corvin asked.

Weston looked over at Corvin, surprised, as if he hadn't even been aware before that someone was sitting next to him. "The river Lethe, yes."

Corvin nodded and looked at Reg. "It is from ancient Greek mythology. A river that flowed through the underworld. Drinking its waters would make you forget."

"Forget what?"

"Forget everything. Your pains. How you got there. Your past life. So that you were just... present. No past."

Reg shuddered. The past was something that she wanted to leave behind. She didn't want it to control her life. But she wouldn't want to forget everything, either. Her past was a vital part of her. The part that kept her anchored and able to remember the things that were important.

"Nothing? Why would you not want to remember anything?"

"Perhaps the people in the underworld were tortured by what had happened in their lives, what things had brought them there. Isn't it better to forget than to remember a life full of pain and misdeeds?"

Reg wasn't sure of that. She looked at Weston to see what his answer was.

Weston's eyes glittered. Reg didn't like his being there or not knowing what his motivations were. The one time he had met her before, he had wanted to be with her mother. To change the past so that Norma Jean didn't die. Reg and Corvin had been able to fight him off, to balance his power, so that he had departed. She didn't know where he had gone or when he had gone to. He hadn't, as far as she knew, gone back to see Norma Jean again. Maybe it was enough for him that he had saved her from death.

Reg looked back at Weston. "Why did you ask about Lethe? What does that have to do with anything?"

"Lethe is here. In this bog."

"The river Lethe is in the Everglades?"

He nodded.

"How could it be?" Reg demanded. "It was in ancient Greece. Or in the underworld. Neither one is anywhere near the Everglades."

"Many things happened when humans changed the flows of the waters in this country," Weston said with a shrug, as if that explained everything. Reg looked at Corvin, sure that he wouldn't be able to make any more sense of this than Reg. But he just shrugged as if he accepted Weston's explanation.

Men draining the swamps in the Everglades couldn't have anything to do with a mythological river being moved around the world.

"It could explain so many people being lost here, or so many strange things happening," Corvin said.

"So could swamp goblins," Reg snapped. "You didn't see Tybalt's storeroom."

He raised an eyebrow questioningly.

"Trust me. He was the cause of a lot of those disappearances."

Corvin nodded slowly. "I won't argue with you, Regina. You are the one who was there. You saw what you saw."

"I did. He had… this room was full of skulls. Row upon row of human skulls. Trophies."

"How quaint," Harrison put in.

Reg glared at him. "It was not quaint," she snarled.

"Oh." He modified his expression accordingly. "No, of course not."

The waitress returned with Harrison's chocolate cake. She was looking nervous, as if she expected there to be more people at the table or that Harrison might already have a piece of chocolate cake. He did things like that, after all, so she was right to expect something else unusual to happen.

"Here you are, sir," she put the plate of cake down in front of Harrison. "Is there anything else I can get you?"

Harrison opened his mouth to answer, but Reg beat him to it. "No, nothing else."

Harrison looked disappointed. The waitress left. Reg looked at Harrison. "She wasn't asking if you wanted *anything* else. Just coffee or something like that." She pushed cutlery toward him as he dipped one finger into the chocolate icing. "You use the fork. Not your fingers."

Harrison sighed and unwrapped the cutlery from the napkin. "Humans are so picky about things that are thoroughly unimportant."

"Yes, we are. I don't want people here to see you eating food with your fingers like a three-year-old. And I don't want you appearing and disappearing out of thin air. Or stealing mermaids."

He rolled his eyes and began to eat the cake with his fork. "These things would only matter to a race confined to linear time."

"Well, we are. So get used to it."

He took a few more bites. "Where is the cat?"

"I didn't bring Starlight with me. He's at home. We didn't think that the Everglades were a safe place for a cat."

"Such as he?" Harrison snorted. "He would not be hurt by the swamp."

Reg didn't argue. She tried not to think of Starlight, afraid that if she let him enter her thoughts, Harrison would decide that she wanted him there and would bring him to her by magic. Something else that would be out of place and difficult to explain. How did a woman with a cat in her arms happen to get into the restaurant?

Reg turned her head to speak to Weston, but his seat was empty. She turned back to Harrison to find out where Weston had gone, but Harrison's seat, too, was empty.

CHAPTER TWENTY-NINE

*C*harming," Corvin said dryly. He slid back along the bench seat to take the position he had been in before Weston's appearance. "Your friends need to learn manners, Regina."

"Well, at least they didn't blow anyone up or make anyone disappear," Reg said, shaking her head. She looked into the aquarium just to be sure that he hadn't taken one or more of the mermaids with him. There didn't appear to be any swimmers missing or anyone upset by a friend's sudden disappearance. "Sheesh. I don't know how you teach an immortal the proper way to behave."

"They are too non-linear."

Reg just shook her head. She took a few more bites of her hamburger and was close to finishing it. She eyed what was left of Harrison's cake. She wasn't going to let that go to waste either. She'd had enough exercise and skipped meals over the past day or two that she didn't have to feel guilty about the extra calories and how her skirts were getting tighter around her waist. She wasn't fat; she'd been too skinny before. But she could only tell herself that for so long.

"Perhaps we should make some plans for tomorrow," Corvin suggested. "Am I to assume that you are going to stay in the Everglades and continue with the search?"

"Why would you assume that?"

"Because I don't think you're the type who likes to give up on a mystery before it is solved."

"Maybe not, but I don't want to be the type who is eaten by a swamp goblin, either."

"I think you're safe in that regard. Well, are you, or are you not?"

"I shouldn't. Not when he lied to me to get me involved and sent us all on a wild goose chase."

"He's young. He's still learning."

"He's older than me. I don't know how old, exactly. The way you warlocks age doesn't make it easy to tell."

Reg thought about it. What was she going to do? Go home or stay and continue the search?

They didn't have a lot of time for the search anyway. They had to have the wizard back to the Spring Games in short order if he were going to get properly registered and ready for the games. She'd never been to the Spring Games before and had no idea what witches and warlocks had to do to ready themselves.

"I suppose we don't have much longer."

"No. A day or two at most. I'm surprised that Damon would even make an attempt. But I suppose he is tempted by the reward money."

"Yeah, he is." Reg frowned. "How is there a prize for finding a guy who disappeared decades ago?"

"It was first instituted when he disappeared. The prize monies have been invested ever since then, growing due to interest and other investments. Since it has been fifty years, they are talking about dissolving the fund and disbursing the monies to some other project. This may be the last year that it is offered."

"So it's Damon's last chance."

"Yes."

Reg blew out her breath.

"You knew about this? That he'd been missing for fifty years?"

Corvin nodded. He shrugged uncomfortably. "I wasn't as interested in Damon's search as in coming to the Everglades. I didn't realize... that he'd misled you about how long Wilson has been missing."

Reg licked the last of the ketchup off of her fingers and pulled Harrison's remaining cake over to her. She took a couple of bites of it and sighed.

"I suppose I'll stay and help, since it's the last chance."

Corvin nodded as if he had fully expected this. "So then, we should start on a plan."

"Shouldn't we include Damon in that discussion?"

"Perhaps. But there's no reason we can't discuss preliminaries now."

"Okay. Maybe it's better that way, since he's been sending me in the wrong direction. Where would you go if you were looking for this guy?"

Corvin considered, tapping the pads of his fingers on the table. "Where would I look? I might start somewhere that magical powers were more concentrated. Like the Lost Village."

"Damon mentioned the Lost Village before. Or maybe it was Tybalt. But I don't know anything about it. Why is it lost?"

"Well, it isn't... it's more of a ghost town. Its former residents disappeared."

"Disappeared where?"

"That's the mystery."

"And you think that since they all disappeared, maybe Wilson's disappearance had something to do with the Lost Village too? That there's some kind of magical force at work there?"

Corvin shrugged. "It wouldn't be the first time that a rift had opened up, causing a series of disappearances or other strange happenings. You know how some places are thought to be cursed after a string of bad luck."

"Yeah. I guess. So how long would it take us to get to the Lost Village?"

"It's not far from here, but we'll have to go through some pretty dense vegetation to get there. If you don't have a good guide, you can wander out there for days."

"Yeah, well, our last guide didn't turn out so good. So what are you going to do this time? Just go out and get some random guide?"

"I'll ask around tonight. The locals should have some recommendations. Then we'll get started early, and maybe by the end of the day we'll have a lead."

"Do you think so?"

His lips pressed together. "No, I doubt it. But I doubt if young Damon has a better plan."

* * *

Reg felt like she had barely closed her eyes when someone was shaking her awake. She squinted in the dim light of her hotel room, trying to make out the shape hovering over her.

"What...? Who's there? What's wrong?"

"Reg, we need to get an early start," it was Damon's voice. "I know you're not normally up at this time, but..."

Reg turned her head to look toward the window and the clock. The window was still dark. Maybe a little lighter than it had been when she went to bed, but not by much. It certainly wasn't morning yet.

"It's not even daylight."

"I know. But it will be soon."

Reg sat up, rubbing her eyes. "Why exactly do we have to get up before dawn?"

"The new guide that Corvin picked was pretty strict about the schedule. If we want to get to the Lost Village today, we have to go early."

"Is he a goblin?"

"No."

"He'd better not be," Reg warned.

"Can I turn on the light for you? Are you going to stay awake?"

"Turn on the lamp."

Damon fumbled around for the switch and eventually got the bedside lamp turned on. It felt like it was going to burn a hole right through Reg's eyeballs. She covered them up, groaning and swearing at Damon. She should have said no to participating in the search. She should have said no to continuing after she found out how he had lied to her. She should have just gone home and told Damon she would see him the next time she saw him.

"I'm sorry." Damon's tone was wheedling. "I brought you coffee. Do you want coffee?"

"I'm going to need more than one."

"I'll get you another one. One before you get dressed and one when we reach the boat?"

Reg reached out her hand without opening her eyes, and Damon put a to-go cup of coffee into her grasp. Reg squinted her eyes open just wide enough to see the orientation of the sipping hole and drank down the first few swallows of the hot, bitter coffee.

"So get out," Reg growled at Damon. "I'm not changing while you're here."

Not that changing was going to involve much more than putting on a bra and changing her t-shirt. And she was going to have to splash some water on her face. That and the coffee should be enough to at least get her on her feet. But she wouldn't be alert and able to carry on a conversation yet. That would have to wait until she was on the boat with her second cup of coffee.

* * *

Reg put out her hand as she approached the boat, and Damon put her next cup of coffee in it. Reg had a sip. It wasn't quite as hot as her first cup had been, so she was able to drink more at a time. Fire in the furnace. Soon she'd be able to talk intelligently. She greeted Corvin, who laughed at her sleepy-eyed demeanor and lack of makeup. She was dressed. What more could they expect before dawn?

Corvin touched her elbow and escorted her onto the boat, making sure she didn't trip over any steps or go overboard. He sat Reg down near the guide. Reg glanced over at the thin, dark-skinned man. Reg wasn't sure whether he was that brown from the sun or due to his ethnicity. She closed her eyes, melting into her chair.

"Are you a swamp goblin?" she asked.

"What? Are you talking to me?" the guide asked uncertainly.

"Yeah. Are you a goblin?"

"No. Of course not."

"Good."

Reg took another sip of her coffee.

It was some time before the sun was above the tree line and Reg felt like it was actually day. Not the time she would normally be getting up in the morning, but at least it was daylight. She watched the sky change color. It was pretty. She understood why people liked the sunrise. But it wasn't something she was interested in getting up to see every day. A sunrise was a sunrise. She couldn't imagine being able to do what Erin did, getting up hours before the sun was up in order to bake bread before her bakery opened every morning.

Every morning.

It was crazy. Anyone who did that had to be crazy. When they had been in foster care together, Reg was the one who was always identified as being unstable and Erin was in pretty good shape. But getting up that early in the morning wasn't normal.

Now that Reg's eyes were open and she was looking around, the guide started his usual patter, telling her about the Everglades and the treasures it hid. Except he didn't mean actual treasures, like the box of gems that Reg had. He talked about natural beauty, species that were near extinction, and the storied history of the place.

You couldn't take those to the bank.

"Tell me about this Lost Village," Reg told him. "That's what I want to hear about."

The guide obliged, going into a long narrative about the village originally inhabited by the Seminole Indians. Until one day, they had disappeared. But that wasn't all. Confederate soldiers had hidden or been lost there. Al Capone had hidden out there during prohibition. People had come and gone, but the village was once more deserted.

It was, Reg thought, an excellent place to start. She didn't know anything about the rifts Corvin had mentioned, but a place with that much history of people disappearing or hiding out was bound to have a pretty big ghostly imprint, and maybe she could learn something there.

CHAPTER THIRTY

$\mathcal{T}$here wasn't much left of the Lost Village in the physical world. But as soon as Reg stepped off the boat, she could feel the ghosts around her. So many ghosts. They all pulled at her, wanting to talk to her or through her. She'd never been in a place with so many spirits before. It was overwhelming. Reg put her hands up, trying to fend them off. Corvin was there beside her and touched her shoulder lightly. Reg drew strength from him, trying to build a shield up around her. She was careful not to draw too much of his energy. She didn't want to leave him weak, but he had offered. At least, she took his touch as an offer.

She had been learning to build a protective shield around herself, and having been in contact with Harrison the night before helped. He had shielded her before, and she had learned a lot about how to construct a shield just from feeling the one he put around her. She had quickly surpassed Corvin in his ability.

After a few minutes, she was feeling better. She could breathe again. She opened her eyes, opened her mind, and looked around at the remnants of the Seminole village.

"You okay?" Corvin asked.

"Yeah. Better." She pulled away from him so that she wouldn't keep drawing on his energy. She could maintain the shield reasonably well. For the time being. "This place is... amazing."

He looked around, expressionless. "What do you see?"

"All of the ghosts," Reg said, shaking her head. She couldn't believe that he couldn't feel them. Anyone who stepped onto the ground there should be able to feel them. "There are so many."

"Indians?"

"More than that." Reg looked around. There were plenty of Seminole ghosts there. But she suspected that most of the village had escaped and hidden, rather than allowing themselves to be decimated. "There are men in uniform too. The soldiers." Unlike the natives, who were mostly calm and peaceful, the soldiers carried a heavily sad and desperate feeling. They were dark and downcast. Some still attempted to fight each other, even though they no longer had the bodies to do so. They fought like shadows, striking out but never touching each other.

And not just at each other; they seemed intent on killing the Seminoles as well—even women and children.

And there were a few scattered gangsters that must have been members of Capone's gang who had been killed while they were still hiding out in the swamp.

"Pretty overwhelming?"

"I can manage with the shield."

She could see Corvin's nod out of the corner of her eye. He still stayed close to her side, which seemed to be irritating Damon. She supposed it was Damon's gig, and he had the right to be irritated at Corvin taking over leadership, first dictating where they should go and who their new guide would be, and then staying at Reg's side instead of waiting for her to ask, crowding out Damon the same way as Weston had crowded Corvin from his seat at the restaurant the night before.

Reg looked around for someone to talk to. She wanted someone safe. Someone who would not try to hijack the conversation to speak through her to someone else, or who would not intrude on how her brain was organized and try to take over to dictate his own ends.

Reg walked around the ruins for a few minutes, just looking around and taking it all in. She could see shadows of the teepees and buildings that had been there at one time, even though they had fallen down and rotted away by that time. She could see how the Seminoles and the others had lived their lives there.

Eventually, she sat down in the middle of the village, in the door of one of the teepees. There a grandmother and little girl had sat, tending a fire, preparing food and hides, making tools with the materials they had at hand. She watched the ghost of the grandmother sewing, fitting garments together for her family, caring for them.

"Grandmother," Reg whispered. She wished she had done more to prepare. She could have learned a few words in Seminole so that she could at least address them in their language, even though she couldn't converse in it.

The grandmother's ghost looked at Reg, smiling patiently. What teeth she had left were worn down to nubs.

"Can you help me, Grandmother? I am looking for a man. I don't know if he ever came through here."

The woman continued to gaze at her, not answering.

"If he came here, it was after you died."

The ghost nodded, understanding.

Reg closed her eyes and formed the picture of the wizard in her mind. She hadn't kept Damon's picture with her, but she didn't need to. She had memorized the face, had tried to imagine what he might look like now. He might still look young, with black hair like he'd had in the picture, or it might all be gray or white fifty years later. And Reg didn't know when he might have passed through the ghost village. Soon after he had arrived in the park? Much later, after he had escaped whoever had kidnapped him? Or was he there in the village too, attracted to the other ghosts by their magnetic pull?

"Who is he?" the grandmother asked.

Reg tried to think of how to describe him in a way that would make sense to the woman in her culture.

"He was… like a medicine man. Someone who could… do things that others could not."

Reg didn't know what kind of wizardry Wilson had performed. Had he had a particular talent or area of interest? Did he dabble? How was a wizard different from a warlock? She might have asked Damon some of those questions before she had started, but she had pretended that she knew what he was talking about and had not asked what she should have.

The old woman nodded slowly as she fed sticks into the fire. "There was a medicine man. More than one."

More than one. Of course. It couldn't be that easy.

Reg went back to the picture. He couldn't have changed that much before he had shown up in the ghost village, could he? She showed the mental image to the grandmother again. "Was one of them this man?"

She considered and didn't say anything for a long time.

"I remember him," the child piped up.

Reg looked over at the little child. "Do you? That's wonderful. Do you know… how long ago it was? A long time ago or recently?"

They looked at her blankly.

"Reg," Corvin spoke, "there is no time for the ghosts. They won't have any way of marking how long ago anything happened."

"Crap!"

Reg tried to stay calm. She was close. Much closer than she had been before. Here was someone who had actually seen Wilson. That was important. She went back to the picture, holding it in her mind.

"Did he look like this? Or did he look older?"

She hoped that the wizard had aged during the time he had been in the Everglades. The question wouldn't be much help if he hadn't changed in appearance.

"Older than that," the child said thoughtfully. "But… not an old man."

Reg tried to make adjustments to the picture she had formed of him. "How did he look? Can you describe him?"

"He did not have hair in the middle," the little girl gestured over the crown of her own head. "And it was spotty. Not just black."

Reg imagined black hair flecked with gray and the little girl nodded.

"Yes. And I don't think he was so tall."

Reg hadn't even realized that she had given the wizard a body and height. She considered her mental image and made what adjustments she could.

"Fatter. Not like a warrior."

Reg felt like a forensic artist working with a witness to a crime. She'd always admired the people that could draw sketches of other people like that.

The little girl turned to the other ghost. "Grandmother? You remember him?"

The older woman nodded gravely. "Yes. He came here in a wind-boat. Made a fire and burned herbs. He did not speak to us as you do."

"He couldn't see ghosts?"

The grandmother looked at the little girl. "He did not speak to us. I don't know whether he had the sight."

The little girl nodded her agreement.

"Did he say why he came here? Was he looking for something? Was he... by himself or maybe running away from someone?"

"No... there were others. The living come here sometimes to look. Most do not make an offering. He at least showed that respect."

Reg nodded. She looked at Corvin. She didn't know if he could hear what the ghosts were saying or if he could understand what was going on by virtue of the connection between them.

"We should burn herbs too," she suggested. "Do you think... I don't know much about plants, but could you and Damon look around, see if there's sage or something?"

Corvin didn't look particularly pleased with being given this assignment, but he was familiar with herb-lore. He nodded.

"You'll be okay by yourself for a few minutes?"

"Yes. I'm fine here and I have a shield."

CHAPTER THIRTY-ONE

The little girl spoke to her grandmother, but in a language that Reg could not understand. She tried to sense what the ghosts were feeling, since she couldn't understand what they were saying to each other. It was strange not to be able to understand them when they could have made her understand. But she supposed they didn't always want to be overheard, just like living people.

The grandmother was nodding slowly to what the little girl said. Her eyes flicked to Reg a few times, but she didn't say anything immediately. She closed her eyes in meditation and just sat there by the fire. Reg didn't know how she could sit so still without moving for so long. Maybe it was easier for ghosts because they didn't have bodies to keep still or muscles that would get sore from sitting in one place in one position for too long. But Reg's mind wouldn't let her sit for that long either. She would be too restless. She couldn't concentrate on one thing for that long.

Reg watched Corvin and Damon when she could see them—moving in and out of the trees, stooping to examine something on the ground, collecting a few leaves here and there. Eventually, they returned with their offerings.

Corvin placed them in front of Reg, telling her what each was. None of it meant anything to Reg. But that was why she was glad to have them with her. She wouldn't have known on her own which plants were appropriate for sacred offerings and which would mean nothing, or stink, or end up insulting the ghosts so that they put a curse on the whole group.

"And I can burn these?" Reg asked. "That's the right way to offer them?"

Corvin nodded. "They can be burned... and I suspect that with ghosts, that's really the only way. It isn't like they can eat or drink them or use them in a poultice."

Reg nodded. Taking each kind of plant in turn, she burned a few leaves of each in her hand, and wafted the smoke toward the ghosts. The other spirits who were gathered around, outside of her shield, quieted and calmed. Maybe she should have done that to begin with, but she hadn't known.

The grandmother bowed with each offering, and sometimes waved her hand through it as if to draw the smoke closer to her, but her movement did not affect the drifting smoke.

She tilted her head. "Ah, sweet bay leaves." She drew a deep breath. She nodded slowly. "You should not burn all of that one. You should take it with you in case you need it."

Reg hesitated. "Are you asking me to take it? I don't want to take anything off of the island, in case..."

"You will not be cursed if you take it with you. It is our gift to you. You will need it."

Reg gathered what remained of the sweet bay leaves. She wasn't sure what to do with them, so she shoved them into her pocket, hoping the ghosts would not think that she was being disrespectful in doing so.

Reg sat after having offered each of the wild herbs. She wasn't sure what to do next. Her shield was growing weaker. She noticed the gangsters and the soldiers were getting closer to her than they had before.

"We'd better leave soon."

Corvin nodded. He glanced up at the sky and then looked at his watch. "It's later than I would like. I didn't expect it to take so long to get here, or for us to be here for so long."

Reg looked around. The day seemed to be growing dusky. How long had they been there? She could have sworn it had been no more than an hour. But time in a place like that could be unreliable. As Harrison often pointed out, humans were limited in their understanding of time. While everyone said that time always progressed at an even pace and could be measured by clocks and watches, Reg wasn't so sure she believed that. Her experiences with time had been... unusual. She wasn't surprised at how quickly the time had gone, and yet at the same time, it was disconcerting and made her feel a little bit off-balance.

"Yes." She started to get to her feet, and paused to bow to her ghostly hosts. "Thank you for talking with me."

"The man had a sickness," the little girl said.

"A sickness. What kind of sickness?"

The girl looked at her grandmother and again exchanged a few words with her in their native tongue. She looked back at Reg. "I don't know the English word for it," she said. "Maybe you do not have a word for it. In our tongue... giant sickness."

"Giant sickness?" Reg looked at Corvin and Damon, hovering close by. "Have you ever heard of that?"

Both warlocks shook their heads. Reg was disappointed. She had hoped that it would be a clue for them. It would be something they recognized, and it would help them to find him. Maybe he would be in a hospital somewhere as a John Doe. Or perhaps he had died. But either way, it would be a step forward. Instead, it was just one more thing to add to the list of things that they didn't know or understand about Jeffrey Wilson.

"Can you tell me about giant sickness?" she asked the two ghosts.

The other ghosts were pressing in more insistently, making goosebumps break out on Reg's arms, neck, and back. She tried to strengthen her barrier against them.

"They talk about the land of the giants," the older woman explained. "A land where the people are very tall like trees and stand all day, or lie on the ground. They wander out of the village into the swamp. You must not let them wander or they may never return."

Reg had a chill. Was that what had happened to Wilson? He had contracted this disease and had wandered away from the others in his group with hallucinations and had never returned? He had probably died, drowned in the river or eaten by a gator, unable to care for himself.

"What can be done about this giant disease? Is it... curable? Does it pass?"

A shrug from the woman. "You must do what you can for them. The best medicine you can. But many do not return once they have wandered into that twilight."

Reg nodded slowly in thanks. She looked at Corvin and Damon. "I guess we'd better go back to our boat. If it's still here. What if the guide thought that something happened to us and left without us?"

"He will still be there," Corvin assured her. "I told him that we might be a long time. He knows to wait."

As they turned and headed back to where the boat was waiting, Reg felt the spirits around her closing in. She turned around quickly. They were reaching, grasping, icy fingers brushing against Reg's skin. They could not take her yet, but they would completely break through her barrier before long. She tried to strengthen it, clutching Corvin by the arm and drawing from his energy.

"We have to stop them!"

"Stop who?"

"All of these ghosts." Reg gestured, then rolled her eyes, exasperated with having to explain. "They all want to talk. They all want to use me. And I can't. They would take more than I have to give. Help me to build up the defensive spell."

Corvin took a deep breath in and let it out slowly. He looked around them, up at the sky, and then around them on the ground. Reg could feel him beginning to weave his spell in with hers, but it was not very strong. It wasn't going to be enough.

"You have a flame?" Corvin suggested. "That might help."

Reg conjured fire between her hands almost without effort and coaxed it into a small fire in the middle of one palm. Small and easy to control, so Corvin could focus on and concentrate his energy on strengthening the spell. It lifted Reg's spirits a little as well. It would keep the icy fingers off of her for a time.

"Thanks."

Damon was walking ahead of them. He looked back, as if impatient for them to hurry up. But Reg couldn't move too quickly. She didn't want the ghosts to sense any haste or fear. No negative emotions that would feed them. She hummed to herself, trying to keep her spirits up. One of the soldiers marched close to her on the right, rattling his saber and making threatening comments toward the others who were around. On her other side walked one of the gangsters, wearing a long coat, a horrible-looking submachine gun cradled in one arm. She could see why no one would have wanted to get too close to the Lost Village while Capone and his men were hiding there.

They got closer to the river and Reg scanned the shore for their little boat. She couldn't see it. Were they farther away than she had thought? She had spent some time scouting out the village before deciding to talk to the grandmother ghost tending the fire. She probably hadn't noticed how far she had walked.

There was fog gathering over the water as the sun got lower in the sky. The two put together meant that it was getting darker very quickly. Reg tried not to betray any fear to her traveling companions, but she didn't like it. She wanted to get back to their boat and out of there.

Along the tree line, lights started to flicker. Reg looked at them. More ghosts? Living beings with lanterns to hold back the night and keep the spirits from chasing them? Was it a vision that only Reg could see, or could the others too?

"What is that?"

Corvin looked toward the lights. "It's nothing. Just foxfire."

"Foxfire. What's that?"

"Nothing you need to worry about. You're perfectly safe. As long as you stay away from the lights."

"How do you know it's foxfire? What does it mean?"

"I've seen it before. It doesn't mean anything. It's just... a phenomenon."

"Is it because of the ghosts?"

"Perhaps. No one has reliably identified all of the factors. It comes and goes as it will."

Damon chuckled. "That's a pun. Will-o'-the-wisp, it's called."

"Foxfire? Will-o'-the-wisp? And it's just... nothing? It's just there?"

"Don't be distracted by it," Corvin said. "Keep going. We need to get to the boat."

"Where is it? I thought we would be at it by now. We didn't walk this far when we came, did we?"

"We'll be there in a minute. It's just a little farther. It seems longer because of the dusk. And because you are tired. You've expended a lot of energy already. Probably more than you realize."

Which meant she had drawn more than she realized from Corvin as well. He too was tired as he tried to help maintain her shield, even though she knew he didn't normally do protection spells out in the open. He'd told her they were much more challenging to maintain in an open area than in an enclosed room. She tried to give it a bit more of a boost. The flame in her hands grew, flaring across the faces of all of the ghosts. They fell back, giving her more space.

Then Reg saw the boat.

CHAPTER THIRTY-TWO

$\mathcal{I}$t would have lifted Reg's spirits if it had been their boat. But the one she saw was not their little airboat, with the guide waiting patiently for their return. Instead, she saw masts and sails rising up out of the fog. She gasped and held Corvin's arm more tightly.

"Holy crap!"

Corvin looked at her with concern, and Damon stopped and looked back, waiting for her to come and wondering why she had stopped moving.

"What is it?" Corvin asked.

"You can't see it?"

"See what?"

"Is it... a ghost ship? You're telling me you can't see that?" Reg gestured toward it. Corvin looked in the direction she pointed. Damon turned and looked blindly in that direction.

"A ship?" Corvin repeated. "No. I don't see a ship. Do you want to show it to me?"

Reg took a deep breath and held it. She tried to push the picture of the ship into Corvin's mind. Even though he was open to her sharing, there was still a point of resistance, like trying to push it through a tough membrane.

"Can you see it?" she repeated urgently.

Corvin gazed in the direction of the ship. He nodded. "Yes. I can see it.

It must be supernatural. There's nothing like that around these days. Even in museums."

Damon was the only one who couldn't see it, but Reg didn't have the energy to try to show him too.

"What kind of ship?" he demanded. "The water isn't deep enough for ships."

"It's like... a pirate ship," Reg explained. "The water around here must have been deep enough back then. Before they drained it."

Corvin nodded his agreement.

"What do we do?" Reg demanded. "I don't want to... walk into trouble. What if they try to touch us or curse us?"

"I think the best thing to do is just to walk by as if we can't see it. If they don't know that we can see it..."

Reg wasn't sure that would make any difference. But she had asked his opinion and he was more experienced in that type of thing than she was. They kept walking, drawing closer together as a group, pretending that it didn't tower over them. Reg dragged her feet forward.

She glanced toward the foxfire burning in the trees. Maybe they should stay there, where there was light and it was safe. She would feel better there with the little green lights than having to walk in the shadow of the ghost ship. She could hear voices calling out over the water. The seamen were shouting to each other. What would they do when they saw her and her company?

It took a lot of energy for a ghost to do anything that affected the corporeal world, but that didn't mean that they couldn't do anything. There had been plenty of times as a child when Reg had been terrorized by ghosts, and knowing that they were real and not just something that had come from an overactive imagination didn't actually help her feel better.

"Do you think... maybe we should just stay away from the water until they go?" Reg suggested.

"Stay on the island?" Corvin gave a bark of laughter and shook his head. "No, we're going to get off of this island as fast as we can, before anything else happens."

"But it would be safer over there in the trees. Where there are lights. We can... just stay there, where it is safe, and then when the pirate ship goes away, we could find our boat."

"No," Corvin repeated firmly. "Don't let the ship distract you. Focus on getting to our boat. It's getting dark and we can't take the chance of getting confused or misled."

"Or what?"

"Or nothing. Our boat is just down the shore. Pretend that the ship isn't even there. Damon can't see it. Pretend that you can't see it either. Maybe he can give you a vision where it isn't there and you'll feel more comfortable."

Reg glanced at Damon. "No. I don't want anything else in my head. Just what's real."

"It all depends on your outlook," Damon said. "If I did, then that would be real to you. It's real to me. And to anyone else who walks along the shore here. It isn't really there. It's just an energy imprint left there long ago. A boat can't do anything to harm you."

"The ghosts on board could. I know, I've dealt with ghosts before."

Damon opened his mouth but apparently couldn't come up with a good argument.

"Just keep moving," Corvin encouraged, nudging Reg forward. "Let's go. We'll be to our boat in a minute."

Reg heard the waves lapping against the shore as if it were the ocean. She heard a splash and knew that the pirates had just put a small boat in the water. They were coming after her. Reg picked up her pace. She wanted to get to their boat before the pirate ghosts could reach the island. She stumbled over a rock and Corvin held her up.

"It's okay, Reg," he told her.

"They're coming."

"They won't hurt you."

Reg tried to get her uncooperative body to move faster. She felt like she was walking through mud. Her feet were slow and heavy. She needed to hurry to get away from the pirate ghosts. Who knew what they would do if they could reach her? She didn't want to hear their words. Didn't want them trying to take over her body or to send messages through her. She didn't want their thoughts in her head.

"Please… hurry."

"We're both here. We're right with you, Reg."

Reg was trying to jump over the plants and grasses, bounding like a goat but still feeling like she wasn't getting any farther ahead. She didn't want to, but was drawn to look back to see the pirates and how close they were getting. The boat cut through the water toward them but had not gained as much as Reg had feared.

"Come on!"

Then finally, they made it around a corner into a little inlet, and Reg saw the airboat waiting for them.

CHAPTER THIRTY-THREE

*G*o!" Reg encouraged. "There it is. Hurry up."

She was sure she was still slower than either of the men, but telling them to go faster. If they went any faster, they would leave her behind.

They all hurried as quickly as possible without tripping, which meant that they were going at a quick walk rather than a sprint. They could only go so fast, contending with the marshy ground, clumps of plants, and falling darkness .

They got to the shoreline, and Reg stopped, looking out at the airboat. It was too far for a jump, or at least to be sure of landing on it. And she was afraid of what would happen if she stepped into the water. Once, it wouldn't have bothered her. So what if she got her feet wet? But since her sirens instincts had been awakened, she couldn't be sure that they would all be safe if she stepped into the water.

Damon made a running start and jumped, making it just to the edge of the boat and pulling himself farther onboard with the rail. He got out of the way and turned to watch Corvin and Reg.

"Just come," he insisted, seeing Reg hesitating at the edge of the water.

Corvin plunged into the water, stopping halfway between the waterline and the boat. He reached out for Reg. "Jump."

"I don't know if—"

"I've got you. Just do it."

The longer she hesitated over it, the harder it would be for her to make the decision or the jump. Reg closed her eyes briefly, gathered her muscles and, holding her breath, jumped toward the boat.

Corvin caught her clumsily and shoved across and up so that she landed on the steps of the boat, with just one toe dipping into the water. Reg scrambled up and looked back at the pirate ship and the pilot boat, edging nearer.

"Okay. We made it. We can go."

The guide was watching them, bemused. He shook his head slightly. "You look like you've been having fun."

He turned the key in the ignition as Corvin clambered up onto the boat, soaked from mid-calves down. By the time they were each in their seats, the guide was pulling the boat out and making a large arc to circle back the way they had come.

"You were a long time on the island," he said conversationally. "I didn't think there was that much to do there. You get lost?"

Reg shook her head. "No. We were just visiting."

He squinted at her as if trying to translate what she had said, then shrugged and went back to driving. Reg looked back at the island. The ghost ship, the foxfire, and the island were indistinct. In a few minutes, they would be out of sight.

Damon rubbed his hands briskly as if they were cold. "Well... that was a waste of time. We're no farther ahead than we were when we started." He shot a look at Corvin. Coming to the Lost Village had, after all, been his idea. And they had wasted a whole day on it.

"Actually, we're farther behind than we were on the first day," Reg said.

The men looked at her, frowning.

"How can we be farther behind?" Corvin asked.

"If the two of you had believed me and listened to me the first day, we wouldn't have had to go through all of this. We would have had him home by now."

Damon tried to start a sentence several times, each time only getting an angry syllable or two out before he stalled and tried to say something else.

"What are you talking about, Reg?" Corvin intervened. "Are you saying that you know where he is?"

"Well, not now. But I know where he was the first day. If we're lucky, he'll be at the hotel tonight. But we haven't been that lucky so far, so I don't really expect him to be."

She wished she dared to take a picture of the two of them gaping at her in disbelief. But sliding out her phone and snapping a picture of each of them probably wouldn't make them happy.

"At the hotel?" Damon said finally.

"I don't know if he was staying there or just came to see the mermaid show last night."

Damon knew that Corvin and Reg had taken in the mermaid show the night before, but not all of the details. He knew that they had agreed on a course of action without him, which had kind of riled him up, but Reg told him that if he wanted to be in charge, then he shouldn't have lied to her from the start and he was welcome to go looking for the lost wizard all by himself.

"You saw him last night?" Corvin asked.

"Yeah. We both did. Remember, I showed you the guy that we'd seen at the Skunk Man Saloon the first day?"

Corvin thought about it, but couldn't be sure. His eyes didn't light up with recognition.

"I just figured it out when I was talking with the grandmother today," Reg explained. "I was trying to imagine what Wilson had looked like when she and her granddaughter saw him, starting with the picture you have and then trying to change it by what she said—going bald, with salt and pepper hair. Fatter. Maybe shorter than I had imagined. And I kept trying to develop that farther. What if that was the halfway point. What if he got balder and the rest of his hair went white? What if he put on a little more weight. And I couldn't get him out of my head. The man we saw at Skunk Man Saloon."

"Did you talk to him?" Damon asked. He grimaced, trying to recall who had been there. But he had clearly discounted everyone else he had seen and had only been focused on Reg and Corvin and getting his dinner. He wanted to get on his way and start looking for the missing wizard in earnest. He didn't believe that Reg had been able to find him with her powers. He had only wanted to hurry out of there to get started on the real search.

"No. I don't think so. Maybe pleasantries," Reg explained. "But it was him. He was sitting right there next to us. Just like I had told you."

"You didn't know where he was when we got off the boat."

"Maybe it was because he was too close. I don't know. But he was there. I took you right to him the first day."

Damon shook his head slowly in disbelief.

"You were right too," Reg pointed out. "You're the only one who really believed that he was still alive."

Damon looked only slightly mollified by this. "I was, wasn't I?"

"Why didn't he ever go home?" Corvin asked. "Why didn't he leave the Everglades? He didn't look like anyone was keeping him here, physically or under some spell. The man you pointed out… he just looked like a tourist."

"It's possible that he doesn't want to go back."

"He would have gone back if he could," Damon insisted. "I've talked to his family. I know he would have. He left a wife and children. Something must have happened to keep him here. If this guy you saw is really Wilson."

"He was. Look at your picture and compare him with the guy that—" She broke off. "Okay, you never saw him or paid any attention to him. But I'm telling you, he's the guy. Corvin thinks so, don't you?"

"Don't put words in my mouth, Regina. I'm not saying that he is, and I'm not saying that he isn't. I don't know." He rubbed his chin. "Hopefully, he's still at the hotel. That would make things much easier. We could get this cleared up tonight."

But Reg knew it wasn't going to be that easy.

* * *

Trying to get details from the front desk at the hotel was like pulling teeth. They didn't know whether Wilson had registered under his own name and they didn't have a current picture of him to show to the clerk at the desk. They couldn't very well show him a fifty-year-old picture and hope that he recognized the man they were looking for.

Reg tried to describe him physically, explained that she had seen him at the mermaid show the night before, but said that he had left suddenly and she didn't realize until later that he had left his credit card on the table. So she clearly needed to track him down before he had to cancel his card.

"Oh…" A look of dawning comprehension spread over the clerks' face. "The Canadian?"

Reg looked at Damon. He nodded eagerly. "Yes, the Canadian. Is he registered here?"

"No. That is, he was, but he checked out last night. Rather unexpectedly. Right in the middle of the mermaid show, like you said. I thought maybe he got an emergency call, had to go home for something."

"He didn't say anything about why he had to leave?" Reg pressed. "Did he say where he was going?"

"No, he didn't say why. He just... seemed rattled. I thought it must have been bad news."

Reg looked at the others. She couldn't think of anything else to ask him. They had a line on Wilson, but it was tenuous. Reg knew what he looked like now, so that would help her to find him. So would the fact that she had now seen him a couple of times. If she'd really had his credit card or something else of his, that would have helped.

"Okay. Well, I'll just hang on to his card, and if you see him or hear from him, you can give me a call?"

He made a painstaking note and had Reg give him her phone number again. "If I hear anything, I'll let you know. I'm sure once he realizes that he left his credit card here, he'll be calling us."

Reg nodded. "Great, thanks."

They went upstairs to their rooms.

"Can you find him again?" Damon asked. "You did once before, and now you know him better, so it should be easier. And he's probably close by. He didn't go back to Canada. He's probably just in a different hotel."

"I'm beat tonight. I don't have the energy to do anything." Reg yawned. "If you want, you can call around to other hotels. If he's registered under his own name, maybe you'll be able to find him without any psychic services."

Damon's expression took on a slightly different cast, and Reg knew immediately what he was thinking. "No, that wouldn't get you out of paying me half the reward. You wouldn't know where to find him if I hadn't already done all of this work. Just because I can't find him until I've had some sleep, that doesn't mean I didn't help."

"Yes," he sighed. "You're right."

Reg looked over at Corvin. "You heard him. I've still earned my fee."

Corvin nodded. "I'll be your witness," he agreed wryly. "If he tries to renege on the deal."

Damon's mouth twisted into a snarl that he tried to smooth out. "I'm not going to renege on anything. I keep my promises." He aimed his sneer in Corvin's direction. "Unlike some other people."

"When have I broken a promise?" Corvin protested.

Reg and Damon both just looked at him. Corvin rolled his eyes and shrugged. "Yes, fine. But it really shouldn't count when it is instinctive behavior." He gave Reg a penetrating look. "Am I right?"

"I... don't know. I haven't figured that out yet." Reg looked away from him, not wanting to discuss it. Damon didn't know the details of her reaction to water, and she would prefer that he not find out.

"I'm going to bed. If you guys want to make calls to the hotels, then go ahead, but I'm wiped out and I'm going to sleep."

"It's early," Corvin protested. "You're not going to go to sleep this early. You won't be able to."

"That might work if Damon hadn't gotten me out of bed before first light. Let me sleep until noon, and I won't go to sleep before three in the morning, but what time was it when you got me up? Five?"

"Closer to six."

"That's crazy. No one gets up that early. Except maybe bakers. And I'm not a baker."

"Clearly not," Damon agreed, chuckling. "Lots of people get up at six."

"*Before* six?"

"Well, some. Maybe not a lot, but... some people."

"Crazy people. Not psychics."

"Why not psychics?"

"Because psychics do seances at midnight or later."

"Ah." Damon shrugged. "Makes sense."

"Most magical practitioners prefer the hours of darkness," Corvin told Damon pointedly. "Most of us do not have nine-to-five jobs."

Reg figured this was meant as a dig against Damon about the way that serious witches and warlocks worked. Damon's security work did tend to be daytime work rather than nighttime work. But Reg knew that Davyn had a daytime office job as well, and he was the head of Corvin's coven. It couldn't be very uncommon. Most of the practitioners she was familiar with had conventional jobs as well as whatever magic they practiced. Other than those who were retired, like Sarah.

"I'm going to bed," she repeated, folding her arms, waiting for them to leave.

"Oh." Damon got it. "Got it. Good night."

He headed toward the door. Corvin lingered, as Reg had known he would. "Is there anything else I can do for you, Regina?" He leaned closer to her, his warm breath on her face. The scent of roses started to waft toward her. "Whatever I can do to help you to relax and regenerate so that you're ready to go tomorrow…"

"I'm relaxed enough without your help. Good night."

He gave her another moment to change her mind, then complied, leaving her alone in her hotel room.

Reg decided on a warm bath before bed. Before long, she found her eyes drooping as she soaked. She climbed out of the tub, pulled on some night clothes, and slid into bed.

And then lay there awake.

CHAPTER THIRTY-FOUR

*I*t was one of those nights when no matter what Reg did, she couldn't find sleep until she gave up on the plan of ever being able to go to sleep that night and then fell into restless dreams, knowing that morning was only an hour or two away and she would have to get up again. She dreamed of being in the swamp again, running away from goblins and cats and Canadians. She didn't know which way to go, where the danger was coming from. She kept waking up, looking at the gradually brightening window, and then falling asleep again, too exhausted to do anything else.

When Damon called, she was in the shower, trying to wake herself up. Sleep had just made her more tired. But she'd at least had a break and a rest from using her powers. While tired, she figured she could still use her psychic powers to try to track down Wilson. Find the Canadian wizard, convince him to go back to Black Sands with them to participate in the Spring Games, and then she could relax, and it wouldn't matter whether she slept or didn't sleep for the next week.

"You up?" Damon asked, hearing the noise of the shower in the background.

Reg wiped her dripping face with the towel. "Yeah, I'm up."

"Great. Breakfast and then we can look for Wilson?"

"Coffee. I don't know about breakfast."

"Coffee, then. Or do you want to combine your drink and your work and read tea leaves?"

"Nope. Need the heavy-duty stuff today."

"We'll bring some up. So you don't want anything to eat? Toast? Eggs?"

"No. I don't eat this early."

It was only a couple of minutes before Corvin and Damon were at her door. Damon handed her a Starbucks cup. Reg inhaled the vapor.

It was in the morning that she was most aware of Starlight's absence. The cat always wanted her to get up before she was ready, and then was always underfoot and demanding to be fed. She missed him and wondered how he was. Francesca hadn't called her to let her know there was anything wrong, so she had to assume that he was fine. When she was done, he would be at home waiting for her to return.

She took a sip of the hot, bitter coffee and nodded. "Great. This should get the engine going."

"How did you sleep?" Corvin asked, giving her a sideways look.

She glared at him. "You put some kind of curse on me when you said I wasn't going to be able to get to sleep early. I was exhausted. That was a nasty thing to do."

"It wasn't a curse."

"The power of suggestion, then. You shouldn't have said that."

He shrugged, looking smug.

They all sat down, sipping coffees and pretending that they weren't covertly looking at the time, wondering when they were going to get started. Reg pushed her coffee away when it was only half-finished. She blew out her breath.

"Okay. Let's do this."

"What are you going to do?" Damon asked. "Did you bring your crystal ball?"

"No. I'm just going to... do like I did when I felt him in the Skunk Man Saloon. Just try to reach out and locate him."

Damon nodded.

Corvin watched Reg with keen interest. He was attracted to her powers, so watching her using them, or feeling it, clearly whetted his appetite. Reg shifted uneasily away from him. Damon was there, and he wouldn't let Corvin do anything, or he would at least try to stop him. But Corvin's powers were much greater than Damon's, and Reg worried that even she and Damon together would not be strong enough to stop Corvin if he let his hunger get the better of him.

"Should you be in here?" she asked.

Corvin raised an eyebrow. "Why not? I'm part of this team. I have been helping all along. Why would you suggest kicking me out of the room now?"

"Because… you look hungry."

Corvin chuckled, but didn't deny it. Reg looked at Damon for support. "Watch him, right?"

Damon nodded. "I will. You don't need to worry about him. Just stay calm and do your thing."

Reg looked at Corvin one more time. But she needed to focus on Jeffrey Wilson if she were going to find him. She had been so close the last time. If she had only known back then that he didn't look like the wizened old man Damon had put into his fake vision, she might have had the chance to persuade him to go to the Spring Games the very first day.

She closed her eyes and rested her hands on her knees, palms up. She focused on her third eye and built the picture of Wilson in her head again. The original photograph, then how the little girl had said he looked, and then the face and body Reg had seen on two occasions. She meditated on his name.

Wizard Jeffrey Wilson. Canadian. Wandering in the Everglades for fifty years.

Why? Because of the illness that the little girl had mentioned? Giant sickness?

She pulled away from the question and focused on what she knew. She had studied the maps of the Everglades several times, and she pictured a big map now, with all of its intricacies. She mentally marked the places she had been. Then the places she knew that Wilson had been. He'd probably been everywhere in the swamp over the years, but she stuck with the ones that she knew.

A pulsing started in the middle of the map. At first, it was barely visible. Just a fuzzy area on the map that began to throb like a heartbeat. But it wasn't in time with *her* heart. Was it the location of the wizard?

Reg studied the map, noting the nearby markings. As she looked and studied, the dot became more clear. Red, with a defined size, blinking on and off. Reg grew more confident in it. She fixed the location in her mind, breathed deeply, making sure that she really knew it and it would be fixed in her mind.

She opened her eyes.

Damon looked at her expectantly. "Well…?"

"Yeah. I saw a location on a map."

"Hallelujah. Close by? If he was here yesterday, then he probably hasn't gone too far."

Reg nodded. "Yeah. Not too far. By the downed plane."

Damon looked at her, then looked at Corvin. His eyes went back to Reg. "Downed plane? What downed plane?"

"You said that there had been plane crashes in the Everglades, didn't you? Or was that Corvin?" Reg looked at Corvin and shrugged. "So, of course there are downed planes."

"Yes. But when they are discovered, the wreckage isn't left there. They are retrieved."

Reg looked at him. "Okay. But… that doesn't mean that they have all been discovered."

"Of course not. But how are we going to find a wreck that hasn't been discovered?"

"The same way I'm going to find a wizard who has been missing fifty years."

Corvin rubbed the space between his brows. "Okay… fair enough."

Reg rolled her eyes.

"So, what do we need?" Damon asked. "A boat, I assume. A guide."

"A boat driver," Reg clarified. "I don't want a tour guide who thinks he knows where I want to go. I want someone who will follow directions."

Damon nodded. "Okay. Yeah. I'll… see who I can find that will fit the bill."

"We'll all go," Reg said, eyeing Corvin again. She didn't want to be left with him. "Then we won't waste any time going back and forth."

Corvin didn't voice any objection. Reg gathered her purse and whatever she thought she might need. She was pretty proud of herself for already being dressed when the warlocks had made it up to her room. Usually, it took a considerable length of time for her to get her proper clothes on, traipsing around half the day in her nightwear, towel, or robe. She looked around the room.

"Should we pack and check out? We shouldn't need to stay here another night."

"Let's hold off on that," Damon hedged. "We don't know yet what's going to happen today. It may take longer than you think. We might still need a place to stay tonight. Then we can head back to Black Sands in the morning." He checked his watch. "In time to get Wilson registered in the Games."

"And collect our reward."

Damon nodded.

Reg grinned. She liked the part about collecting their reward. And now that she had located Wilson, she was sure it was in the bag.

CHAPTER THIRTY-FIVE

*I*t took longer than expected to get a driver that Reg approved of. They all seemed to be good ol' boys who thought that they knew everything and that Reg should just sit back and let them take her on a tour of the most interesting places in the Everglades. Even those who said that they would take her where she wanted to go still *thought* they knew better than she did, and Reg didn't want to have to deal with their oppressive attitudes while trying to get a fix on Wilson. And that meant it was almost noon before they even stepped onto the boat.

"It might be a late start, but this time we know where we're going," Reg insisted when Damon looked like he was at the end of his rope because it was taking so long.

"Yeah."

He could stay back at the hotel with *his* doubts too. Reg had difficulty pushing her feelings down and keeping quiet about it. It was Damon's gig. His contract. Not hers. Not Corvin's. Damon cast the single vote.

They all settled into their seats. Reg sat closest to the driver and gave him instructions as they drove out into the open water. If the boggy, grassy river could be called open water.

"Where exactly are we going?" the driver asked, hands resting lightly on the instruments.

"I'm just going to direct you."

"There really isn't anything interesting in this direction. Are you a botanist?"

"A botanist. I don't even know what a botanist does."

"They come out here to study the plants. Grasses that are apparently different somehow than all of the other grasses. Little flowers and marsh plants that have special properties or are endangered species." He shrugged. "I don't understand all of it. I just take them where they say they have to go."

"Well, same with me. I'm not a botanist, but I just need you to follow my directions."

He nodded and kept driving, following her turn-by-turn directions.

Until he didn't.

The driver shook his head when Reg pointed to a right-hand branch. "Nothing over there. It's a dead end."

"That's the way I want to go."

"It's a dead-end," he repeated. As if she hadn't understood him the first time, and saying it more loudly would somehow get through to her. "You can't go that way."

"Then I want to go into the dead-end," she told him icily. She stared at him and held his gaze until he was the one to look away.

"Okay," he said finally and turned the idling boat right.

Into the dead end. A few hundred feet into the inlet, and then Reg could see walls of swamp all around them except the way they had come in. The driver looked at her for instructions. Reg stared at the impenetrable walls of vegetation.

"Go as far as you can," she told him. "Right to the shore."

Another eye roll, and then he inched the boat forward. Damon and Corvin both stood up, trying to see whatever it was that Reg was on to.

Except that she hadn't seen anything. There wasn't anything to see.

They got to the end of the dead end. Reg stepped to the edge of the boat, then jumped to the shore with a mucky splash. The mud was up to her ankles, and the saw grass again did its best to cut through clothes and any exposed skin. She pulled herself up the embankment, grabbing hold of whatever branches and vegetation she could. Damon and Corvin jumped off behind her, and the three of them made their way up to the higher ground with grunts and muttered curses when a branch would break or a misstep would mean falling to their knees onto the foul, marshy ground.

Reg stopped to take a break, looking back behind her. She could no longer see any sign of the boat. Corvin wiped his face with the back of his arm.

"There isn't any sign that anyone else has been through this way," he pointed out.

Reg looked at the ground. No footprints ahead of them. None but their own behind them. "Well, maybe there's another way in. He might have gotten onto the shore at another place, or maybe even from the other side. I don't know. But I know he's this way."

Corvin pulled out his phone and looked at it, tapping a few times.

"We're not going to go any faster with you checking the time," Reg snapped. "And I doubt there's any signal out here."

"Taking coordinates. I don't want to get lost and not be able to find our way back here."

"Oh. Okay."

He had a point there. With how disoriented Reg had felt the night before trying to find their boat, it was probably a good idea. There was no guarantee that she would be able to get them out just because she had gotten them in. The Everglades was that kind of place.

It swallowed people alive.

That reminded Reg of alligators and other large predators, and she looked around carefully to make sure that there weren't any suspicious-looking logs nearby. She didn't want to run into Jock the Croc.

Crocodiles didn't seem nearly as scary after being faced with a swamp goblin and Bigfoot, but she wasn't going to take any stupid chances.

"Okay. Let's keep going. This way."

She rechecked her mental map and corrected their course slightly. They were getting close. Not quite there, but very close.

"What would he be doing out here?" Damon's voice was querulous. "This is… the middle of nowhere."

"The driver said there are rare plants out here. Maybe he's looking for some ugly orchid. Or one of those plants that only blooms every fifty years and smells like a dead body. How do I know? Maybe he needs a rare ingredient for some magic spell he's been putting together."

"He missed it blooming the first time and had to wait fifty years for it to bloom again?" Damon demanded, heavy with sarcasm.

"Maybe he did. If he was stuck halfway and couldn't finish his spell…"

"Why wouldn't he go home for the intervening fifty years? Come back and try again next time?"

"You're the one who knows magic. Maybe he wasn't allowed to leave the park between gathering the first ingredients and the one he couldn't get. Maybe that's when he got sick. Who knows!"

Corvin looked at the two of them. "If you children are finished quarreling..."

Reg scowled at him. "What?"

"I think there's something up here." He pointed.

Reg and Damon turned together to follow the warlock's outstretched hand. Reg first thought he meant there was something alive up there. Something dangerous. Her heart beat hard and she searched the trees for a man-shape. Or the shape of a large cat. Or a crocodile, though she didn't think that a crocodile could have crawled that far from the water.

But there seemed to be something under the trees. A large, dark shadow. What? A house? A big fallen tree?

More like a UFO. As they walked toward it, Reg could see the sun glinting off of the metal body every now and then. It didn't look like a plane. Not until they got right up to it. It was caught in the middle of the grove of banyan trees, the trunks and roots growing in weird shapes around it as if they were pulling it down into the ground. Reg couldn't see both wings, mostly just the main body and a bit of the tail. It was close enough to touch, but she didn't reach out to touch it. She knew by the weight in her stomach that the bodies of the pilot and passengers were still inside, their energy imprints still in the jungle growth so many years later.

"What is it?" Reg asked.

"A plane," Damon offered.

Reg glared at him. "I think I know it's a plane. I mean... what kind? Where—or when—is it from?"

Corvin walked around it, examining it from other angles. He didn't touch it either, which surprised Reg a bit since she knew that he collected artifacts. But maybe that was only artifacts imbued with power, and he had no interest in any of the remnants of this crashed plane.

"World War II era," he said. He noted the markings on the tail section. "I think... this might be the Lost Patrol."

Reg stared at it. It was so big to be a lost object, and yet, so small when she considered the scale of the Everglades. It had remained lost for decades, even with people looking for it. And there it was, the trees consuming it.

Damon looked around. "You said that Wilson was close to the lost plane. So, where is he?"

Reg glanced around. She considered her mental map. But like before, she was suddenly stymied. Now that she was close, it was like the focus was off and she couldn't pinpoint the Canadian's location anymore.

"Umm…"

"Don't tell me you lost him again."

"Last time, that meant that we were practically on top of him," Reg shot back. "So let's take a look around and find him."

"There isn't anyone here."

"He's close by. We're really close." Reg walked a similar circuit to the one Corvin had followed, but looking outward from the plane this time instead of toward it. She looked for any movement, reached out with her mind for any flicker of Wilson's consciousness around her. She had circled twice, each one a little wider; then she saw something else in the trees.

CHAPTER THIRTY-SIX

The man Reg had seen twice before was walking through the trees, scratching his head and looking at a brochure or map he held in front of him. He was dressed in light-colored clothing, not nearly as filthy as Reg's were after crawling and stumbling up from the shoreline to the plane. He wore a wide-brimmed white hat. His face was still pale like a tourist's. Not brown after years in the sun. But then, he was wearing a sunshade. Apparently it worked.

Reg walked toward him and called out as if they were old friends. "Jeffrey. Hey."

He looked up from his map and smiled. "Oh. Hello." He studied her face. "You look familiar…"

"Yeah. The Skunk Man Saloon and then the mermaid show last night."

"Oh. Were you there?" His lips pursed. "I don't have the best memory for faces anymore."

"Yeah. I recognize you."

"Did we talk?"

"Not really. You're from Canada, right?"

He nodded, giving her a polite smile. "Yes, that's right."

"What are you doing out here? You're kind of in the middle of nowhere."

"So are a lot of places in Canada."

Regina indicated their surroundings with a gesture. "But I bet they don't look like this."

"No," he admitted. "Nothing like this."

Reg was keeping an eye on Corvin and Damon in her peripheral vision. They were not approaching, but seemed okay with her making the initial contact and trying to put Wilson at ease.

"How long have you been here?" Reg asked.

"Here? Not very long. Just today."

"And in Florida?"

He looked at her, his eyes cloudy. "What is happening here? Do I know you?"

"Sort of." It was probably best if he thought that she was at least an acquaintance. "You've been here for a long time, haven't you? In Florida, I mean. In the Everglades?"

"I don't know. There's a lot to see here."

"Yeah. There sure is. But you've been here for a *really* long time."

"No... I don't think so."

"Have you looked in a mirror? Do you look the same as you did when you first came here?" Reg turned toward Damon. "Do you have the picture?"

Damon approached slowly. He looked relaxed, but Reg could feel his spiking anxiety. They didn't want to do anything that would make the Canadian wizard run. They didn't want to take the chance of losing him. Damon handed the photo to Reg. She showed it to Wilson.

"This is you, isn't it?"

He studied the picture. He frowned and shook his head. "No... I don't think so."

"That was fifty years ago. You've changed since then. But this is you."

"Fifty years?" Wilson laughed. "I don't know who you are, lady, but you've got it all wrong. I'm just here for a vacation."

"You left fifty years ago and never came back. You left your family behind. And you never called or wrote or did anything to let them know that you were okay." Reg held the picture in front of him again. "This is you."

He touched his face and then his fringe of hair, then pushed his hat aside as he felt for the large bald patch. He frowned and shook his head. "I think you're mistaken, young lady."

"Why don't you come back to the hotel with us, and then we can work it out. If it's just a case of mistaken identity, then…" Reg shrugged. "No worries. But if you are Jeffrey Wilson." She indicated the picture. "This Jeffrey Wilson, then you need to come back with me."

"Back to the hotel? I don't want to go to your hotel."

"It's the one that the mermaid show was at last night. Or we can go to your hotel. You have your ID, don't you? Your passport? Driver's license?"

"Of course I have ID."

Reg looked back over her shoulder at the plane wreck, which Wilson's eyes had fastened upon. "Do you remember that? Do you remember when it crashed? Or hearing about it after that?"

"That's a Grumman Avenger. I remember flying one in the war."

"Yeah. That one has been crashed here all that time."

She let him consider how corroded and overgrown the aircraft was. If he had been in the park for fifty years, he had been there almost as long as the plane had. And he could see what kind of shape it was in.

"Those boys," Wilson said softly, looking at the plane.

"Did you know them?"

"No. I don't think so. But how could I just ignore them? They had wives, families. People who have been looking for them."

"And you have people who have been looking for you."

"No… I don't think so."

"You have been missing for fifty years. They never knew what had happened to you. We need to let them know."

"I would know if it had been that long."

"You see how long that plane has been here. The whole jungle has grown around it. And the whole world has grown around you. Come with me. We'll sort it out. We'll help you figure out where to go from here."

Wilson hesitated. "You seem like a very nice girl, but none of this makes any sense."

"Why are you drawn here? Because it's one thing in the park that has been here as long as you have. The one thing that makes sense. Cell phones and computers and color TV's… smart cars and microwaves and video recorders… so much has just kept on developing while you've been here. It's time to pull you out of the swamp."

"I still don't believe you."

"What year do you think it is?"

He frowned and shook his head. "I don't know. That kind of thing stopped mattering… a long time ago."

CHAPTER THIRTY-SEVEN

*W*ith continued coaxing, Reg managed to get Wilson to agree to go back with them to civilization. He didn't indicate that he had a boat and driver waiting for him somewhere. Reg didn't know if he had the skills to teleport himself across the swamp or if he had just forgotten where he had left his boat. But once she talked him into going back with her, he was amenable to going in their boat.

They retraced their path back to the waiting boat and driver. The driver made no attempt to hide his astonishment at seeing them come back with a man who hadn't gone with them initially. His mouth gaped open and he stared openly at the wizard who looked like a retiree tourist that had just stepped off the plane.

"Who is he?"

"This is Jeffrey Wilson," Reg told him. "That's who we came for." She blinked. "Didn't you think we would find him?"

"Well... to be honest... no. There's nothing over here. What was he doing? Did you drop him yesterday?"

Not that Wilson looked like someone who had just slept in the swamp.

Reg just smiled. "We would like to head back to our hotel now."

Wilson shook his head. "Not *that* hotel," he insisted. "Somewhere else."

"We'll hit a coffee shop or something close by," Reg told him. "Is that okay?"

"I don't want to go to that hotel."

"Okay. We won't. But why not? Did something there scare you?"

Maybe he had an innate fear of mermaids. Or water. Reg had to admit she'd had a certain amount of trepidation sitting next to that huge tank of water. It seemed sturdy enough, but if one of the walls had failed... if someone ran into the side or fired a bullet into it... she could drown sitting next to it.

"Yes. I don't know." Wilson shook his head, confused. Was that what the ghost of the little Seminole girl had meant when she talked about his sickness? Some kind of dementia? She could understand his being confused about how long it had been since he'd entered the park. A lot had happened since then, and she was pretty certain that there had been magic involved. But not being able to remember what had scared him a couple of nights earlier? He knew he was afraid of something at the hotel.

* * *

Wilson got agitated at the thought of getting anywhere near Miami. After some discussion, their driver suggested a fruit stand in Homestead where they sold milkshakes, a popular tourist attraction. Wilson seemed eager to go there, so the driver changed his course and headed south. After they disembarked, a quick Uber ride got them to the fruit stand, and they each ordered milkshakes and sat down to talk, hoping that Wilson would be more cooperative in a relaxed setting.

Reg could see his aura start to change as he took the first few sips of his fresh mango milkshake. He had been very anxious before, which had increased his confusion. The colors of his aura started to warm. Reg gave him a little while, just making small talk and asking him about what sites he recommended they should see or restaurants they should visit.

She could see, out the corner of her eye, how impatient Damon was. But he would have to wait until Wilson was ready to talk. It was one thing to find the guy. It was another to get him to the Spring Games. Reg could see that wasn't going to be a "given."

"Have you ever been to the Spring Games?" Reg asked him. "Damon was telling me about it, and it sounds like a lot of fun."

"I was going to go one year," he said. "I was invited to participate.

But… I don't know what happened." He looked puzzled. "Maybe that was just a dream. I don't think that really happened."

"You were invited," Damon agreed. "But you disappeared. You never showed up for them."

"Why would I be invited? Those are… it's the magical games, isn't it? I'm not…" He gave an embarrassed little shrug. "I'm not magic."

Damon's mouth dropped open. "You're one of the most powerful wizards ever!"

"Me? No. I keep telling you; you must have me confused with someone else. Maybe there is a Jeffrey Wilson who is a wizard, but you're mixing us up. I'm just… well, I'm retired now. I don't do anything."

"What *did* you do?" Reg prodded, sensing that he didn't know.

"I was a… oh, it was so long ago now, it doesn't matter anymore."

It was like he had forgotten who he was. Reg was sure they didn't have the wrong person. How would a non-practitioner of magic have heard of the Spring Games and known what they were? How had he gone to the site of the plane crash without hiring a boat? Why had she immediately homed in on him when she had started her search?

Something clicked in the back of her brain. She looked at Wilson for a few minutes, then switched her gaze to Corvin.

"What was it you were talking with Weston about in the restaurant."

He shook his head. "What? I don't recall. The conversation was all over the place."

"About forgetting."

He frowned.

Reg kept her voice low as if by being quiet, she could avoid upsetting Wilson. "You were talking about someone forgetting everything that had happened to them."

"I don't know if that has any bearing on this situation. That was a mythological reference." His voice transformed smoothly to his lecturing voice. "While there is truth to many of the mythologies of the world, you can't take them at face value. The stories change over the years. Sometimes drastically."

"What was it? What myth?"

He considered. "Uh… Lethe. The river Lethe."

"And the river Lethe became the Everglades river, right?"

"Well… no. Your *friends* said that it was in the park, not that it had become the Everglades river."

Wilson and Damon were listening, looking puzzled.

"But they said it was here. And if it's here, do you think that it could have affected the memories of… someone we know?"

Corvin glanced at Wilson. "Perhaps. I wouldn't want to jump to conclusions, but it's always possible."

"You think it's a coincidence that Weston showed up as soon as I saw Wilson in the restaurant and then starts talking about Lethe? And when he left, Wilson was already gone. The concierge said that he left in a hurry. And he doesn't want to go anywhere near the hotel again."

Corvin addressed Wilson. "Well? When you were there during the mermaid show, did you see anyone that you knew? Or someone who made you feel scared or uncomfortable?"

"I don't know."

"Why did you leave?"

Wilson shook his head, his eyes wide. "I did not want to be there."

Damon was frustrated and impatient. "Can you read him, Reg? Find out what he knows and doesn't know? What happened to him?"

"Not without his permission." Reg looked at Wilson. She tried to keep her voice pleasant and reassuring. Beside her, she could feel warmth exuding from Corvin. Not aimed at her this time. He too seemed to be trying to relax the former wizard. "Mr. Wilson… Jeffrey… do you want me to do a reading for you? I'm a psychic, and I could help you to get this sorted out, so you would understand better what has happened to you. I could read your palm or your aura. If you can get tea here," she looked at the menu at the order kiosk, "then I could read tea leaves for you. Whatever you prefer."

"A psychic?" Wilson said doubtfully. "I don't know about that. Most of the psychics I've met have been… well… not actually real."

"I found you, didn't I? I came here and used my powers to pinpoint your location. That's how we knew where you were, even though you were out by the wreck and no one else could find you there."

"You did that?"

"Yes. That's what I do." That was one of the things Reg did. Sometimes. But he didn't need to know that finding lost persons was not one of her main pursuits.

"But if I don't know what happened, then how will your trying to do a reading help?"

"I might be able to figure it out. Right now, you're limited by what's in your conscious mind. I can probe further… maybe find out what's hidden in your unconsciousness. All of those things that happened to you, they're still in there somewhere." Reg gave her head a little shake. "They don't just disappear one day for no reason."

"Maybe they do."

Reg shook her head. "I don't believe that. Why don't you let me try? What harm could it do?"

"I don't know. It could… I don't know; you could put something in my head. You could… cause damage. I don't know if you're one of those creatures who can absorb other people's powers."

Reg glanced at Corvin.

"I'm not." She promised Wilson. "I won't take anything away from you. I'll only see what I can find out and then I'll tell you. That's what you want, isn't it? To find out where you came from, why you've been hanging around here for so many years?"

"I haven't been here for that long. I told you. You have me confused with someone else."

"Then prove it. Let me see for myself."

Wilson banged down his milkshake cup. "Fine. Do whatever it is you want to do. You'll see that I'm not lying to you. I'm not the guy you're looking for. You're just desperate to make someone fit the mold."

CHAPTER THIRTY-EIGHT

*R*eg waited for Wilson to settle down. She didn't really have to. Since he had consented, she could begin probing around in his consciousness immediately, and it would probably be easier while he was so emotional. But she wasn't going to take advantage of him. She wanted to make sure he understood what he was saying before she started.

"You want me to do it?" She asked. "A reading?"

"Yes."

"I need you to start breathing deeply. Make sure that you're taking a long breath in, hold it for a few seconds, and then push a long breath out. Nice and slow, and even, and calm."

He rolled his eyes, and Reg was ready for his complaint about why she couldn't just go ahead and do what she had said, without all of the fake rigmarole. If he were a wizard, then he probably had a pretty good idea that there was no need for window dressing. She might need to focus and meditate, but he didn't.

But he was still pretending ignorance of the unseen world and forces around them. Or he really couldn't remember what he had once known and been. So he didn't argue, but closed his eyes and started breathing with Reg, following her instructions. His body gradually became looser. His aura cleared. Reg focused her brain and sat across from him, sending out gentle feelers toward him.

His defenses were still up. Reg waited and breathed, just exploring the outer edges of his consciousness and waiting for him to relax.

If he were a non-practitioner, he certainly had strong defenses for one. Which just helped to convince her that he wasn't telling the truth. Or he didn't know the truth. Because he was *definitely* magical.

"Just breathe," she urged quietly. "It will be okay. I'm not going to do anything that will harm you."

"This is silly."

"It's not silly. And you know that, or you wouldn't be resisting so hard."

"I could help you," Corvin offered.

But Reg didn't want to overcome Wilson's defenses by force. She wasn't using all of her power and failing; she was just waiting for him to relax and cooperate. Using her full strength and a boost from Corvin would be like... Reg didn't even know what to compare it to. She had no intention of using force to get what she wanted. That would leave lasting damage and trauma. Wilson had to cooperate, or she would not get in.

"Do you want to hold my hands? That would help." Reg put her hands in the middle of the table for him to take.

Wilson didn't at first. He just sat there staring at her, not believing, not letting her in.

The warlocks were impatient, moving around and hovering in a very distracting way. Reg jerked her head at them. "You guys. Take a walk."

"I want to hear what he has to say," Damon objected.

"He's not going to say anything; I'm going to read for him."

"There's no difference. I want to be here. I want to see and hear."

Reg shook her head. "Go look at souvenirs."

"Reg. I think one of us should stay here in case you need help," Corvin suggested.

"I don't need any help. I can do this on my own without the two of you supervising and hanging over me. Just give us some space."

She outwaited them; both eventually walked away from the table in dissatisfaction. Reg nodded.

"Good. Now it's just you and me."

Wilson looked after the other two. "Where are the other men?"

"They're just going to wander around. Check out some of the stores. I didn't want them in the way."

"No. Not them. The others."

"Which men?" The only person Reg could think that he might be asking about was the driver of the boat, and they had taken their leave of him. They wouldn't be seeing him again.

"The ones who were at the show last night."

"Oh." Reg sighed. "Weston and Harrison."

He nodded. "Where are they?"

"I don't know. They don't… take physical form very often. Not around me, anyway. I only see one of them every now and then. And they don't really go anywhere. They just… disappear."

Despite his insistence that he wasn't magical, Wilson seemed to take this new information in stride. He nodded slowly.

"So right now…?"

"They're not here. But we should stop talking about them if you don't want to see them, because I don't want to call one of them accidentally."

"You can do that?"

"That's what usually happens." Reg started to give a more full explanation, but that meant remembering other times when she had called Harrison, and telling him how she did it, and she would just end up calling him by accident. So she immediately moved the conversation in another direction. "Tell me what things you've seen here in the Everglades. Describe some of your favorite places to me."

"Oh, that's a hard one. There are so many fascinating places in the park. I don't know where to start."

"Skunk Man Saloon?"

"Well, when I'm just hanging out at the bar with the guys…? Yes. Definitely. Low stress, lots of ambiance. And I like the cheesy pictures."

"In the menu? All of those ugly old black-and-white Bigfoot pictures?"

"Not Bigfoot…" He waggled his finger at her. "Skunk Man. Not the same thing."

"But the same species, right?"

"I don't know. It can't be established by science unless we have samples for comparison."

"You want to capture him?"

"No, no. Just compare things like hair, skin, body structure. A thorough scientific discussion…"

"Have you ever seen him?"

"Who?"

"The Skunk Man."

There was a flash of something in his eye and then it was gone. He shook his head. Reg tried to dig further. He was more relaxed and discussing things he liked was helping him to open up to her.

"Are you sure? You never saw him?"

He'd been in the Everglades for fifty years. She'd been there for only a few days. What were the chances that he had never seen Etienne or one of his kind? Even though Etienne kept to himself, other creatures knew where he lived, and Wilson had, Reg suspected, the ability to move from one place to another, maybe even unconsciously. It seemed unlikely that he had never seen a Bigfoot. And Etienne had admitted to meeting a wizard thirty years before.

"I think I would remember that," Wilson asserted. But again, it was followed by a flash of doubt. Reg pried at it, trying to separate those little flashes of doubt, bring the memories back to the surface. She thought about Etienne herself. His size and shape. The way he talked. His kindness and quietness. She remembered him eating out of the hubcaps and putting them carefully back in his cupboard. All of the little details she could remember.

His Hershey's bars in that little cupboard.

Wilson's head twitched. "What was that?" he asked suddenly.

"A memory," Reg suggested.

"No, I can't remember. This was more like..." he reached for the words. "Something that was there... and then it was not."

Reg nodded, probing further. It seemed like the closer she got, the more fuzziness she encountered. Just like when she had used her powers to find him, but when she had gotten too close, suddenly lost the signal and couldn't pin him down.

As if someone didn't want him to remember or be found.

She recalled again how Weston had appeared when she noticed Wilson in the restaurant. How Wilson didn't want anything to do with the two men she had been with that night.

Why?

Because they'd had something to do with his memory loss.

They were part of the reason that he hadn't been able to leave the Everglades for fifty years.

"Remember Lethe?" Weston had asked, chuckling to himself, probably able to see Wilson over Reg's shoulder from where he was sitting. Was it a prank, then? Causing an old wizard to lose his memories? To forget his whole life?

"Lethe," Reg said aloud, getting a feeling for the word.

Wilson looked at her. "Lethe. What's that?"

"Those men that you saw me with. Did they ever give you a drink? Or put something into yours?"

"I... don't know. I don't remember that."

Reg looked at his scattered consciousness from his perspective. All of his memories and powers were so widely dispersed, it was difficult to close in on one thing. Everything remained tantalizingly out of her reach. And out of his.

She backed off, not wanting to push him any further.

CHAPTER THIRTY-NINE

*Y*ou see?" Wilson said, his voice tinged with regret. "There's nothing there. I don't know who the Wilson you are looking for is, but I'm not him. There's nothing for me to remember. I don't have any wizardry. You should go back to your Spring Games and forget about me again, like everyone else."

"Everyone hasn't forgotten you. That's why there is still a reward being offered for your safe return. Because people do care and want to help out."

"But you can see that there's nothing to do. No way for you to help out."

Reg wasn't ready to give up yet. She turned around to look for Damon and Corvin, and when she couldn't see either of them, she called Corvin on her cell phone.

"Reg?"

"You can come back. We didn't really get anywhere."

Corvin and Damon were back in a few minutes. They sat down at the table. Corvin looked at Reg.

"Didn't figure anything out?"

"Well... I'm still trying to sort it out. I think... that he did drink the waters of Lethe. I think that's what Weston was saying that night when he showed up. He wanted to check up on what I was doing because I was in the same place as Wilson. He remembered giving Wilson the waters, or enchanting him, or whatever it was that he did. And he didn't want me undoing anything."

"That would mean that you *can* undo it."

Reg nodded slowly. But she couldn't think of any one action that would help to restore Wilson's memory. She could get further in a reading than she had done so far. But that didn't mean it was the right thing to do or the proper way to go about restoring Wilson's memories. What if she did manage to pry that door open by sheer force of will? What kind of permanent damage would that do?

"In the mythology, is there any way to counteract the effects of the river of Lethe?"

"Hmm." Corvin rubbed his beard, thinking about it. "No... there was some talk about another spring that could reverse the effects, but that always seemed a little bit too... pat for me. Like the 'eat me' and 'drink me' in *Alice Through the Looking Glass*. One makes you bigger; one makes you smaller. Lethe makes you forget and another spring makes you remember." He shook his head. "I never put any stock into that one."

Reg imagined trying to go to all of the different springs and inlets in the Everglades to gather a few drops of water of each, to try to give Wilson the antidote he needed. It would take another fifty years. Maybe that's what he had been doing for the past fifty years. Wandering through the park, looking for the water that would restore his memory.

"There isn't anything else?"

"Sorry. No."

Elbows on the table, Reg rested her face in her hands. She rubbed her temples and tried to come up with something else.

"The Seminole said that he had giant sickness. Do you know the cure for giant sickness?"

Corvin shook his head. "I don't know much Seminole medicine. They didn't sound too encouraging about being able to cure it. They said that some people get over it," Corvin looked over at Wilson, his voice low, "but that most never return from the twilight."

"There has to be a way. I know he still has memories. I can see them now and then. Just flashes, very fast, but they're there. Something is still there."

Corvin shrugged. "I believe you. But I don't know what you can do about it. I don't know if you can do anything."

CHAPTER FORTY

$\mathcal{W}$e don't need to cure him," Damon pointed out. "We just need to bring him to the Spring Games."

Reg took a deep breath and looked at Wilson. "How would you like that? A vacation for a couple of weeks. Get away from the Everglades and watch the Spring Games. You said you would like to be able to go."

Wilson shook his head slightly. "I told you, I'm not magical. So I wouldn't be able to go." His eyes went to Corvin and to Damon. "They wouldn't let a non-magical person go, would they? They don't do that. They don't open it up to regular people."

"I could get you in," Damon reassured him. "Whether you think you have any power or not, I promise, I could get you in."

"For how long? They wouldn't be fooled for long. Then they would kick me out. Maybe punish me too. Please go ahead and do your own thing and leave me out of it. I've had enough…" He broke off, frowning and not able to finish the sentence.

"You've had enough of being punished?" Reg suggested. "Did you do something that made the two men punish you? Or even just one of them? Why did they make you forget?"

"I don't know. I have no idea." Wilson's face was flushed. "What would make someone *like that* angry enough to punish me this way?"

Reg didn't have any more idea than Wilson did. Corvin shook his head.

"They don't need much provocation to do something like that. Arachne was punished for thinking she was better at weaving than Athena. Men were killed in order for the immortals to steal their wives. Or they were targeted for being strong or brave. Not just if they were boastful, but if someone else boasted *about* them…"

"So you're saying, it could have been anything. It wouldn't have to be something really offensive. Just something that Weston decided to retaliate about one day."

"Or Harrison."

"I don't think that Harrison would…" Reg trailed off. She liked her "Uncle" Harrison. He had protected her and kept her safe. He had asked what she needed. He'd helped her when Starlight had been sick and with so many other things. But she knew he was also careless with human lives. He followed the few rules that the immortals had set down, like not doing anything to harm another immortal and not having offspring with a human. But as far as the humans' societal laws and guidelines Reg tried to explain to him, he was just amused.

So of course it could have been Harrison who had cursed Wilson just as easily as Weston. She saw Weston as the bad guy and Harrison as the good guy, but Francesca had warned her all along that no good could come of being too close to an immortal.

"It isn't fair," she complained. "I don't understand why the immortals have to poke around in human affairs and screw things up like they do. And if they do, they should at least acknowledge it and try to set it straight."

"Don't call him," Damon warned.

Reg realized that she had been thinking about it. Knowing how great the immortals' powers were, she knew that they could reverse Wilson's amnesia and open the doors to his memories once more if they chose to.

But Damon was right. Asking them for something was bound to back-fire like it always did. Making wishes or using magic for one's own ends always seemed to result in something terrible happening to balance the benefit. Or something that was ten times worse than the benefit; it didn't seem to be balanced.

"I won't."

"Come to the Spring Games," Damon urged Wilson. "If you decide you don't want to be there, or someone says that you shouldn't be there, then you can come back here. But can't you give it a try?"

CHAPTER FORTY-ONE

*I*n the end, they wore him down more than anything. Maybe after being in the Everglades for fifty years, Wilson was just ready to move on to something else. Reg knew she would have been bored long before that. No matter how many interesting creatures and plants there might be in the park, she didn't think she could have stayed for more than a few weeks before getting tired of it. Marshes just weren't her thing.

There were a lot of logistics. They needed to pick up Wilson's things, go back to the hotel in Miami to get the company's things, and Damon had phone calls he needed to make before showing up at the Spring Games with Wilson. There were the magical equivalent of affidavits and other legal documentation to be sworn and filed.

They decided to drive during the night rather than spend another night at the hotel and risk losing Wilson again, since he wanted to go nowhere near where he had seen Weston and Harrison.

It was a long trip and Reg knew that she was being irritable and unreasonable by the time they reached the end of the road. All she wanted was to go home and go to bed. Damon could take care of everything else. He could put Wilson in his spare room and file all of the rest of the paperwork he hadn't managed yet. He could collect on the reward and just bring Reg her half when he had it.

Sarah had left the outside light of the cottage on for her. Reg felt so glad to be home again that she could have knelt down and kissed the doorknob. But she didn't. She opened the door and stepped into her little home, letting all of her stresses and troubles fall away. She was home, and that was all that mattered.

Starlight jumped off of her bed in the bedroom. Reg heard him thump to the floor.

"Starlight! I'm home! Come see me."

Starlight came dashing through the kitchen and to the door. He rubbed against Reg's legs, making inquiring purr-meowing noises. He wound around her so affectionately that she was hardly able to take a step. She didn't want to kick him or to push him out of the way.

"Star, you wouldn't believe how much I missed you! No more quests for a while. I need to be home in my bed with my cat!"

He continued to vocalize and rub against her. Reg dropped everything else on the floor and picked him up, cuddling him against her face.

"Do you know that you helped me in the swamp even though you weren't there?" Reg asked him.

He rubbed against her face, and Reg told him all about the panther who had been curious about Reg's memories of her house cat and had followed her in the swamp and helped her out when needed.

Starlight squirmed to be put down, and when he jumped with a plop to the floor, he started meowing and rubbing against the refrigerator. Reg understood what that meant too.

"You're hungry? I'm sure Francesca and Sarah have already been by to feed you. Probably more than is good for you."

But he kept telling her how he was starving. She gave in, finding some tuna in the fridge and putting it into his dish. When she put it on the floor for him, Starlight wasn't there. Reg looked around, irritated. "Hey, I thought you were hungry?"

She found him digging into her duffel bag to see what she had brought home for him.

"I didn't bring anything. It's just all the same stuff as I took with me. Except that it's sweaty and dirty now." Which, of course, was perfume for cats. The smellier, the better.

Reg went over to her duffel with Starlight's hindquarters sticking out, and pulled him free.

"Hey. I got you tuna. Eat your tuna."

He tried to grab something from within the bag as she drew him out of it, and when she saw his face, his mouth was slightly open, like it was when he smelled something funky—getting high on her stinky clothes, no doubt.

Then she saw the leaves inside the duffel bag and was immediately concerned. "Oh no! You're not supposed to be getting into stuff like that. It might be poisonous to cats!"

He squirmed to get out of her grip and huffed when he landed on the floor. He looked at her bag, his mouth still open slightly, then went to the kitchen to eat his tuna. Reg bent down and picked up the leaves that had been left in one of her pockets. She examined them, trying to remember where they had come from and why she had them.

A few minutes later, Reg was knocking on Sarah's back door. She heard Sarah's invitation to "come in," and entered. She knew that Sarah had said numerous times before that she could just go in, but didn't feel comfortable with that. She found Sarah in the living room, sitting in a comfy chair with a cup of tea beside her and a book in her lap.

"Ah, you're back," Sarah observed. "How was your trip?"

"Well… it was eventful."

"And did you find Mr. Wilson?"

"Yes. I did. He's with Damon. I'm going to let him handle all of the red tape. I've done my part."

"Good for you. That must feel good."

Reg nodded, uninterested in that line of discussion. She sat on the couch close to Sarah and held out her hand with the leaves in it. "Do you know what these are?"

Sarah looked at the leaves, then bent over to smell them, not touching them. "I would guess… sweet bay leaves. Laurel. Did you get them in the Everglades?"

"Yes. Corvin gathered some herbs for us to do a smudge. For the Seminole ghosts. That was one of them."

Sarah nodded. "That's a good choice."

"They told me that I should keep some of this one. In case I needed it."

"And you want to know what you're supposed to do with it."

"Yeah. That, and whether it would be poisonous for Starlight. I don't want him to get into anything that might hurt him."

"They could be. But probably he would just smell or it and leave it alone. They are quite pungent, and the leaves very sharp. I can't imagine him wanting to eat any amount."

"Okay. Yeah. So what do you think I'm supposed to do with them?"

"Like most herbs, they have many applications. They were one of the sacred herbs of the Seminoles. But they didn't really have prescribed uses for each plant. It was up to the medicine man or woman to discern what a patient needed and then prepare the remedy. Maybe something to be eaten or drunk, maybe a poultice or a totem. It would depend on what the practitioner thought the best application was."

"So when she gave it to me, does that mean she thought I needed to take it? She didn't tell me what to do with it, just said that I might need it."

"What did you go to her about? Were you sick or did you have any concerns at the time?"

"No... we went to the Lost Village to see whether Wilson had been there, or if they might know anything about him."

Sarah thought about that. "So... what's wrong with Wizard Wilson?"

"I don't know if there is anything wrong with him, other than that he doesn't remember anything. I think... that Weston gave him the waters of Lethe to make him forget."

"Ah."

"The ghost said that... he had giant sickness. Is that what she meant? She said that people with giant sickness go to another land, and wander in the woods. Could she mean... did Weston actually take Wilson to another land to give him the waters? To the underworld? And Wilson did wander— for fifty years. We found him near a plane crash, one that has been missing since the Second World War. But I have no idea how he got there."

"Then perhaps this herb is what he needs to treat this giant sickness."

"But she didn't tell me how to use it."

"Then I would start with the most basic methods. Maybe a smudge and a tea. See if either of those makes a difference to his memory."

CHAPTER FORTY-TWO

*R*eg decided she wasn't going to go out again that night. She wanted her own bed and her own space for a while, and it wouldn't make any difference whether Wilson got his memories back that night or in the morning. Or if he didn't get them back. In fact, he would probably rest better if he didn't have a flood of memories about his former life and his family to deal with. It could be pretty traumatic to suddenly remember everyone and everything he had left behind.

So she felt justified going to bed without informing the others that she might have a remedy for Wilson's amnesia. She had a warm bath and then got into bed, Starlight cuddling up against her and purring away loudly. Reg scratched his ears and chin.

"I missed you too. I hope you weren't too upset about me being away for a few days. Francesca and Sarah took good care of you, right?"

He just kept purring, and Reg didn't have any feelings of reproach or anger from him, so she supposed he was okay with having been left alone.

She fell asleep quickly to his soothing, rumbling purr.

* * *

Her early bedtime made it easier for Reg to wake up at a somewhat reasonable hour of the morning. She texted Damon as she went through her morning rituals of putting on the coffee, feeding Starlight, and eventually finding clothes for herself for the rest of the day. It was a while before Damon responded, so maybe he was having a slower, "recovery" morning as well.

He texted that he and Wilson would come by in an hour or two so she could try the bay leaf remedies.

Reg was dressed and had replenished her coffee levels by the time the two men got there. Starlight was asleep, sprawled on his back in a patch of sunshine. He opened his eyes curiously at the arrival of the guests, but then just squirmed to get some more of his tummy in the sunbeam and purred quietly.

Wilson looked around. He seemed agitated and uncomfortable. Reg had expected him to be happy to be out of the park, but maybe it was too far out of his comfort zone for him to be able to relax. He looked as if someone might jump out of the woodwork at any moment and attack him. Reg did her best to make him feel calm.

"There's no one else here, just you and me and Damon. And the cat. You don't mind cats, do you?"

Wilson cast a glance over at Starlight as if he weren't quite sure.

"I don't mind," he confirmed after a moment. Starlight opened one eye partway, then closed it again.

Reg motioned for Wilson to take a seat, but he continued to pace anxiously. Reg let him walk. Damon sat down on the couch.

"So, Damon told you that I have a Seminole remedy that might help you with your memory?" she asked carefully.

"Yes." Wilson turned and walked back across the room again. "But there isn't anything wrong with my memory. The two of you think that I can't remember because I don't have your Jeffrey Wilson's memories, but that's just because I'm not *your* Jeffrey Wilson."

"Don't you think it's a little strange that two men named Jeffrey Wilson would get lost in the Everglades?"

"I wasn't lost; I was touring. Just seeing the sights. Assuming that I'm the same Jeffrey Wilson as the one who disappeared there fifty years earlier? That's the theory that doesn't make any sense."

"So you remember things from your past. Your childhood. Your family. Everything that has happened to you."

There was a slight hesitation, but very slight. "Yes," Wilson insisted. "I remember everything."

"How long were you there, in the Everglades?"

"Just a few weeks. Nothing out of the ordinary."

"How did you know where the plane wreck was?"

"I just stumbled across it. What's surprising is that no one else ever did. Sure it's a big park, and not everyone goes off of the trails, but someone should have found it long ago."

Someone should have, Reg agreed, but they hadn't. Only Wilson had found it. And she had no idea when he had found it or how he got there when he wanted to visit it. Despite his assertion that he wasn't the wizard Jeffrey Wilson and didn't have any magic, she knew something was going on there. There just wasn't a good non-magical explanation.

"But you're willing to try this remedy."

He shrugged. "Sure. Why not. If it will convince you that I'm not the guy you're looking for…"

He might say that was why he was willing to try the remedy, but Reg doubted it. He wasn't going to take an unknown Seminole remedy just for the sake of proving who he was. He didn't want to get his hopes up that it might be the answer. He was protecting himself in case it failed.

"I don't know the way the sweet bay leaves are usually prepared for this," she warned. "It may take some experimenting… and I don't know if it is the solution or not. Sarah suggested smudging and a tea. Does that sound okay?"

He shrugged and nodded. Reg took some of the dry bay leaves in her hand and kindled a small fire.

She knew that as a brand-new firecaster she wasn't supposed to be lighting fires without Davyn there to help temper them, but she'd used her fire a few times in the Everglades and nothing bad had happened.

Wilson's eyes widened at the sight of her kindling and holding fire in the palm of her hand. Reg let the flame die down and the leaves started smoking. She waved the smoke around. She turned in a circle and offered it at each of the four points of the compass, unsure whether the spell required her to offer it in a specific direction. Then she stood close to Wilson and waved it in his direction. He reared back a little, but then inhaled the woodsy, savory smell and seemed to relax a little. His shoulders dropped down. He inhaled again, then looked at Reg, shaking his head.

"It's nice," he said. "But I don't… I don't know anything I didn't know before. Nothing has changed."

Reg nodded. She was disappointed, but she had known that there might be no change.

"We can still try the tea," Damon pointed out.

"Right," Reg agreed.

She moved into the kitchen, where she disposed of the ashes. She had already crumbled bay leaves into a teacup for the second part of the experiment. They were surprisingly sharp and tough. She'd gotten a little cut on her thumb trying to break them up into small enough pieces for the tea. She should probably have gone to the big house to ask Sarah for her mortar and pestle thingies to crush it properly. But what was done was done.

Reg turned on the electric kettle. As it was heating, she gestured to the small amount of lemon juice she had collected by squeezing fresh lemons from the tree in Sarah's front yard. "Sarah said that lemon juice would make it more palatable. I couldn't believe how good these fresh lemons smelled. Like those lemon drop candies. But I know they won't be sweet like that."

Damon and Wilson nodded politely. The kettle started to whistle. Reg poured water over the bay leaves and then added a little bit of the lemon juice. She took it over to Wilson.

"Just let it steep for a few minutes first. If it needs more lemon juice, just let me know…"

He took the cup from her and looked down at the tea. The tea smelled similar to the smudge smoke, only more floral, and was almost overpowered by the smell of the lemon juice. Reg worried that she had put too much lemon juice in it. She didn't want to make Wilson drink something so mouth-puckeringly sour.

"I can get you some honey to go with that."

She gestured to the coffee table where she would typically put down the tea service. "Do you think you can relax enough to sit down for a few minutes?"

Wilson walked over to the couch and sat down at the opposite end from Damon. Reg put the tea things on a tray. "Do you want some tea?" she asked Damon. "I didn't even think to ask."

"No. I'm fine."

They watched Wilson, trying to look as though they were not staring at him. Maybe the effects of the smoke were delayed, and they would start seeing changes in a few minutes. When he drank the tea, would it have an immediate impact? Would it be dramatic, or would his memories come back bit by bit?

Or maybe nothing at all would happen and she was just kidding herself.

Starlight suddenly sat up, ears perked, voicing a little meow. He was looking past Reg, and she immediately looked behind her to see what he was looking at. Harrison. He was wearing something that looked like a prison jumpsuit but appeared to be made from light green silk.

Wilson gave a little yelp of surprise. He looked at Damon and Reg, searching for an explanation. Damon cocked his head slightly, eyeing Harrison with suspicion. Reg felt bad for Wilson; she knew that he was afraid of the immortals—or at least, she suspected it—but there was nothing that she could do to keep Harrison from entering her home. Wards wouldn't work against him, and she normally wanted him to be able to come and go, so she had never asked Sarah or Corvin if there were something that would keep the immortals out.

"Uh, Harrison… it's not a good time."

He raised one brow and looked at her. He glanced around the room in a circle, taking in her other visitors.

"Regina." He sounded disappointed instead of cheerful like he usually did. "You should not interfere with things that you know nothing about."

"What do you mean? How am I interfering?"

Of course, she knew what he was talking about, but she wanted to stall him until she could figure out what to do.

"This is not your domain."

"This is my home."

"Not that." He made a motion sweeping any talk of her house to the side. "This." He pointed to Wilson.

"Damon hired me to find him. I'm just doing my job. Why? What does it matter to you?"

"The wizard is a danger."

"A danger? How? He certainly can't be a danger to you!"

Even when Corvin was at his most powerful, he had needed the help of Reg and the others in order to defeat an immortal. And then it had been a close thing. One wizard who couldn't even remember having powers couldn't be a threat to Harrison.

"You should not get in the way of things you know nothing about," Harrison said sternly.

Which was precisely what Reg had been doing ever since she had moved to Black Sands. How was she supposed to learn anything if she didn't get her hands dirty? No one was going to be able to teach her all of the things she should have learned as a little girl if there had been other practitioners to guide her. She had to explore and find them out for herself.

"She hasn't done anything wrong," Damon argued. "We're just trying to help someone out."

There was a low growl from Starlight. Reg turned and looked at him, surprised. Starlight was looking at Wilson. Wilson had done nothing but take a sip of his tea. He lowered his teacup to look at Starlight, then took another sip. He grimaced, and his eyes went to the tea service Reg had placed on the coffee table. Honey. He definitely needed honey for the sour concoction. Reg moved closer to get the honey and hand it to him, but she was stopped as if by a force-field. Still grimacing, Wilson made himself take a few more sips.

Reg swallowed. Damon leaned forward, watching eagerly. Reg looked at Harrison. He just stood there looking at her, not explaining what she had done wrong.

"What?" Reg demanded. "I'm just trying to restore his memories. You might think it's hilarious to take away someone's powers, their memories, their whole life, but it isn't. It's wrong."

"How do you know that?"

"How do I know what?"

"How do you know that it is wrong?"

"Because taking all of that away from someone *is* wrong," Reg insisted. She couldn't think of how to explain to him how devastating it was to a human being to lose everything that he had. To lose his *self*, not just possessions.

Wilson put his cup down on the tea tray. It was empty other than a little liquid and the dregs. Reg was not close enough to read the leaves properly, but when she glanced at them from that distance, she had an immediate sinking feeling. Something was very wrong. She felt like the sun had gone behind a cloud. Like twilight was descending upon them in the middle of the day. All of the light gradually going out of the room.

Wilson gave her a smile that was unlike any she had previously seen on the Canadian's face. Not the vague, affable smile of the retiree tourist. Not a friendly smile directed at someone who had helped him out.

Instead, it was knowing. Cunning. Almost predatory. Reg looked at Damon, her eyes wide, looking for his direction.

But Damon didn't seem to have figured out yet that Harrison was right; Reg had made the wrong decision.

CHAPTER FORTY-THREE

hat did I do?" Reg asked Harrison. "I'm sorry. I didn't know…"

"Everything was fine as long as he did not remember," Harrison told her. "He was… muzzled. But now… we will have to deal with him."

Damon looked from Damon to Harrison. "What do you mean, muzzled?" he demanded.

"The immortals are the ones who should be muzzled," Wilson growled. "How is it we are still allowing them to control our lives? We're not pre-industrial Greek shepherds! We have technology, magic, and overwhelming numbers. Why should they have any say over us?"

Reg had to admit feeling much the same way about the immortals. Especially when she and the others had vanquished the Witch Doctor, another of the immortals. Humans far outnumbered the immortals and could overwhelm them. There seemed to only be a handful of immortals still in existence. For all she knew, Weston and Harrison could be the only ones remaining. But they took it upon themselves to try to control the lives of the mortals they had contact with. Interfering with the lives of Reg and her mother. Taking away Wilson's memory because of whatever slight they had perceived.

But Wilson clearly didn't mean this to be just an airing of grievances. He intended to take action. Reg couldn't get any closer to him due to the shield around him. How strong was he? As strong as Damon and the people in charge of the Spring Games had thought? Strong enough to take out an immortal or two?

"Not in here," Reg said. "I don't want any violence in my house."

Wilson sneered at her. "You don't want any violence? All of this is your doing. I'm only here and free because of you."

"I didn't do that so that you could hurt anyone. I did it because I thought you deserved to have your life back. Your memories. I didn't do it because I wanted you to... do whatever it is you are thinking of to the immortals."

"Then you should have asked more questions and not been such a stupid little girl. Wandering around in the Everglades, interfering with everyone's lives. You shouldn't have done it if you didn't know what you were doing."

Reg nodded slightly. She could see that now. She had trusted Damon, had believed that he and the organizers of the Spring Games knew what they were talking about. She'd thought that an old man wandering around the Everglades needed to be rescued. She hadn't asked for the proof. She didn't have any idea when she started out that the missing wizard had been gone for fifty years.

She had trusted the vision that Damon had put in her head. She had assumed that it was an accident or illness that had made Wilson lose his memory. When she found out that Weston and Harrison had been involved, she had assumed that they had gone too far and had just been interfering in human affairs without regard to the lives they would affect.

Wilson got up off the couch. He didn't shuffle like an older man now. He stood much taller than she expected and had strength and alertness in his eyes that she hadn't seen before. Ignoring Reg and Damon, he walked toward Harrison. Harrison didn't look cowed. He made no move to protect himself.

Damon moved as to get up off of the couch, but stopped, looking confused and concerned.

"I may have lost fifty years," Wilson said, "but that's nothing compared to what you are going to lose. How do you measure the amount of time an immortal loses when he is destroyed?"

"No," Reg protested. "He's not the one who took your memory away. That was Weston. Harrison was just a bystander."

Wilson rolled his eyes at her. "A bystander?" he laughed. "So this one has seduced you, has he? He took a shine to you, and now you'll believe whatever he tells you. You'll wait on him hand and foot like the Nubian mistresses he's had in the past."

"No. I just... he helped to protect me. And I know he's not the one..."

"You don't know anything. You weren't there. Ask this one whether he had anything to do with it or not. He'll tell you the truth. These ones don't care who knows the atrocities they have performed."

Reg looked at Harrison, but she didn't ask him. She didn't want to know the answer.

Wilson took another step toward Harrison. There was a streak of light and a boom. Reg blinked. Starlight had somehow put himself between Harrison and the wizard.

"Star..." Reg's voice failed. She didn't want anything to happen to her familiar. He was powerful, she knew, but strong enough to fight a wizard like Wilson? Reg edged closer to Starlight and Harrison. She had no clue what she was going to do, but the three of them had to be able to stop Wilson. He couldn't fight an immortal, a being like Starlight, and Reg all at the same time. As when they had fought the witch doctor, he wouldn't be able to watch all fronts at the same time. He wouldn't be able to battle all of them effectively.

"Don't come any closer," Reg told Wilson, making her voice as hard and inflexible as possible. "This is my home and Harrison won't come to any harm in it."

Harrison made a vague gesture toward Starlight, and a tall man in armor stood there instead of the cat. Harrison's eyes flashed toward Reg, and she felt Weston's protective spell drop away.

He scrambled to re-establish the barrier. Reg fought back with one of her own, putting it around Harrison and Starlight, but they both shook it off.

"No, Reg," Harrison raised his hand to signal to her. "Leave us free to act. No fetters."

"I didn't—I wanted to protect you."

"No." Harrison gazed at Wilson. "You thought Weston's waters of Lethe a punishment? They were a gift. For fifty of your mortal years, you have had happiness, unadulterated by greed or vice. Contented to go from one place of beauty to another and enjoy all that the river lands had to offer. Do you think you will be rewarded for your brashness again?"

"See here—" Damon started, and was silenced by a flick of Harrison's hand.

"I don't want your kind of happiness," Wilson snarled, "I want the kind that I make for myself."

"You will never achieve that."

"I can if you and your kind will stay out of my way," Wilson growled.

"No. Humans who are full of avarice always want what they cannot have. They are never happy with…" Harrison's eyes stared into the distance, "…chocolate cake."

There was an iced cake on the counter that hadn't been there before. Harrison jabbed a finger into it and licked off the cake and frosting. "You can never achieve this."

"I don't want a cake," Wilson snapped. "I can go to the grocery store or bakery any time I please to get a cake."

"It's no different from anything else," Harrison said reasonably. "Money. Gems. Power." Gold coins and gems covered the counters, surrounding the cake. Reg saw a crown and a scepter among them. Harrison went through her drawers and found a salad-serving fork. He used it to scoop out a large amount of cake, which he tried, but failed, to cram into his mouth. He stood there, wiping crumbs and frosting off of his face. "Corporeal things. You will never succeed in getting them all, so you will always want more. And a state of *want* is the opposite of happiness."

Wilson raised his hand as if to strike, irritated and impatient with Harrison's declarations. "Enough of your dramatics," he insisted. "We didn't meet here for a philosophical discussion. You know that I am just as powerful as you, and I will not abide you interfering in human lives anymore." He waved his hand and Harrison appeared to take a body blow. Harrison flinched and pulled back, but his expression didn't change. The soldier who stood where Starlight had been struck out quickly, his arm curved slightly and head cocked to the side like a cat playing with a mouse. Wilson took a shocked step back and his eyes flew to the soldier.

"Who are *you?*"

Reg knew the answer to that but didn't bother to answer.

If Harrison didn't want a protective envelope around himself or

Starlight, then maybe the opposite would be helpful. Reg tried instead to wrap one around Wilson.

He didn't seem aware of what she was doing at first. He flicked a couple more blows at Harrison, who didn't fight back, and Wilson was, in turn, a plaything in the soldier's paws—or hands.

Becoming aware of her efforts, Wilson turned suddenly to Reg in a fury. "You interfere again! Why would you do this? It is not your fight! I was going to leave you alone because you reawakened me. But for that stupidity—"

Reg held firm to the protective spell. She was glad that she'd decided to stay home the night before and get a good sleep before giving Wilson the bay leaves. If she'd done it the night before while she was still tired, who knew how long she would be able to maintain the protective spell. But feeling fresh and strong, she felt confident she could keep the little pocket around Wilson secure.

Until he really started to push back. The attacks he'd made against Harrison and the soldier had only been experimental, tests against their power to see if they would react and how much power he had after having been dormant for fifty years.

Did not using his magic for fifty years mean that he would be stronger because it had built up over that time, or weaker like an atrophied muscle or lost habit?

She didn't know how strong he had been before Weston had taken away his memories, but she guessed that the answer was that he had not lost in power during the time he had been held in the Everglades. Trying to keep him inside the protective barrier was as hard as trying to keep Harrison there would have been. She could tell that her spell was not going to hold for long.

"Harrison…"

He watched her curiously. Reg thought he was more interested in seeing her growth and development than he was in controlling Wilson.

"I can't hold him. I thought I could, but he's very strong."

Harrison nodded. "I don't know if I've ever seen a stronger human."

Reg cursed under her breath. How was she going to hold him? Or to convince Harrison to do something about him? Harrison always seemed more interested in food and human culture than he was in protecting the world from powerful beings. She looked at Damon, but he appeared to be immobilized, either by his own shock at what was going on or Harrison's magic.

"Listen," she told Harrison. "You need to stop him. If I let him go, he might kill all of us. Maybe not you, but me and Damon and Starlight."

Harrison frowned at that. "What do you want me to do?"

"I don't know. What can you do to stop him?"

Harrison took a couple of steps closer to Wilson, studying him. Wilson was unable to move from the place Reg had trapped him. He pressed against the spell with his own magic. Strong natural magic that made her wonder whether he had immortals in his bloodlines, or if he were able to steal the powers of others as Corvin did.

"The easiest way would be to kill him," Harrison suggested. "Humans are very frail. A stopped heart or cutting or blocking the flow of blood…"

"I don't want you to kill him; I just want you to stop him. Make him forget again. We'll put him somewhere he can't be found this time."

"That was what we thought the last time. If you can't lose him forever in the Everglades, then where could you lose him?"

"I don't know. Under the ocean?"

"You said not to kill him. Humans need air to survive. Just a little bit of water in the lungs and they expire." He chuckled. "Instead of respiring. You get it?"

"Harrison!"

"I don't have the waters of Lethe. And perhaps that was not the best way to keep him out of our way. Sooner or later, someone was bound to help him. Or he would help himself just by chance."

"Can't you take away his powers?"

"Some of them. But other power exists… simply as part of the organism. Without it, the organism ceases to exist." Harrison studied Wilson like a bug under a microscope.

"Well, take some of it away; he's tiring me out."

Wilson's struggles became considerably less. His face turned a shade redder, and he scowled at Reg. "I will regain what I have lost! You can't take my power away."

It was too bad Corvin wasn't there, Reg thought fleetingly. He would have been happy to drain Wilson's power. But then, she didn't want Corvin getting any stronger either. Was it true that power always corrupted? Or did it only corrupt those who were susceptible, who gave in to its pull?

Reg had some ability to pull from others' powers as well. She had been strengthened by Corvin several times and, when desperate, had drawn the energy from a crowd. She concentrated on Wilson, feeling his power pulsing beneath the surface. She experimented whether she could bleed it off using the shield she already had around him. There was a damping effect, his power dimming and the shield strengthening. That was a good idea. The more he pushed, the stronger the shield around him grew.

The soldier paced, his eyes on the quarry. Harrison watched, his face impassive, absentmindedly sucking icing off of his fingers.

There was a surge in strength from Wilson and a corresponding strengthening of the shield. Wilson's body sagged suddenly, and the sudden cessation of his fighting back against the protective shield made Reg jolt in surprise, just like if she'd been pushing him physically and then he suddenly stepped out of the way. She nearly let the shield go, surprised and immediately worried that she had gone too far. Harrison had said that he could only take so much strength from Wilson before his body would fail.

Of course that was true. Reg knew that her physical stamina and her powers were inextricably intertwined, with her physical condition affecting her ability to access her powers, and her powers sapping her physical strength.

She moved closer to Wilson. Had she taken too much? Had she told Harrison not to kill him and then gone ahead and done it herself?

"Are you okay?"

She tried to read Wilson's suddenly ashen face, stepping closer again. She could feel Starlight's warning, feel him cautioning her and pulling her back. He had seen this behavior in prey before. A sudden freezing or stillness, feigning injury and death, followed by bolting or a renewed attack.

Reg kept the shield in place as she got closer, trying to evaluate Wilson's condition. What he'd said was true. She just kept playing with her powers without really knowing what she was capable of. Experimenting on the world around her. Maybe gaining in strength herself at the expense of others. Not just power-hungry wizards like Wilson, but those who might be innocent bystanders too. She had no intention of hurting anyone else, but she'd learned early in life to take what she needed to survive, putting her own needs ahead of anyone else's.

Wilson glared at her, but he looked a lot more like the man she had found in the Everglades. Less like the powerful wizard who had threatened to destroy them all. His shoulders were slightly hunched, his head down.

"You can't do this. Sooner or later, you have to let me go."

That was true. She couldn't keep him in a bubble forever.

"Promise you won't do anything to hurt any of us."

His eyes glittered. "I won't hurt you."

She didn't believe him. And even if she did, he hadn't said he wouldn't hurt any of them, only that he wouldn't hurt Reg.

"Any of us," she insisted.

He scowled. "Any of you."

"Swear it on your powers."

He was silent.

"If you want me to let you go, then swear on your powers that you won't hurt any of us."

"Fine, I swear it."

Reg waited.

"I swear on my powers I won't hurt any of you," he muttered angrily.

Was it enough? Reg looked at the soldier. He made no sign. She looked at Harrison. Did it make any difference at all what Wilson's words were? Could he lie and just go ahead and do whatever he liked anyway? Was swearing on his powers enough to bind him?

"Harrison?"

Harrison gazed at Wilson and shrugged. "Perhaps."

His level of unconcern was unsettling. Reg knew from what Harrison and others had said in the past that he really didn't care what happened to humans. But she knew that he had great affection for Starlight. And possibly some feelings toward Reg. He took another chunk of cake on his serving fork and nibbled at it, waiting.

"You promised," Reg reminded Wilson. "You promised on your powers." And then she dropped the shield.

CHAPTER FORTY-FOUR

*J*t was a relief to be able to let the shield go. It had taken a lot of power to be able to maintain it. It was like putting down a heavy weight after having to hold it out in front of her for an extended length of time, a favorite punishment of one of her foster families.

Wilson looked around at them one at a time, weighing his options. He was, Reg knew, reduced in his powers. But she didn't know how long that would last or how much it would limit him. And if he tried to attack one of them? Would the universe prevent him from using his powers in a way he had sworn not to? Did the oath bind him or not?

"You will live to regret this," Wilson told Reg.

He looked at the others. Harrison, in particular, drew another long glare. Wilson would never forgive him for being one of the immortals who had cursed Wilson for fifty years, no matter how Harrison spun it.

"You will leave here," Harrison said.

It was more in the flat tone of an observation than a command. Wilson looked at him for a minute, and then he was gone. Reg steadied herself on the back of a chair and looked around, waiting for a renewed attack. There was no sound. There was no sign of Wilson anywhere.

Damon moved, standing up suddenly, and then sitting back down when there was nothing for him to do, no one for him to fight. "Okay… where did he go?"

Harrison shrugged. "We do not need him."

Reg let out a measured breath. "Well... *I'd* like to know if I have to worry about him coming back here. He wasn't too happy."

"He won't ever be happy again," Harrison speculated, "now that he knows who he is."

"He really was better off without any memories? Not knowing who he was?"

"Better off," Harrison repeated, and he shook his head, indicating he didn't understand what Reg meant.

"He was better wandering the Everglades, not knowing who he was, than having his memory restored?"

"Definitely better," Harrison said firmly, nodding.

Reg sighed. "This stuff is so confusing. I thought I knew what I was doing, but it turns out... I didn't have a clue."

Harrison's nod was sympathetic. "Most humans don't," he consoled.

"What if he comes back?"

"It will be some time before he gets his strength back, and you continue to grow in your powers. He did give his oath. Perhaps that will be enough."

"But you don't think so."

"You are never safe in this world, Regina. That is the nature of being mortal. You could be killed tomorrow stepping in front of a bus. Drinking poison. Tripping over your cat." He gestured to Starlight, once more sitting where he had been, washing one of his back feet, toes spread wide. Starlight stopped and looked at Harrison and then Reg.

"Was he... did you turn Starlight into a man?" she asked Harrison.

"You simply saw another form. You should not assume that a being will always be in the same form."

Reg blinked, looking at her cat. "That was weird."

She turned her attention to Damon. He flushed pink.

"This whole thing... was my fault. Do you believe me when I say that I didn't know that he was like that? I just... I just thought he was lost and I could get the reward."

"I guess any reward is out of the question now."

Damon nodded, looking abashed. "I'll have to check the language to make sure, but yeah... I don't think just finding him and letting him go fulfills the terms of the reward. He has to actually participate in the Spring Games."

Reg gazed out the window, making sure that Wilson wasn't there, right outside the house, waiting until they were off their guard to attack again. But the person he wanted to harm the most was Harrison, and Harrison never left by the door.

"I don't think having him participate in the Spring Games would have been a good thing, would it?"

"Uh... no," Damon agreed. "That probably would have been a bad idea."

"They must know what kind of a person he was before he disappeared. Didn't they understand how powerful he was? What he could do to them? Why would they want someone like that to participate?"

"They must not have known. And since then... most of the people who were in charge of the Spring Games back then aren't involved in it anymore. It's only an eighteen-year election period."

She would have expected a position like that would be a two or four-year term of service, but she supposed that with the slow aging process and long lives of the magical practitioners, two years would hardly have been a blink.

"So it was just a publicity thing. To get people's attention."

"I suppose so."

"Harrison, do you think—" Reg turned to speak to him, but he was no longer there. The piles of gold coins and gems were gone. All that remained was the half-destroyed chocolate cake.

Happiness, at least as far as Harrison was concerned, was a chocolate cake.

EPILOGUE

$\mathcal{M}$orning, Reg," Sarah greeted, as Reg made her way out of the bathroom, robe wrapped tightly around her.

Reg yawned. "Morning." She blinked hard, trying to get her eyes adjusted to the bright sunlight. "Is it still morning?"

"It is." Sarah looked at her watch. "For… almost another hour."

"I'm up in good time, then."

Sarah laughed. "I brought you your mail. And you have a delivery from Amazon." Sarah put the box on top of the kitchen island.

Starlight meowed piteously, looking up at Reg from in front of his bowl of kibble. Which was of course, not empty. Reg leaned down to scratch behind his ears. Then she plucked a pair of scissors from a drawer and tackled the tape sealing the Amazon box. Curious, Starlight jumped up to find out what was in the box.

Sarah stayed around for long enough to see Reg pull a 36-count box of Hershey bars out, followed by a box of 48 packets of Quaker apple cinnamon instant oatmeal. Sarah raised her brows.

"I didn't know you like oatmeal. You hardly ever have anything but coffee and leftovers for breakfast. Or lunch. Whatever it is."

"I don't. I hate oatmeal. This is for… a friend."

Sarah frowned, looking at the Hershey bars and oatmeal. Then she gave a little smile. "A friend in Everglades National Park?"

"Or maybe… two friends."

"I see." Sarah nodded understandingly. "Well, good for you, Reg. Good for you."

Did you enjoy this book? Reviews and recommendations are vital to making a book successful.

Please leave a review at your favorite book store or review site and share it with your friends.

Don't miss the following bonus material:
Sign up for mailing list to get a free ebook
Read a sneak preview chapter
Other books by P.D. Workman
Learn more about the author

Sign up for my mailing list at pdworkman.com and get Gluten-Free Murder for free!

JOIN MY MAILING LIST AND

Download a sweet mystery for free

PREVIEW OF MAGIC AIN'T
A GAME

CHAPTER ONE

*Y*ou should print up some flyers or brochures for the Spring Games," Sarah told Reg, as she bustled around tidying up. The older, gray-haired woman opened the planner on Reg's kitchen island to review her appointments.

"I don't have anything to do with the Spring Games," Reg said, frowning and rubbing her sticky eyes. "Why would I print flyers for it?"

"It's a good time to get those tourist dollars! People come from all over to watch the games, and they love to get in on the action and get a psychic reading or some other taste of the unseen world."

"Oh." Reg nodded. She tripped over Starlight, her tuxedo cat, on her way to the coffee machine. Even though it wasn't early by Sarah's standards, it was still before noon and Reg wasn't quite ready to take on her day. She had never seen the Spring Games. Damon had described them as a sort of magical Olympics. Witches and warlocks from around the world gathered to participate in friendly competition to pit their magical abilities against each other.

Reg herself was still just learning about the unseen world. She'd had various encounters with abilities and magical beings that she had always assumed were only the stuff of fairy tales. But apparently, the magical races were just as real as Reg's ability to read people. What she had always assumed was a talent for cold reading was, apparently, actual psychic ability.

And then there were the ghosts. She had grown up being told that the voices she heard and people she saw were either the results of vivid imagination or mental illness. It had never occurred to them that she simply had sight that others did not. There wasn't anything wrong with her brain—or not that, anyway—it was just a paranormal ability that most of the world did not possess.

But she still had a lot to learn, and she was looking forward to the Spring Games not just for entertainment value, but to educate herself more in what was possible in the magical world.

"You really should take advantage of the opportunity," Sarah pressed. "It will be a good time to pick up some more clients outside of Black Sands as well as locals."

"But if they're not here, I'll only be able to meet with them once," Reg pointed out. The real bread and butter was in repeat clients. Those who came back again and again to learn more about their future or their past, or to communicate with lost loved ones.

"You can do phone contacts. Lots of psychics do phone readings."

"Oh. I guess I never thought about that."

"Sure, it's big business. You even see advertisements for them on late-night TV, running up against all of the dating app commercials."

"I always thought those were just scams. Another way to get money from lonely hearts." Not that Reg was averse to a good con. Scams of one kind or another had kept her off the street in her lean years before moving to Black Sands. "They always seemed sort of sleazy."

"That's why I didn't recommend going that way. But getting face-to-face contacts here during the Spring Games and then converting them to phone clients who you talk to once a month or even once a week, that's good business. And they've seen you face to face, so they are far more likely to keep in contact with you, rather than calling a hotline when they have a problem."

Reg watched the coffee dribble into her mug, eventually pulling the mug out a second or two too soon, impatient to get the mental boost she needed. Coffee dripped onto the counter. Starlight jumped up to the counter to watch the growing puddle.

Reg took a few sips of the hot coffee. "I'll do something up on my computer then," she agreed, "and then get it over to the printer to make some copies. What do I do, just... hand them out to anyone I see at the Spring Games?"

"Pretty much. Anyone you talk to or who is sitting close to you. Don't worry about offending; people are there to see magic. They love to get a little taste of psychic powers for themselves."

Sarah was Reg's landlady. She was the one who rented the cottage in her back yard to Reg at a price that she had been able to afford when she first came to Black Sands, penniless but for her haul at the last town she had stopped in to make some ghostly contacts and maybe to leave with a few pieces of jewelry that people didn't need anymore. Sarah was a witch and lived in the big house at the front of the property, and she had taken it upon herself to help Reg establish her business, keep the cupboards and fridge stocked, and do anything else around the cottage that she thought needed doing.

So far, she had never steered Reg wrong. If she said there was money to be made off of the tourists coming to see the Spring Games, then there was.

Sarah was the only other person who knew about the gems hidden in Reg's cottage. She knew Reg didn't need to grow her psychic services business. But she kept Reg's secret. Reg did not want it to become known that she had valuables secreted away.

"I haven't seen Damon over lately," Sarah commented. "Are the two of you... on the outs?"

Reg considered her response carefully. "We were never actually that close... he helped me in my trip to the dwarf mountain, I helped him in his trip to the Everglades... so we're even now. I don't think we'll be seeing a lot of each other in the near future. Besides, he's busy with security for the Spring Games, and I take it that's a pretty big responsibility."

"He will be busy with that," Sarah agreed, puffing out her cheeks and then blowing out the air in a whistle. "It's really too bad that you couldn't find that wizard for him. That would have been a big deal."

Reg nodded. "After fifty years, though, who could have expected to find him?" she said in a neutral tone.

"Ah, well, I know young folk and their magical quests. It doesn't really matter how impossible they are."

Sarah, though gray-haired, did not look anywhere near her age. She claimed centuries, though Reg wasn't sure if she believed it. Sometimes she wondered how much of the time the supposed witches and warlocks of Black Sands were just putting her on, seeing how much she would believe. She'd seen a lot of weird stuff, so she knew it wasn't all made up. But she couldn't help wondering if she was just as naive a mark as she had ever targeted herself. Regardless, anyone under sixty, or who looked under sixty, was definitely 'young folk' to Sarah.

"I don't think you'll see Damon around here any time soon."

Sarah nodded. "Just as well. The two of you always were a little rocky."

Reg wanted to like Damon, she really did. He was handsome and funny and seemed like a nice guy. As Sarah said, they had gotten off to a rocky start, with Damon disregarding Reg's feelings. They had become closer during and after the road trip to the Blue Ridge Mountains. But Reg couldn't let go of how he lied to her, not just with words, but by putting visions into her head that were impossible to differentiate from actual experiences or psychic visions. She couldn't trust him or anything that happened when she was around him.

And there was the fact that as a diviner, he could tell whenever she lied, which under normal circumstances, was pretty often for Reg.

It was pretty hard to have a successful relationship under those circumstances.

CHAPTER TWO

*R*eg thought that the new flyers for the Spring Games looked pretty good, if she did say so herself. She tapped the edges to the coffee table to square them up and set them down in a pile. She looked at Starlight, who was snoozing in one of the wicker chairs that caught the afternoon sunshine. Starlight opened his blue eye to look back at Reg.

"I think I've done pretty well today," Reg told him. "I got these all put together and printed so I'll be ready to hand them out at the Spring Games. I could have just sat around all day in my pajamas thinking it was too late to get them done, but I didn't."

Starlight closed his eye again and started to purr. His aura was cool colors, relaxed and unbothered by her chatter. He was good at reading her moods and was probably happy that she was calm and relaxed instead of worrying about any of the things that could go wrong.

And there were a lot of things that could go wrong. Reg wasn't in charge of the Spring Games, she didn't have any role to play in it, but it could still affect her. If one of the powerful beings that she had encountered recently decided to show up at the Games and disrupt things, it could have long-reaching effects. That wouldn't be her fault, of course. But she still felt a sense of dread in the pit of her stomach.

Because if one of the powerful beings that she had encountered *did* show up at the games and cause chaos, injuries, or death, she couldn't help feeling like she was a little bit responsible. It wasn't her job to go around banning or binding magical creatures, but if she had the ability and didn't, then that was sort of like a doctor walking away from a traffic accident, wasn't it?

But what if she only thought that she might have the ability to stop them but was afraid to put her powers to the test? Or if she was afraid that doing so might harm her, so she didn't get involved or didn't put all of her power into it? There were a lot of less powerful and more vulnerable victims out there. If she chose not to lay it all on the line, what did that say about her?

That she was wise?

Or that she was a coward?

The phone rang, jolting Reg out of her dark thoughts. She picked up her phone and looked at the screen. It was Officer Marta Jessup, a friend. Or as much of a friend as a police officer could be to a con man. Jessup was too honest to let Reg get away with much of anything, but did try to look the other way when she could. Reg didn't know if she was too naive about Reg's somewhat checkered past to believe that she would do anything really wrong, or if she knew too much about Reg's history and knew that sooner or later, she would. And she just didn't want to have to be the one to report it.

Jessup had already been disciplined for losing evidence in a case that she had involved Reg in. She probably shouldn't have asked for Reg's help in the first place, but she had, and Reg had been able to locate Jessup's missing person, but things had gone much farther than that. Reg's involvement always seemed to go a bit beyond what anyone else was willing or able to do.

So their friendship was a fragile one. They tried to spend girl time together and not to get involved in each other's cases. Each looking the other way and pretending that there wasn't a conflict.

Reg swiped her phone. "Hey."

"Are you all set? Jessup asked.

"Um… all set." Reg really wasn't sure what she was supposed to do to prepare for their night out. She hadn't exactly been given any instructions. "I thought… it was just a celebration. What am I supposed to do to get ready?"

"Oh, it is. Just a… not a party, exactly, but a… celebration or observance. Yes."

"Then what am I supposed to do? I thought we were just going to get together and… get some drinks, watch the floor show, whatever. I'm not exactly prepared for anything else."

"You don't have to prepare anything. Just show up. We'll show you want to do."

"Which will be what?"

"Nothing to worry about. You've gone to Easter parties before, haven't you?"

"Easter parties… no, not really. Maybe when I was a little kid, but I don't remember. Certainly nothing as a teenager or adult. What exactly happens at an Easter party? I don't suppose we'll be bobbing for hard-boiled eggs."

"No, but we might color some eggs. You've done that before, haven't you?"

Reg could remember a couple of disastrous attempts at dying eggs using a grocery store kid's kit. It looked perfectly simple but had always ended up in spilled dye, fights with foster siblings, and tears.

"Not… exactly what you would call successfully," she said with reluctance.

"Well, maybe there will be egg dying. There will be other stuff too. Maybe planting flower seeds or bulbs, prayers and chants, blessings over the upcoming season. Stuff like that."

"I'm really starting to wonder if this is for me. You know that I'm not into all of the spiritual stuff."

"You don't have to be. There will be food. Sarah is bringing some baking, and so is Letticia. I don't know who else. But that's always good. And there will be some kind of show for the kids to watch. Just come and hang out. You don't have to participate in anything that you're not interested in or comfortable with. Trust me, you know that my powers are pretty… dim, even when compared with the least powerful of witches. I'm not there to do anything, just to participate and have a good time. Celebrate the upcoming spring equinox together."

"I don't know. What about clothes? Should I dress up? I didn't even ask Sarah if there's some kind of dress code."

"It isn't a sky clad ceremony," Jessup said, her voice teasing, "so clothing is not optional."

"I know that!" Reg's face got hot, embarrassed even though there was no one there to see her. "I mean… is it like a ball? Or a garden party? Do I need to wear something pink and frilly? Or is it just casual? Are people going to be wearing blue jeans?"

"I don't suppose anyone will be wearing blue jeans, but there isn't any prescribed dress. People will be wearing things all over the spectrum, from dressy casual to formal garden party. What you wear normally, your gypsy skirts and headdress, is perfectly acceptable."

"Are you sure?"

"Yes, I'm sure."

There were times that Reg wished she had Damon's gift of divining. She would really like to know whether Jessup was being completely honest or was just trying to calm Reg down. She didn't want to be *handled*.

"What are you going to wear?"

"I don't know. Dress slacks. Some kind of blouse. I'm not a frilly person, so it's not going to be some kind of Easter froth. Just something… spring colored with nice lines."

"Okay." Reg felt a little better about that. As long as Jessup was telling the truth about what she was planning to wear and didn't show up for the party with thirteen crinolines layered under a Little Bo Peep dress.

"And should I bring something? I didn't bake anything. I could boil some eggs for the egg dying or pick something up at the bakery."

"No, the food and activities are all handled. Just bring yourself."

"So that's tonight, and the actual equinox thing is during the opening ceremonies of the Games?"

"The opening ceremony of the Games is during the equinox," Jessup corrected.

"Yeah, whatever. That's when the equinox is."

"More or less, yes. Just a couple of days, and we will be experiencing the most *balanced* time of the year. A very important date on our calendar."

"Because day and night are the same length."

"That is one of the measurements we use. But other things come into balance during that time too. Light and dark, good and evil. A sense of peace and security."

"Seems sort of strange to have a competition in the middle of all of that. Doesn't it sort of contradict the whole 'peace and balance' thing?"

"There are those who believe so," Jessup admitted. "One thing that the police force will be doing is trying to keep any protests under control and make sure they don't interfere with the games or people's private ceremonies."

"There are protests?"

"There are protests in connection with any big event."

"They are protesting... what? Spring?"

Jessup laughed. "They're protesting the Spring Games being held over equinox, like you said. That it's supposed to be about balance and cooperation and peace, and the Spring Games are about competition and singling people out for awards. But I don't see why you can't do both. The games are fun. It isn't like they take over our lives. We enjoy watching them, seeing people show off what they can do; no one gets really hard-core competitive about it."

Reg wondered if that was true. She'd seen the real Olympics, and things got pretty competitive there—athlete against athlete and country against country.

"How are they run? The games? Do they split people up by country?"

"Countries are an artificial construct that doesn't follow magical traditions. The teams or competitors tend to be split more by kinship than by geographical location."

"So... fairies against fairies, or fairies against pixies?"

"There aren't a lot of different magical species participating. There will be some fairies, but I don't think I've ever seen the pixies take part. But more along the lines of... covens that follow certain traditions banding together and competing against covens that follow other traditions, or that trace their ancestry or heritage back to a particular witch or warlock or family."

"It's mostly witches and warlocks?"

"Yes."

"But no one we know? Sarah isn't in it?"

"I don't know who is or isn't in it, really. Not Sarah. Not as far as I know. She's not interested in competing, just in enjoying the celebrations."

Sarah was retired. Sort of. She still used magic, but she didn't seem to sell a particular service or kind of magical assistance. She helped Reg set wards that would keep Corvin and other dangerous practitioners away. She gave Reg tea or helped to treat her when she wasn't feeling well. Brought her soup and other food, knowing that Reg tended to just forget about meals and constantly graze on junk food.

"And making cookies."

"She makes good cookies."

"I know Letticia does. I've had hers before."

"Yes, she's a good baker."

"I can't believe she can do that in her little wood-burning oven. It must be really hard to keep it a constant temperature."

"A little bit of magic probably helps."

* * *

Magic Ain't a Game, Book #11 of the *Reg Rawlins, Psychic Investigator* series by P.D. Workman can be purchased at pdworkman.com

ABOUT THE AUTHOR

Award-winning and USA Today bestselling author P.D. (Pamela) Workman writes riveting mystery/suspense and young adult books dealing with mental illness, addiction, abuse, and other real-life issues. For as long as she can remember, the blank page has held an incredible allure and from a very young age she was trying to write her own books.

Workman wrote her first complete novel at the age of twelve and continued to write as a hobby for many years. She started publishing in 2013. She has won several literary awards from Library Services for Youth in Custody for her young adult fiction. She currently has over 60 published titles and can be found at pdworkman.com.

Born and raised in Alberta, Workman has been married for over 25 years and has one son.

* * *

Please visit P.D. Workman at pdworkman.com to see what else she is working on, to join her mailing list, and to link to her social networks.

* * *

If you enjoyed this book, please take the time to recommend it to other purchasers with a review or star rating and share it with your friends!

facebook.com/pdworkmanauthor

twitter.com/pdworkmanauthor

instagram.com/pdworkmanauthor

amazon.com/author/pdworkman

bookbub.com/authors/p-d-workman

goodreads.com/pdworkman

linkedin.com/in/pdworkman

pinterest.com/pdworkmanauthor

youtube.com/pdworkman